Love MD

DEVON ATWOOD

Copyright © 2023 Devon Atwood
Cover art copyright © 2023 GRBookCovers by Gabriella Regina
Cover copyright © Cottage Hill Publishing House
Poetry by Christian @scruffylookinbookherder
Edited by Marios Pagonis

Cottage Hill Publishing House
P.O. Box 1181
Lyman, WY 82937

First Edition: November 2023

ISBN: 9798861450249

Books in the Love and Other Jobs series by Devon Atwood:

Love Rx

Love MD

Love Esq. (Coming Soon)

Love JD (Coming Soon)

For the spunky pranksters.

Trigger Warnings: Non-consensual restraint, dubious consent edging, and some very light BDSM content with safe words used throughout. Enjoy!

ONE
June

D r. Brady saw my bra.

And then I set him on fire.

All in all, the whole debacle had been his fault, and after I got over my embarrassment, I was going to make him pay.

I woke up earlier that morning with a glow stick in my ear, and it really didn't set the mood for me. I sat up, startled, and batted at my ear. In my half-awake haze, I wondered if the cockroaches in our apartment complex had finally mutated off their steady diet of hard seltzer and pot and were there to eat my brains.

"What the fu —"

"Happy Birthday!" A high-pitched voice sang in my ear. Lizzette, my roommate, pulled the glow stick from my ear and waved it in front of my face. "Birthday shots at StellaVibe!"

Lizette—or Liz—had two modes: Party girl with no job, and party girl with a job. At the moment, she was in "no job" mode, and she'd been driving me insane for days. In two weeks, she would leave for Miami to chase after some famous DJ and club hop her way to "DJ Bunny" bliss. All of that was made possible, of course, by her doting parents, who believed Liz was God's greatest gift to dance clubs everywhere.

I groaned, shoving her away and pulling a face at the glow stick. "Like twenty decibels down, babe. What are you talking about?"

"StellaVibe is hosting a *neon* show tonight," she screeched, her words rapid fire and trilling with her Argentinian American accent. "Can you believe that? *On your birthday!*" Liz leaped off my full-size mattress and started to beatbox techno music. Poorly.

I groaned, rubbing my eyes with the heels of my palms, and then looked over at the clock. I gasped and threw my cherry blossom print comforter off my legs, stumbling out of bed. "Jesus *Christ*, Liz, I'm like forty-five minutes late! You couldn't have stabbed my head half an hour earlier?"

"We're gonna get *crunk*," she continued, dropping it low— again, poorly—and ignoring my distress.

"Not if I get fucking fired," I snapped.

She sobered, standing. "You really should do something about your potty mouth. It's going to get you fired."

I gave her a glare.

"Relax, birthday girl. I got your coffee to-go, your outfit is right here, and I made you a peanut butter and jelly sandwich for breakfast." Lizette smoothed her sleek, black hair away from her face like she'd been awarded the title of Miss Birthday BFF Salt Lake City. Honestly, she had the perfect, perky tits for beauty pageants, so... believable. "And I called your boss to let him know you're sick today. Which is why you'll be late. You're welcome."

"You did *what?*" I gasped. *Oh no. Oh very much no.* "Liz, please tell me you're joking. Brady will see through that."

"He can't prove you're *not* sick," she countered with scrunched-up brown eyes.

"He's a doctor," I reminded her bluntly. And an ass. Dr. Amos Brady, the Grumpasaurus Rex with a medical license, barely tolerated me as an employee, let alone a *lying* employee. I was probably one mistake away from getting fired, and I wasn't even a bad scheduling operator. I got a little spacey when I had a vision for an art piece I wanted to get home to and work on, but for the most part, I stayed incredibly tolerant of his gruff lectures.

"Okay, okay, I'm joking," she soothed. "Relax. You think I would call your boss? You make him sound like a terrorist." She shuddered.

"He is," I growled, grabbing the outfit she'd laid out on my bed and wiggling my way into it. "And the day you call my boss and tell him I'm sick," I continued, my voice muffled as I pulled the white lace blouse over my face, "is the day I have to move back in with my parents. Because he'll fire me."

"Okay, okay, sorry," she muttered, staring at her manicured nails. "But you're still going out tonight, right?"

"If I don't get fired," I said, pronouncing each word clearly and spearing her with a wide-eyed look.

"Packed you a lunch, too," she added.

"Fine. Thank you. I love you and appreciate you. Where are my shoes?"

She held them up with a beauty pageant smile.

I managed to get my wild hair in a messy bun, and three minutes later, I had my lunch bag, backpack, keys, and coffee balanced precariously in my arms as I threw myself into the seat of my clunky silver sedan. It, like my job, was on its last, sputtering legs. But they both had to hang in there because I had no money.

As I sat in traffic with my scalding-hot coffee in one hand and my phone in the other—it was standstill traffic, don't give me that look—a text pinged in from my mom.

Mom: Happy birthday, beautiful!

I smiled, clicking on the message to type a quick reply before traffic moved up.

June: Thanks, mom! I got the flip flops you sent. GLITTRY!

Mom: Lol. I knew you would like them. But they shed so keep them outside. Luv u

Traffic crawled forward, and I let my phone clatter to the middle console before moving up again. I sipped the coffee, willing it to wash away my headache and clear my gunky lungs. Salt Lake City had horrible air, especially in the summer, and like everyone else, it bothered my airways if I sucked in the smog too deeply. That morning, my seasonal allergies and the pollution had conspired to wrap their phlegmy tentacles around my lungs, and I struggled to breathe worse than usual as I made my way through traffic slowly.

My phone dinged again, this time with a "happy little trees" Bob Ross ringtone. That would be Instagram. I checked it at another stoplight and realized it was a private message to my art account.

Archer Holmeyer: Hey! I saw your stuff—great work. I'm looking for an artist to paint a mural in my daughter's room. What do you charge?

Elation trilled through me. *Okay, maybe this day isn't so bad after all.* I would have to wait for a quiet moment in the office to reply with my rates, but an art gig? Those didn't come along often for me.

I had graduated from the Ellis Art Institute three years before, and I loved my art, but I didn't fit into the fine art space. Teaching wasn't exactly my thing either, so I hadn't decided what to do with my talents yet. I painted solely for myself and posted the paintings on Instagram hoping to catch the interest of clients. Occasionally, I got commissions or interest in my watercolors and oil paintings, but a mural would be a first for me.

Feeling lighter, I finished the drive and turned into the parking lot of a long, modern, orthopedic surgical center situated at the heart of the medical district. Traffic hadn't been so bad that morning, so miracle of miracles, I ended up only five minutes late.

I liked my job a lot; it had great hours, decent pay, and had been easy to learn. I had a desk with a squishy chair, and the office smelled like vanilla and antiseptic. Too good to be true? It was. They had a really hard time keeping scheduling operators longer than six months.

Because my boss was a dick.

I drew in a steadying breath, pulling on all my patience reserves and reminding myself that the salary was worth it. They bought me takeout every Friday. The benefits were choice. And hey, Dr. Brady was only human… ish. He might actually have been part gorgon; it was hard to be sure. But the worst he could do was fire me, and then I'd get to find a new job with a boss who didn't act like he lived in a lair and drank virgin blood for breakfast. *Silver linings, June. You got this.*

Plus, it was my birthday. What could go wrong on my birthday?

I breezed into the office with my favorite white purse on my shoulder and a determination to be perfectly cordial and non-combative with Dr. Brady. As a birthday gift to him. Because I was a goddess of love and generosity, and no six-foot-brooding-tall, dark, and handsome neurosurgeon was going to steal that from me. It wasn't his fault he had the bedside manners of a petulant chimpanzee. He had to have been born that way. Or maybe he had been scarred by a tragic lover in his past. I would work extra hard to be charitable and understanding of his unfortunate demeanor.

I slid my purse to the floor beside my desk, which curved along the wall of the posh waiting room furnished with masculine touches. My two co-workers and fellow receptionists already had their computers up and running. Katherine had a murky-looking smoothie of questionable contents at her elbow, and Maxine sat primly in her chair, clicking away at her schedule in her crisp, three-piece white suit and bright aqua pumps. I looked down at my outfit and cringed.

I had thrown on whatever Liz had put together without looking, and I had some regrets. For starters, my pants were a size too small and borderline yoga pants. But they had pockets, so they were work pants, right? But then my top. Oh, God, why hadn't I looked at my top before now? I had thrown on a white lace shirt, which was normally fine, but I'd worn my hot pink bra underneath, and the lace had a keyhole opening in the back that exposed the pink bra strap.

I snatched up the navy blue cardigan I kept on the back of my chair and prayed I didn't sweat to death trying to cover my unprofessional stripper bra. Why did I even own that thing?

Before my butt could hit the chair, a message on our inter-office communication software dinged on my desktop. With a sigh, I clicked the mouse, typed in my password, and pulled up the feed.

Dr. Brady: My 9 on 6.13 is supposed to be Andrews' patient, not mine.

I massaged my temples, plunking myself in my chair and pulling up the multi-colored schedule. In our orthopedic surgical center, there were nine MDs and several PAs along with an army of nurses and two anesthesiologists. Each of our doctors had privileges at the three surrounding hospitals, and managing their schedules between their own surgical center, the hospitals, and the clinic, could sometimes be a logistical nightmare.

However, I scheduled patients for Brady, Andrews, and Collins, and only one of those three doctors made me want to walk in front of a semi.

I pulled up the green tab for Dr. Brady, checked the patient notes and file from behind my desk, and then sent him a brisk — but patient! — message.

June: The referral from his GP named you, Dr. Brady, for localized neck pain.

I frowned at the patient's notes, trying to understand why we had such a large file for him.

Dr. Brady: Andrews and I know this patient — he has a new GP but it's a shoulder problem.

How the hell would I know that? I thought with a flash of annoyance. *No, June. Patience. Now you know. Just fix it and move on.*

Dr. Brady: I emailed you his detailed records and history this morning.

I just got here, asshole! I scheduled it according to his referral. Jesus.

June: Okay, I will fix that. My mistake.

I pulled up Mr. Larsey's file, found his phone number, and dialed it. It rang twice, and then an elderly man answered. "Hello?" he asked.

"Hello, this is June Matthews with the Salt Lake City Orthopedic Care Center. Is this Gordon Larsey?"

"Oh, yes," he said brightly.

"Mr. Larsey, I apologize for this, but I had a miscommunication with scheduling you yesterday. I was told that we need to schedule you with Dr. Andrews, does that sound right?"

"No," Gordon said, and his voice took on a hard edge. "You've done this to me every time! I need to see Dr. Brady for my neck pain."

Patience. Patience. "I understand, Mr. Larsey. I saw the referral, and we are so happy to get you taken care of. Sometimes our medical team consults within the center, and given your records and previous scans, Dr. Brady and Dr. Andrews feel very confident that Dr. Andrews can—"

"I want to talk to your supervisor," the patient snapped.

I swallowed a sigh. "Of course," I said brightly. "Let me put you on hold."

Katherine glanced at me, her black-lacquered nails doing a tap dance on her keyboard. "Carla doesn't have the patience for that first thing in the morning."

"Neither do I," I muttered. Before I could go in search of Carla, our office manager, another message pinged through the portal.

Dr. Brady: I need MRI for J. Kauffman. Was supposed to come in yesterday.

I had absolutely no control over how quickly imaging centers and outside services sent files to our office, and he knew that very well. I ignored his message and hopped out of my chair, patting my unruly, red curls in their messy bun, and straightening my cardigan—like a marginally tidy appearance was going to help Carla's mood when I told her she had a cranky patient to deal with at 8:08 in the morning.

I found Carla in the nurse's station, organizing patient files for the day so each doctor could find their correct files at the correct time. A stylish forty-something woman with dark skin and full lips, Carla completely personified the gorgeous corporate maverick ideal. She kept her hair natural and curly, and I could easily imagine her on a high rise somewhere, sipping a dry martini and laughing with her socialite friends.

And really, Carla was the boss I wish I had. In a way, she was everyone's boss, but I wished I could defer to her directly. She'd been reading a "leadership book" for the last week and a half, and although she shouted corny things like, "Transparent is trusting!" and "What we do matters, but who we help matters more," the idea that she cared about our potential as staff made me feel all cozy inside.

That said, she wasn't a morning person.

"Good morning," I said brightly.

Carla gave me a once-over. "Why do you look like someone forgot the boba in your boba tea?"

Accurate. Still stings. Thanks so much. "I have a Mr. Larsey who wants to be scheduled with Dr. Brady, but Dr. Brady says no, and he wants him to be scheduled with Dr. Andrews."

"And you told him this?" she asked, double-checking some files against her schedule on Dr. Frazier's file holder.

"Yes, and I already scheduled him with Dr. Brady because that's what the referral from his GP said, but apparently that was a mistake. And now he wants to talk to my manager."

"Lord alive," she muttered, slamming down another stack of files. She gave me an exasperated look. "It's too early in the morning for this."

"It is," I agreed, tapping my hands together nervously.

"I'll handle it." She picked up her leadership book off the counter. She'd been carrying it everywhere like a preacher and her bible. "Double check with Dr. Brady. Always."

"Got it," I said, stretching my mouth uncertainly.

She clacked away in her black stiletto heels, and I blew out a breath. Crisis one averted. No big deal.

Jackie, the blond nurse just to my left, gave me a sympathetic face. Patients were, arguably, the best and worst parts of our jobs. When I returned to my desk, I had three other messages from Dr. Brady.

Dr. Brady: MRI?

Dr. Brady: Keep my sched free on Thurs next week after 2. Thank you.

Dr. Brady: Kauffman is my 11 today. Need MRI.

"Maybe you should send a nurse to take his blood pressure," Katherine suggested. Her bright, unnaturally red hair had been pulled into a retro-styled finger wave updo, and she had on a wispy shawl—her signature style. Katherine read palms on the weekends, but I didn't need my life line read to know it had a rocky trajectory lately.

I sat down hard and tapped back with unnecessary force.

June: Will call the imaging center when they open at 9. Will clear your sched.

I immediately blocked off his hours from two to five on Thursday, blowing out a relieved breath that he had either checked beforehand, or I'd gotten lucky and he had no patients booked that day.

The rest of the morning went by in a blur. Between all three doctors and their patients, sorting out their files and faxing off requests for records, and filing new patient paperwork, I was starting to really sweat under the cardigan that was less than appropriate for early June. I decided I was definitely going to get myself a cupcake for lunch. It was my birthday, and I wasn't sure where I would find a single cupcake, but I would buy it. Because I'd earned it.

After giving a patient their stack of forms to fill out, I got another message from toned and tetchy Dr. Amos Brady.

Dr. Brady: Come to my office.

Katherine leaned over, her soft, wide cheeks sucked in with exaggerated concern for the drama unfolding on my computer screen. "Oooh," she said, ending on a high pitch.

I gave her a manic smile. "It's fine. Maybe he just wants to wish me a happy birthday." Katherine snorted, rolling her blue eyes and turning back to her computer.

Dr. Brady didn't wish anyone a happy anything. I constantly took complaints for his brusque bedside manners, and if he wasn't the most talented spinal surgeon in the city, he'd probably never get referrals. But he was the best.

And the actual worst.

I re-routed my calls to Maxine and slumped off through the office door to the nurses' station in the back. Dr. Brady's office had been tucked away in the back with the other MDs, and I wound my way through the long hallways, past the lounge and exam rooms to where his door stood open to his modest-sized office.

He had a window overlooking the parking lot out back, and his desk, shaped like an L, took up a good majority of the office. He had his diplomas framed on the wall beside the window, and absolutely zero personal pictures or mementos anywhere to be found. I was absolutely certain he spent his weekends watching C-Span reruns and skinning helpless animals.

His looks told a jarringly different story, though. Even in a lab coat and dress shirt, the smoothly defined contours of his biceps strained against starchy, white fabric, as if begging to be free and rubbed down with tanning oil. His glossy, dark brown hair had been styled in a soft wave that flicked charmingly over his left ear, and his eyes, dark like coffee beans, stared at me under the hard, black slashes of his straight eyebrows. He had a little scar on his chin, just under his perfectly kissable, bronze lips, and I could sharpen my charcoal pencil on his razor-sharp jaw.

I knocked on the door frame and gave him my most winning smile. "Hey, Dr. Brady. What's up?"

His square, million-dollar finger tapped a file on his desk. "Kauffman's MRI."

Dread thwacked me in the chest like a paintball to the ribs. "Ah. Right. I did call the office, but they said they'd have to get back to me."

"And did they?" he asked. His voice tickled up my arms, low and deceptively soothing.

"Ah, no."

"Did you follow up?" He leaned back in his chair and folded his hands over his stomach.

I tried to keep my attention on his face and not the tantalizing peek of his perfect body under the outline of his white shirt. "I didn't."

"June," he said, scowling, "I can't treat Mr. Kauffman if I don't have his records."

No shit, Sherlock. "I can follow up with them now, but—"

"But it's 10:45 and the patient will be here any minute," he finished, still scowling.

Patience, June. Patience. "Okay, well, faxing only takes a minute. I'll get through to them and explain the situation. I can have it by the time you see him."

"You hope," he pointed out with a frown of consternation. "I thought the barrage of reminders I sent you this morning would be enough, but maybe I need to start writing things on your forehead. You can check it during the dozen bathroom trips you take instead of making calls."

My mouth popped open. The voice in my head chanting *patience, patience* started to hiss, *payback, payback.* "How do you—I don't take—"

"Spare me," he said, rolling his eyes and standing from his desk before grabbing the file in front of him. "I have a conference call with UCHealth, and then I'll see Kauffman. With his MRI."

I pressed my lips together hard. "Maybe *you* should call the imaging center, Dr. Brady, if you're that concerned."

He laughed, a short bark that filled the office. "June, are you really suggesting that you're so bad at your job, you need the MD to take over for you?"

You toad-skinned, limp-dick, maggot-brained —

"Do better or go home," he added with one last contemptuous look before breezing past me in a cloud of woodsy cologne and antibacterial soap.

I felt my curls start to shake with my anger. Sweat pooled under my arms, and my heart beat furiously because I did about as well with confrontation as I did with insults to my intelligence. I got it a lot — red, curly hair, big, green eyes, and a small frame. I looked like a pocket doll, and people generally assumed I had plastic for brains, too.

I blocked his path, scowling furiously. Dr. Brady stopped, his dark eyes widening in surprise.

"You just went through four receptionists in less than a year — so you tell me. Do you want me to go home?" I challenged.

He considered me, his eyes roving over my features, his one hand in his lab coat pocket and the other cupping the file. Finally, he said, "I'm not your nanny, Ms. Matthews. Go home if you want, or you can stay and do your job. It's up to you." He stepped around me and disappeared toward the conference room.

I shook like a jacked-up washing machine. "That *pompous —*" I started to seethe, but stopped when Carla breezed by with a clipboard and her "leadership book."

She gave me a suspicious look. "What did he say?"

"Nothing," I ground out. I cracked my neck and marched down the hall toward my desk. "If he wants diligence, I'll give him diligence."

TWO
Amos

I saw my receptionist's bra, and then she set me on fire. Somehow that ended up being my fault, but as per usual, that's how my luck turned out.

Maybe the fussy patients and overly sensitive receptionists had been right to complain—I did give off crotchety neighbor vibes. But I didn't think it was so extreme to expect my receptionist to do her only job.

The anger that radiated out from her tiny frame was almost enough to make me feel some guilt. Almost. But I got the feeling that June Matthews responded better to a little uncomfortable nudging rather than gentle coaxing. She might not like it, and she might not have been pushed a day in her cushy, middle-class life, but she would respond to it, and we would both move on with our lives more content with our jobs and more aware of our roles in the workplace.

If she didn't, she would leave, and I would find someone else.

Although Andrews and Collins would probably kill me. They liked June. She had a cute, friendly artist vibe that made our patients feel at ease, and she had learned the system pretty quickly.

Her enormous, Pixar-like green eyes stared at me, wide with incredulity and shimmering with unadulterated hatred. *Sorry June. You're about as terrifying as a baby panda. Keep trying to intimidate me, though. It's entertaining.*

I breezed by her, hoping our interaction would spur her toward more efficient pursuits, and headed for the conference room. I heard her mutter something under her breath, and I felt my lips twitch up. She'd get there. It wasn't like I was asking her to survive residency. I shuddered at the memory.

In our small conference room, Andrews lounged in an office chair. He had the back tilted as far down as it would go, and he kept his eyes closed and hands resting on his stomach when I entered. The man looked like he ate an apple and a healthy puff of oxygen every day, and his long, string bean fingers had interlocked over his concave stomach. I knew he ate—I saw it. But the man was as stressed as they came. He had like a million kids—okay, seven—and worked as some kind of volunteer clergyman for his church in all his non-existent free time.

He opened one brown eye hesitantly. "You're interrupting my five-minute nap."

If I remembered right, his wife had just had a baby four months before. I didn't imagine he got a lot of sleep. "The future of brain imaging waits for no man," I said with some amusement.

With a sigh, Irving Andrews sat up straight and rolled his chair to the oval conference table. We had a phone set up at the end, and in a minute or two, my colleague at UCHealth in Colorado would call to discuss using their MRI 3T to add some necessary data to the study we'd been working on since my fellowship.

Our real ace in the hole, a doctor and the closest person I could call to a friend, Dr. Cade, had left the city to live in some small town in Idaho near his brother. But the man was brilliant, and if Andrews and I could supply the funding and obtain the right equipment, I knew his brains would do the rest.

"The NIH grant was a no-go," Irving said, rubbing a long hand over his thin face. "Although, no surprise there."

I scratched my hairline, taking a seat next to him. "Yeah, that was a slim chance. Melanie didn't seem hopeful even when she wrote it. There's still the CANN grant. Melanie has that almost finished."

"Yeah, I just wish we had better news for Cade, but here we are."

The phone rang, but at the same moment, I got a ding on my work phone from our inter-office messaging system. Andrews motioned for me to get it and answered the phone on speaker.

I looked at my screen while Andrews and Sterling greeted each other.

June: A. Hernandez just finished her bloodwork. She says schedule for a month?

My brows snapped together. What kind of question was that? If I'd written on her papers that I wanted to see her in a month, then that's when I wanted to see her. She didn't need to confirm that with me.

Dr. Brady: Yes.

"… we got your proposal, and we'd love to schedule you, but we didn't hear back about your funding requests," Sterling said.

Andrews gave me a "here we go" look. "It looks like our NIH grant fell through, but we're working on the funding. Can you schedule us in the meantime?"

Sterling sighed over the other end. "I really wish I could. The demand has been pretty high, though."

"We're working on it," I said quickly. "We can cover forty percent, but the rest has to come from our grants. We've had bad luck with them falling through."

"Well, it's tight competition," Sterling admitted. "We're old friends, Amos, so I'll hold your spots for a little bit, but when will you know?"

"Not sure," I admitted, fiddling with my phone. "But I'm going as fast as I can."

"Okay. We all want this research to take off, and you and Cade are rock stars over there. Let's make it happen."

I smiled slightly to myself, but then my phone dinged again. I opened the app.

June: It's 4 weeks and 2 days from now. Is that ok?

How had she gotten worse at her job in the last ten minutes?

Dr. Brady: I don't care. As long as it fits the sched.

June: Just making sure!

I got a little wiggle of suspicion in my brain, but then my attention pulled back to Sterling as he began his update on the research he'd managed to compile, and the peer-reviewed studies on the cusp of publishing in journals around the world. Our research centered around connectomics, which aimed to map the neurons in the brain with precise, measurable images. We needed to use the latest technology to back up our claims, but getting the use of MRI 3T machines wasn't like renting a carpet cleaner. It was expensive and hard to schedule in ample time blocks.

My phone dinged.

Starting to feel the heat of irritation creep up my neck, I checked it again.

June: Got the MRI. Your 11 is here.

Dr. Brady: Stop texting me everything you do.

June: I'm using the bathroom. If that's ok?

Little twerp, I thought with pure vexation poking my temples. *Fine. Play games.*

Dr. Brady: No, it's not.

June: Already going. I'll update you later.

"Jesus," I muttered.

Andrew gave me a questioning look while Sterling continued his excited rundown of their progress. I shook my head. I could handle June.

And I certainly would.

June: Kauffman says appt. ASAP?

Dr. Brady: What does the paper say? YES

June: Your 6 on Friday canceled.

Dr. Brady: I can read a schedule, thnx.

June: Going to the bathroom.

June: It's almost my lunch, but I got F. Rocks MRI in.

June: M. Duschene called and wants to reschedule for 7.13. So I did that.

June: Bathroom break again lol.

June: Going to lunch. Maxie has my calls.

I'm going to strangle her, I thought darkly as I sat in my office, clicking through emails and trying to ignore my phone. June had been texting me nonstop for over an hour, and I thought I might hear that text tone in my dreams.

Reluctantly, I stood from my desk to go retrieve my salad from the staff lounge. June might be there, and she might end up with a grape tomato shoved up her nose if I got too close, but risks had to be taken. I'd done an extra thirty minutes of leg day that morning, and not only did I fully regret it, but I was also ravenous.

As I passed the nurses' station, I caught a wisp of conversation that almost caused me to pause and eavesdrop.

"… always redoes it! Like I can't manage!"

"I know, oh my God," the little blond nurse whispered to her black-haired coworker. "It's like they think we're all morons."

I frowned, continuing past them to the lounge. June and I hadn't been the only employees in the surgical center with disagreements—a general air of discord hung heavy in the clinic, and I noticed the constant frown between Carla's eyebrows as she looked from employee to employee, consulting her new book on leadership for solutions. It had been a long winter — lots of snow and wind, and it had only let up recently. Maybe the sunshine would put everyone in a better mood.

I turned the corner into the staff lounge and then immediately froze.

June had her cardigan off, and I realized why she had been wearing it. Her white, lace blouse clung tightly to her generous curves, and the back had a giant keyhole exposing the milky skin of her back and the garish, twinkling rhinestones on her hot pink bra. Even through the sides of the lace top, I could see the hearts and bling through the material. She looked like Office Stripper Barbie. And could her pants get any tighter? Were those even work appropriate?

She was bent over one of the tables in front of a cupcake. There was a single candle in the middle of the frosting, and she had an old box of matches that failed to light with every strike. I had entered somewhat behind her, and she looked up just as my eyes had finished raking over her figure.

Her gaze squinted distrustfully. I scowled. "What, Matthews?"

"Stop staring at me."

"I'm not staring," I said in monotone, and walked past her.

"Yes, you are," she replied with an accusatory point. "I'm hot. Leave it alone."

"You're the one drawing more attention to your stripper bra," I pointed out.

June's face went strawberry red. "Are you for real?"

I held up a placating hand and went to the fridge. "Forget I said anything."

June bent back to her task after one last, dubious glance over her shoulder at me. "Stupid, ancient matches," she muttered, striking another one that flared briefly before dying.

I reached for the fridge handle, watching her with a mix of curiosity and wariness.

"Light," she growled. *Strike. Hiss. Fizzle.* "Goddammit!" she shouted.

"June," I snapped. Cursing was my least favorite form of communication in any setting, but I absolutely would not tolerate it from *my* employee during work hours.

She rounded on me. "*What,* Brady?" As she spun, the unlit match flew out of her hand. In the middle of the table, a stack of napkins had been placed in a metal container. Somehow, the smoking, unlit match managed to find just the right waft of oxygen as it flew through the air, and as June faced me, eyes wide with consternation, the napkins erupted into flames behind her.

She inhaled sharply, whirling around to face the table. "Oh my *God.*"

I surged for the counter and grabbed a water bottle someone had left sitting there. But June had an even worse idea and lunged across the table to grab the napkins and… what? Throw them in the air like a bomb in an action movie? I didn't get the chance to find out what she *had* planned to do because she grabbed the napkins, swung toward the sink, and immediately realized that fire *burns*, and she let go with a shriek.

The flaming box of napkins flew right for me, landing hard on my shoe. The hem of my pants lit on fire.

June screamed.

I screamed.

The nurses ran in like a flock of dazed geese. I uncapped the water and doused my foot and the napkin holder. Smoke sizzled around us, filling the air with acrid, black smog.

June stared at me with her hands over her mouth. I glared at her.

An eruption of noise and chaos flooded through the staff lounge as everyone clamored and wanted to know if I'd been burned and what had happened and how my pants caught on fire.

I had eyes only for the chaotic mass of red curls and shocked, pink features of June Matthews. I threw the water bottle on the ground and shook my burned, soaking pant leg before storming up to her. "What pea-brained, *childish idiocy* were you doing in an office lounge *with fire*?" I heard myself roar.

The small crowd gasped. June's moss green eyes welled up with tears.

"Dr. Brady!" Carla barked from the back of the pack.

I clenched my jaw with resigned regret. Okay, so I hadn't meant to yell. But she could have hurt herself—or worse, the surgical center.

I looked over at the assembled crowd made up of nurses and the other receptionists, along with Dr. Black and Dr. Buchanon. Carla nudged to the front of the throng with her sharp, dark eyes pinned on me and her arms folded. I gestured toward the table. "We can't have fire in a medical facility."

"We don't talk to one another in this way, Dr. Brady," Carla snapped. Although her eyes did flit to June with some consternation. I put my hands on my hips. Seriously, how was I the one at fault here?

June sniffled, and a tear leaked out of the corner of her long-lashed eye. "I'm sorry. It's just… It's my birthday."

My internal groan echoed the sympathetic gasps of the nurses and staff. I might as well have wrapped her with rope and left her in front of a train. Villain mode activated.

"Were you harmed, Dr. Brady?" Carla asked briskly.

I looked down at my pant leg. The fabric on my black trousers had been singed and ruined beyond repair, but my skin barely smarted. "I'm fine," I clipped.

"Good, then I'd like to see you in our conference room."

I resisted the urge to sigh, and taking a step forward, I held out a hand to June. "Let me see your hands, first."

"Did she touch the fire?" Jackie gasped.

"She threw it at me," I said with no small amount of acidity.

"I'm fine," June said, and clasped her hands against her breasts again. Was it my imagination, or had her fear suddenly turned back to malice? A little shine of defiance lit in her eyes, and I mentally tucked that away for later. What had I done to her, exactly? She was the one who had lit me on fire.

"Staff meeting," Carla declared.

"Can't we just meet here?" Dr. Nayar drawled. She was, if possible, even more no-nonsense than I was, and had a breadstick from her lunch in her hand and a sour expression on her dark brown lips.

"Fine. Those who aren't here will get the announcement via email." Carla took a few steps back, putting her tall, thin frame further into the lounge near the corkboard along the back wall. She pulled on the hem of her navy blazer. "There have been *several* unsavory exchanges between personnel of *all* kinds," she said, hooking me with her gaze. I glared back sardonically.

"And I have become concerned about our team effort and staff morale," Carla continued. "As such, I have discussed it with Dr. Frazier and Dr. Vasquez, and we have agreed that a company retreat would do wonders for our collaborative spirit." She held up the leadership book like a preacher giving a sermon. "When we are willing to risk adventuring into the wilderness, and even becoming our own wilderness, we feel the deepest connection to our true self and to what matters the most."

I wasn't the only one who rolled my eyes.

"We've arranged for a retreat in the wilderness," Carla said, her tone leaving no room for argument. "And every employee will attend."

I didn't see how staying at some hotel in the woods, getting buzzed every night off cocktails, and sitting in a circle with our planners was going to do anyone any good, but if it pulled the attention off my growing "criminal record" in this place, then so be it. Frazier and Vasquez had controlling shares as partners, so if they had planned it with Carla, then there was little I could do about it.

"We have already booked a weekend in Jackson Hole, Wyoming." She gave us all a death glare. "There will be cabins. And hiking. And I don't care if you hate the outdoors. We need it."

A few groans came from people scattered throughout the crowd, but most of the employees seemed thrilled.

"When?" I asked, putting a hand in my pocket.

"Clear your weekend for June twenty-fourth through the twenty-sixth," she said. "The office staff will work hard to clear your work schedules, and we will make this happen because this," she said, gesturing to the room as a whole, "is not going to fly."

I had a date with a tennis player that weekend. Figured.

"If you can't find childcare," Carla continued, addressing the room beyond June and me, "please come speak to me. We will do everything we can to help you find arrangements. Okay?"

A murmured response rippled through the gathering, and then they dispersed. June gave me an accusatory scowl.

I raised my eyebrows. "What?"

"This is your fault."

I felt my expression slam back down. "How?"

"You were looking at my bra, and you made me uncomfortable, and then you *yelled* at me."

"You're wearing a shirt that shows your underwear. How is that my fault?"

She gasped, looking at Carla. "Are you hearing this?"

Carla examined her nails. "You are both terrible. Teamwork, Matthews and Brady. Teamwork."

Oh, I wanted to work June, alright. I wanted to work her to the bone until she dragged her tired little pixie body home and cried to her mommy and daddy every night about how horrible her mean boss was.

I also wanted to see her bra again, but I forced myself to put that aside.

"I can work as a team," June said, lifting her chin a fraction. "I always do."

"Right, if the team is neolithic and oh-for-ten on the leader board," I growled.

"Stop," Carla snapped. "Out of the lounge. Both of you."

I grabbed my salad from the fridge, and without so much as another word, I banished myself back to my office. Teamwork? I could do teamwork. I'd make Matthews captain of Team Work Until You Cry. I wasn't going to put myself under the guillotine by firing another scheduling operator. By the time I was done with her, she'd be begging to leave.

THREE
June

I had definitely underestimated Dr. Brady's potential for entering his villain era. My mistake had been thinking he perpetually lived in a state of evil, mustache-twirling depravity, but I had been so very wrong about that. It got so much worse.

It wasn't just the soft, barking reprimands if my lunch ran a minute later than it should have, or the increased workload of moving his patients from the end of June to July for the retreat. No, actually, the worst part was the Digital Initiative. Dr. Brady had informed me the day after the "incident" that we would be digitizing every record in the surgical center from 1999 to 2015, and he thought I was the perfect one for the job.

But could I do this thing during normal work hours? No, he'd said. I would be paid overtime, of course, but it needed to be done outside office hours, from five to seven in the evening. Lately, he'd been pushing it to more like nine.

How, you ask, could he enforce such a thing?

He stayed late every fucking night. If his surgeries didn't run long—which they usually did—then he went to the physical therapy gym and worked out for obscene amounts of time. Then he'd come back to his office, shower, and smelling like cinnamon, he'd sit in his office doing paperwork. If I tried to leave, he would *strongly suggest* I stay as long as he did to ensure the Digital Initiative got done before we left for our retreat at the end of the month.

Even on the Friday everyone else had been approved to leave and travel to Jackson Hole, Dr. Brady had sent me a text reminding me that he had a last-minute surgery that day and that he would need me to come in and update the patient's records.

I knew for a fact that he could easily do that himself, but I was at the whims of a madman.

As I punched my foot through the pantleg of my jean shorts, Liz watched me with uncharacteristic concern. "Girl... I do not feel right leaving you like this." She leaned against the wall, studying me and twirling the pull strings of her corset bralette. She wore it over jeans that had been so purposefully shredded all the way up to her coochie, I wondered why she wore them at all.

She had slicked her long, black hair into a high ponytail, and her bangs covered half her eyes. She looked like a model with her glossy, caramel lips, and I looked like a camp counselor who'd been mauled by a mountain lion.

Liz was headed for Miami, having paid her rent for three months, and fully intended to DJ Bunny her way through every club in the city. Over the course of two weeks, she had watched me slowly decay into a dry-skinned, dull-eyed, pathetic, moaning zombie.

I hiked the shorts up, buttoning them around my waist and over my belly button. I'd chosen a cut off, T-shirt-style crop top, and I looked down to survey my outfit. Oh, my God. I'd actually lost weight. I *never* lost weight. I had the body of a thirteenth century English peasant that stayed stocky and plump to survive the harsh winter famines. Apparently, all it took was a relentless work schedule and a domineering, cranky boss to shed some pounds.

Liz gasped. "*Guuurl.*"

"Oh, my God," I moaned, patting my soft belly. "Look at this. Look what he's doing to me."

"I am gonna report him," she said, chewing gum loudly and inspecting her long, coffin-shaped nails. "Report him to the BBB or something."

"Does that apply to doctors?" I asked weakly. "I don't think it does. I watched this documentary about a surgeon who literally butchered people on his operating table for *years* and no one did anything about it. I doubt they would care how he treats his secretary."

Liz gasped, "Wait, shit, wasn't that guy a neurosurgeon?"

The blood drained from my face. Oh my Hell, was I working for Jack the Ripper? I looked around my filthy bedroom, scattered with unwashed clothing and a fine layer of dust. The psycho killer had worked me so hard, I hadn't had any time to clean it. "You think he's a murderer?" I wondered in a hollow voice.

"Shit, girl," Liz stood, shaking her head. She took my shoulders in her hands. She smelled like fancy perfume and hair gel. "We've got to find you a new job. I'll tell you what—come to Miami with me. The place I'm staying in is *gorgeous*. I'll tell Papi all about your abuse and he'll fly you out. Swear to God."

I sighed, letting my head fall. "I can't. You know I can't."

"Oh, what, the mural thing?" she asked incredulously.

Yeah, the mural thing. I'd actually managed to land that gig with the dad who wanted his daughter's wall painted. I had told him that as soon as my workload decreased—it *had* to, eventually, right?—I could take some time to sketch up a mural and send it to him for approval before coming to his house. I had tried to sketch it on the weekends, but I was so drained, I mostly slept and watched HGTV.

Liz clicked her tongue. "Well, maybe you should talk to *his* boss at this retreat thing. The bastard has to lighten up at some point. What did you do to piss him off, again?"

"I set his pants on fire," I said sullenly. Liz pulled a face like that was actually pretty bad. "Yeah," I sighed. I shoved my feet into my worn canvas shoes and bent down to pick up the pink duffel bag at my feet. I'd already packed everything else I would need for the camping retreat thing in the back of my car. "I'm sure he'll get over it."

"Just get even," she snapped her fingers. "Get. Even. Look at you. He wore you *down,* girl. You can't let a man do you dirty like that."

I sniffed, frowning. "You're right."

"Hell yes, I'm right," Liz said, curling her lip. "Get him. I'll text you ideas. We'll make him wish he never messed with the red-headed temptress June. You're feisty, babe," she reminded me.

I lifted my chin. "I *am* feisty. And I've got like a six-hour drive to think of ways to make him miserable."

"Get it," she said. She took my shoulders again, this time from behind, and marched me out of the small, outdated bedroom to our tiny living room/dining room/itsy bitsy kitchen combo living space. "Give him hell, June."

It only took us ten steps to reach the front door, and I turned to give her a hug. "Thank you. I'll make him miserable. I promise."

"Yes," she said, squeezing me tightly. "That's my girl. Text me as soon as you get to this woodsy thing they're making you do."

I snorted. "Okay. Fly safe."

On the drive to the surgical center, I let my anger simmer. Dr. Brady had worked me so hard, I'd forgotten to be mad at him. But I was mad now. Hell yes, I was mad. And I'd find a way to get even with him. I ran through ideas in my head, daydreaming about finding a way to get him chased by a bear in the woods or dunked in a muddy lake. Oooh, he would hate that. He was always so clean and perfectly pressed—I would have bet my next overtime check that he had OCD or something.

Were bear pheromones a thing? Where did one buy pheromones? I could douse all his clothing in it and watch from a safe distance while he got chased down.

Wait, was that murder?

No, no, no, I reasoned. *The bear is the murderer. You'd be the… instigator.*

It was probably a good thing I had no idea where to get pheromones, on second thought.

As I pulled up to the center, I got a coughing fit, interspersed with sneezes and gagging, and I rummaged around frantically in my car for a loose fast-food napkin. The further we got into summer, the worse my allergies got. The news had said the pollen was bad this year because of all the rain and snow we'd gotten in the winter, and I knew from experience that the smog over Salt Lake City could get nasty. Whatever it was, my allergies were not having it.

After coughing until I half expected to find brain matter on my tissue, I blew my nose, popped an allergy pill, and staggered my way to the dark, empty building.

What an absolute asshat. No one else was here, and I should have been on my way to Jackson Hole, but instead, I had to update a patient's chart with information easily available to Dr. Asshat. He had probably finished the surgery early this morning and was halfway to Jackson Hole by now.

Cursing my boss under my breath, I unlocked the front doors and stomped over to my computer at the front desk. The AC kicked on just as I sat in my chair, making me jump and look around the deserted building. It was kind of creepy with the lights off and no one else around.

In fact, most, if not all, of the medical district tended to shut down on Fridays, and we often remained the only busy building because we had too many patients and not enough doctors. Dr. Brady had been known to fit some in on Saturdays, too, probably because he'd sold his soul to a demon in exchange for a medical license. Only soulless servants of the Demon King would *want* to work on a Saturday.

Hurrying, because the darkened building was starting to give me dystopian zombie movie vibes, I clicked into the portal, entering my username and password, and rushed to finish the inane task. I clickety-clacked my way through it, glancing around nervously and picking at my chipped nails while I waited for things to load.

Finally, I finished, and with an assertive *tap* of the enter key, I logged out and let the screen go dark.

Rolling my lips between my teeth, I sat back in my chair and swung back and forth, surveying the tomb-like silence of the medical practice. Odd, how full of life it usually was, and I had never really noticed.

I glanced over my shoulder at the shadowed hallway that led back to the exam rooms, and then further back, the MDs offices.

A slow, evil smile crept up my face. Dr. Brady's office was back there. And he was miles away.

I hopped up from the chair, grabbing my purse and tiptoeing down the hallway, as if there was anyone to hide from anyway, and then fast walked my way to his office. It would be locked, but he had given me the keys to the building the night before.

Big mistake, mister.

When I reached his office door, bearing the practical black and white placard that read "Dr. Amos Brady," I fished the set of keys from my purse and flipped them on the ring one by one until I found the one with duct tape labeled "Brady."

Score.

I unlocked it tentatively, stuck my head around the door, and peered inside. Perfectly tidy, quiet, and dark, his office sat there with arms wide open, just waiting to be vandalized. Or snooped. Or something. I didn't know what I wanted to do, but it was his *private office*. There were so many possibilities.

I flicked on the lights and started to explore. Lots of degrees and certificates. Boring. Medical files piled in neat little stacks. Super boring. A gym bag with perfectly washed and pressed workout clothing and some travel-sized toiletries. Not even a condom in there.

Gasp.

Was he an LDS bishop or something? My parents were Mormon, and I did love them for it, but the devout members followed strict rules. Not that I had jived with the religion as I grew older, but I knew their culture better than I knew actual laws. No "canoodling" before marriage was one of the rules.

Come to think of it, Dr. Brady hated cursing, too, and everyone in the building knew to watch their mouths around him. Another Mormony thing.

I had to know. If he really was a bishop, which was a sort of volunteer pastor for the local branch, there would absolutely be evidence. A Book of Mormon, a Jesus poster… picture. Whatever.

I went to the desk and opened drawers, looking for missionary pamphlets or a book by one of the main church leaders called apostles. In the drawer just below his keyboard, I found a yellow leather book that looked like it cost *a lot* of money. It had a bee stamped on its cover.

Bingo. That was definite Mormon shit right there.

I snatched it up and plopped my butt in his sleek, black leather computer chair. It hissed, lowering smoothly, and I rubbed the slick arms. "Oooh," I whispered in awe. Nice chair.

Launching my feet off the floor to send the chair spinning, I opened the book to the first page. I expected to find scripture passages, church meeting notes, or maybe a journal — another LDS custom — but that was not at all what I had found.

It was a poem.

> *You set me out to*
> *chase perfection,*
> *And forced me to be framed within your image,*
> *You taught me not to grieve her,*
> *Saying I must, "Be A Man"*
> *And after all that I've Accomplished*
> *I still cannot find a single prescription*
> *that will cure your lack of pride in me.*

My jaw dropped, and I slammed my feet on the plastic floor guard. Dr. Dark and Surly was a poet. I turned the page and found another one.

The simple way you smiled,
How it crinkled up your nose,
The complicated way you're brilliant,
And your mind keeps me on my toes,
The effortless way you dance like dust in sunbeams,
warms me to my core.

I gasped out loud. *Is this about a girl?*

I turned another page, launched myself into another spin, and kicked my legs straight out in front of me while I spun and read his poetry. It was so innocent and beautiful. I'd read a lot of poetry — the artist bunch and all — but his was so unassuming. So real. He just wanted to record what he felt. That, or there was some weird Cyrano shit going on here and someone was writing poems for him.

The chair stopped suddenly, jolting me to the side. I sucked in a surprised breath.

Dr. Brady had his hands on the arms of the chair and leaned over me with a dangerous glint in his chocolate eyes. "Matthews," he said, his voice low and husky like he hadn't used it all day.

My breath froze in my lungs. I shrank back in the chair, gripping the book in my shaking hands.

Fuuuuuuuuuuck.

He smelled like cinnamon and was dressed in a black, athletic T-shirt that stretched across his broad shoulders enticingly. His biceps flexed as he leaned closer to me, nearly putting us nose to nose. "What are you doing?"

An inarticulate sound escaped my throat. He plucked the yellow journal from my fingers, scowling. "I, uh," I stammered.

Dr. Brady slammed the book closed with one hand and then leaned around me again, pressing the book between his enormous hand and the chair arm. "You, what?" he challenged softly. His body caged me in, fully preventing any escape from the chair.

I wonder where he'll hide my body, I thought.

"Matthews," he snapped.

I jumped, lifting my eyes to his. "Yeah?" I asked weakly.

"I asked what you're doing."

I swallowed hard, drinking in his long lashes and the dark, slashing eyebrows that looked like they'd been painted with the steadiest, fading stroke of a paintbrush. "I'm... snooping," I admitted, dazed.

"Hm," he hummed, narrowing his eyes.

Wait, wait, wait, I thought with sudden alarm. *Why are my nipples getting hard? What is this? Shut the fuck up, body. We're in danger of being killed, not screwed.*

"You're going to be late if you don't get your rear end out of my office, in your car, and up to Jackson Hole."

I glanced down at his toned arms, still trapping me. "I, uh, you've got your…" I faltered. *Sir, you have your well defined, sexy arms dangerously close to wrapping around my body. And for some bizarre reason, there's a hormone monster inside of me that wants you to.*

He didn't move. "Something wrong?"

Sense sparked to life inside of me when I registered his tone. I lifted a scrunched scowl up to his now amused expression. "Oh, very funny." I swatted his arm. "Get off me."

Dr. Brady caught my hand and wrenched me to my feet with alarming ease. I would have crashed into him if he hadn't caught me by my upper arms in a firm grip. He lifted me slightly, so unconsciously strong, he brought me to my tiptoes. "If I find you in here again, you're going to regret it, Matthews."

I scoffed with confidence I didn't feel. "Oh, you'll do *what* exactly?"

He leaned forward slightly, sending a shiver down my arms. "Fuck around and find out, June."

I gasped. "You cursed."

He released me and then nudged my ass with his knee, propelling me toward the door. "Get out of my office."

I stumbled through the doorway, my heart screaming in fear, and nearly tripped in my haste to get as far away from that mortifying encounter as possible. Was he allowed to manhandle me like that? Wasn't that some kind of HR violation even if we had been outside work hours?

No, actually, more importantly, what kind of weirdo did it make me if I enjoyed the thrill of getting caught by him? Like, I was terrified and embarrassed, but there was just *something* about it that had felt different than our other encounters. Sexier.

I shook my head, skip-walking down the hall and then out the front doors. It was the adrenaline, I decided. Nothing else could account for my reaction.

FOUR
Amos

I'd almost had a stroke when I had seen June in my office. First
of all, she was the least sneaky spy in the history of spies. She
had left the light on—the only light in the building—and the
door wide open. And I'd heard the roll of wheels and squeak of
the chair spinning long before I had actually found her.

When I did, my first thought had been panic. She'd had my
journal in her delicate hands, and while her chair spun in a
smooth, rapid cycle, she'd stared at the page with a surprised look
on her face. As far as I could tell, anyway. She had been going tilt-
a-whirl fast, and I didn't understand how that didn't make her
puke. But my anger nearly fizzled out when I saw her legs
outstretched in front of her, wide apart like a kid on a tire swing,

and my annoyance was replaced with a twinge of something else. Something that admitted she was… cute?

I struggled to banish that thought and channel my outrage that she would dare to snoop in my office, even if I'd been an absolute a-hole to her for three weeks.

Thankfully, I managed to put some kind of fear into her pocket-sized body. She pushed my buttons like no one else did, and the urge to control her went beyond boss and employee. It was compulsive. Maddening.

The smell of her fruity bodywash and the little sheen of sweat glistening on the curve of her cleavage had distracted me completely. It was the most messed up cocktail of anger and lust I'd ever experienced. Something about June dressed down in shorts and a crop top made me want to see what she looked like on the side of the pool wearing next to nothing.

Dangerous thoughts.

Ironically, I'd come back for the notebook, intending to use my forced downtime to think and get some creativity on paper. I didn't care if June read my poetry — it was published for anyone to read if they looked up my name. But I *did* care that she had thought to snoop in my office. If I had to guess, she had been looking for a way to retaliate.

I wasn't about to let her get away with that.

I turned off the lights, locked the door, and headed out to the parking lot before I pressed the fob on my shiny sport utility vehicle. I loved that car. It was brand new, glossy, gunmetal gray, and upgraded to the nines. It had way more space and luxury than I really needed, but wasn't that kind of the point of luxury? I did it because I could.

I turned up a song by Halocene to full blast before I pulled into the gas station and filled up the tank. I wasn't a fan of road trips—too much time to think and no way of being productive. Who enjoyed that? No one could possibly enjoy that.

I got myself a water and some jerky before heading off into the middle of the West Coast's buttcrack. No offense, Idaho, but why? Why even live here? Cows and dirt.

There was nothing to look at before I got to Wyoming where I knew, at least, snow-capped mountains and green hills waited. Until then, it was a lot of flat, boring scenery punctuated with a few mountains through lower Idaho before I branched off to the remote Route 34.

As I nodded absently to a Theory of a Deadman song, I recognized a little silver sedan on the side of the road. Its hazards were on, and there didn't seem to be any other cars within sight of it on the deserted, old highway. I knew that car, but it couldn't be. Silver sedans, even old, beat-up ones, were a dime a dozen.

Then again, it could be June's car. Was her luck really that abysmal? June did seem to end up on the wrong side of the lucky coin toss more often than not, but surely her car wouldn't break down in an area with no cell service, miles from the closest gas station.

I slowed down, checking behind me, and then pressing my hazards lights to crawl up behind the car to make sure the driver was alright.

Sure enough, I'd seen that plate before. It was June.

I put the car in park and saw her eyes flicker to me in her rearview mirror. She immediately disappeared, ducking down. I snorted to myself. Like I hadn't seen her already. I put my sunglasses in the compartment next to my sun visor and undid the seatbelt. Everything in my car made satisfying whooshing sounds, which somehow never got old. I opened my door after checking that we were alone. We were. Frighteningly. Then I walked to June's side and leaned against the window frame.

She had her head against the steering wheel, and her windows were all the way down. She rotated her face to me, still keeping her forehead on the steering wheel. "Hey," she said.

I looked around the interior of the car. It was a disaster. A girl bomb of used water bottles, college sweatshirts, paint tubes and brushes, fast food wrappers, and unopened bills had exploded all over her worn fabric seats. It smelled like acrylic paint and potato chips. I gave her a confused look. "What happened?" I meant the car, but a good portion of my brain meant her life in general.

"I forgot to get gas."

It was even worse than bad luck. She was an airhead. I gave her an eyebrow raise. "For real?"

"Yeah," she said weakly.

I sighed, looking around at the deserted, arid landscape. Nothing for it. "Roll up your windows, grab your stuff, and lock the car."

She straightened, tapping her chipped, short fingernails on the steering wheel. She looked like she wanted to argue.

I opened her car door. "Okay, leave your windows open and doors unlocked. I'm sure you're right and no one will bother stealing this dumpster anyway."

She gave me an outraged look. Her wild, red hair had been clipped away from her face with a desperate-looking claw thing held together with springs and a prayer. Sweat beaded her brow and down her neck, sliding down her shirt, as if daring me to look. I didn't. I focused on her dark green eyes and the interesting fluttering thing her lashes were doing while she thought about the situation. Finally, she said, "Fine."

"I'm so glad you came to the only inevitable conclusion here," I muttered dryly. "I'll open the back for you."

"You're *so salty*," she said in exasperation, turning to her right to gather up some junk I had assumed was just trash. They were art supplies, apparently.

I made my way back to the SUV, punched a button on my key fob, and leaned against my door, waiting for her to lock up her car and gather her stuff.

She had a lot of stuff.

Eventually, I got tired of waiting, and I walked back to her, wrenched most of the bags from her arms, and towed everything—including her—back to my cool, shaded car so I could get out of Idaho's kiln.

"Wait, I need my—"

"I'll buy you one in town," I snapped.

"My laptop!" she finished with a little growl.

"Fine, get the laptop, but let's go."

She jogged back to the car, and with her generous, round rear end hanging out of the car door, her muffled voice shouted, "Aren't we coming back for the car, though?"

She couldn't pay me enough to make this drive again for her junkyard on wheels. I checked my smart watch, which was set to an analog display. "We're late, June," I said. "We can get it on the way back." I felt a bit guilty for making us so tardy, but I had needed to get that surgery done today. My patient had been in horrible pain, and I couldn't postpone her treatment for a stupid retreat. She was a seventeen-year-old kid who had fallen off a rock wall and could barely sit straight without crying. Carla could wait for that.

"They'll tow it!" she said frantically, straightening from the car and giving me a crazed look. "I can't afford that!"

"So, remember gas next time," I shot back heartlessly. I wasn't going to pretend like forgetting to fill your car with gas before a five-hour trip made any sense whatsoever. She gave me a downcast look. I sighed, ending it on a growl. "I'll call the local PD and tell them why it's there, and then I'll explain that we'll be back for it. Okay?"

"Okay," she said, but her face didn't seem to agree with her words. She really hated me. Which was probably for the best because my body was doing funny things with her in close proximity, and I didn't need a nightmare like June Matthews in my fantasies.

She climbed into the seat next to me, and her eyes bounced all over the new car. Then she patted her hands together in a nervous, silent clapping gesture I'd seen her do before.

I retrieved my shades from the compartment. "Seatbelt," I reminded her. She turned fast, zipping the belt down and clicking it into place. I gave her a sardonic look. "I'm not going to demand a pound of flesh for giving you a ride to Jackson, Matthews."

She gave me an irritated glance. "I'm not afraid of you, Dr. Brady. I just don't like owing people favors."

"Amos," I said, putting on the sunglasses and switching off my hazards. "And I like it when people owe me favors. I like to collect on them," I added with a grin.

She mimicked me silently, turning to look out the window. "Whatever."

Little brat, I thought with a flare of amusement. I made sure the road was clear, and then I stepped on the gas.

June gave a soft squeak of outrage as I gunned it to sixty in less than four seconds, and her hands jumped out to the side, grabbing whatever she could as I plastered her body against the seat. Her left hand grabbed my forearm, but she didn't seem to notice as we climbed to seventy in a blink.

When I leveled out, barely managing to keep from snickering, she rapidly unclamped her hand from my arm and wedged them both between her bare, pale legs. Trying really hard not to smirk, I turned up my music again.

She gave me a reproachful glare. "Very funny." I shrugged, schooling my features into a smooth mask.

June listened to the Amaranthe song for a minute, and then she got an incredulous smile that dimpled her one cheek. "You like *girl rock*?"

I bristled. "It's heavy metal."

"It's a Swedish girl band," she insisted, still smiling like she'd found a pair of my underwear in the clinic waiting room. "It's ABBA for goths."

I narrowed my eyes. "Okay, snarky, what do *you* want to listen to, then?"

She pulled a pair of wireless, rose gold headphones from her small backpack between her feet. "Not rage queens of darkness. I have an audiobook," she said primly.

"You read smut, don't you?" I teased.

Dark red crept up her cheeks. "It's romance," she muttered.

I felt my grin widen. "Oh my God, you read porn."

"It's not porn!" she protested and snapped her headphones to her ears. I wondered if she could hear through all that springy hair.

I tried to wipe away my half grin. "Sure, it's not."

She ignored me until we made it to Star Valley, and then suddenly, she lowered her headphones around her neck and stared in wonder at the green, towering mountains and gentle ripple of hills and farms. We crawled through small, touristy towns, and then, as we rounded a bend through a canyon, she shouted, "Stop the car!"

I fought the urge to panic. "What's wrong?" I asked calmly.

"Stop, stop, stop!" she urged, looking over her shoulder at me and then turning back to the window, hands plastered against the glass.

I cringed at the finger marks she left behind. "Okay, okay, chill out." I pushed the hazards button again and pulled off the road. There was a generous shoulder, at least, and before us, the mountains had opened up, making way for distant, white-tipped monoliths and craggy towers of red and gray stone around us.

Before the car had even come to a full stop, she opened the door and tripped out.

"Hey, whoa, Jesus," I said, slamming the car into park, and hurrying after her.

She fell onto her knees, but quickly righted herself. She had a sketchbook and black pencil, and immediately started to sketch with staccato scratches and swooping lines. Her eyes stayed riveted on the scene before us, only jumping down to her sketch pad briefly while she tried to replicate the shapes and contours of the majestic Teton Mountains.

I watched her for a minute and then bent over to get a look at her knees. She had a scrape on her right shin that was bleeding, but she paid it no mind. I rested my hands on my hips. "How long is this field trip going to take, Matthews?"

"Shh," she said. I watched as the random shapes and sharp outlines began to take on the appearance of mountains. She dropped expert shadows, and then like the wave of a magic wand, turned a five-year-old's impression of mountain shapes into hyper-realistic sketches. She coughed into her arm, rattling her chest with the intensity of it, and then inhaled with a wheezing sound.

I gave her a speculative look. "You okay?"

She coughed into her arm again, eyes still on the mountains and pencil moving fast. "Allergies," she muttered absently.

She did seem like the type of woman who forgot to take her allergy pills. Figured. I looked around, taking in the view as we approached evening. The air was clear and cool with a slight breeze rolling off the mountains that filled my senses with crispy, snow-scented air.

June had trees and smaller plants sketched out by the time she turned around with an apologetic smile. "Okay, sorry. I really want to paint this later. It's gorgeous."

"If we stop every time you like a mountain," I said, holding out a hand to guide her back to the car, "we're going to get there after midnight."

"I've never been up this way," she confessed. She had the sketchbook pressed to her chest like she didn't want me to see it.

I had watched her draw the whole thing, but okay. I hooked a hand around her elbow before she got in the car. "Hold up, Monet. You're going to bleed on my leather seats. Wait here."

She looked down at the gash that ran down her shin. "Oh," she said.

I leaned around her to open the passenger-side door, keeping a grip on her with my left hand and then reaching into the glove compartment to pull out the travel-size first aid kit I kept on hand. I wasn't sure why I kept a hold on her arm while I did that.

Maybe because she felt like a loose coil liable to spring away at any moment.

Or I wanted to shake her. Hard to say for sure.

I steered her to the open passenger-side door and had her lean against the seat. I kneeled in the biting gravel, and my well-worn hiking shoes crunched as I shifted my weight to get a good look at the scrape. It was impressively deep for something she'd done tripping over her own feet. I glanced up at her from below.

She gazed back, her expression wavering between sheepish and wary.

I felt something dangerously close to infatuation wriggle around inside my chest, and quickly looked back down. Blood. Wounds. I could handle those. I unzipped the red first aid kit and found a cleansing wipe. Gently, I swiped around the gash, cleaning up the blood that had wept all the way down to her dingy white canvas shoes. I ripped open another one, this time focusing on the debris that clung to the broken skin.

She sucked in a breath, and her leg twitched away from me.

I placed a hand under her smooth calf and pulled it back down with a stony glance upward again. "You play stupid games, you win stupid prizes," I said, quoting my jerk father.

"Do you ever say anything remotely pleasant?" she shot back.

I cleaned the rest of the wound, keeping a hand on her calf when she tried to jerk away, and gave it a good once-over. Oof, that was deep. She'd been a millimeter away from needing Steri Strips. Which I did not have in a car first aid kit. Instead, I smeared it with antibiotic ointment and let it be. "Put more of this on it tonight before bed," I said, giving her the ointment. "But otherwise, leave it alone."

She took the small, yellow tube and hitched herself onto the seat. "Thanks."

I zipped up the first aid kit, giving her a slow blink. "You're a mess, Matthews."

"Thank you," she said, like she was accepting an award.

I tossed the kit back into the glove compartment, started the car again, and stole another glance at June as she stared lovingly out the windows.

Suddenly, I wanted her to look at me that way.

And that was really stupid.

FIVE
June

I couldn't believe I'd gotten myself stuck in a car with Dr. Cranky Pants. I mean, yes, he'd stopped so I could sketch that stunning summer mountain spread, but he had looked straight up pissed the whole time. We were already late, so I didn't see why he had to look like he'd swallowed a bag of sour gummies. Then again, I'd have been equally annoyed if he'd pulled over to brood at the mountains. Or whatever he did in his free time.

At least his air-conditioned car made breathing easier. As soon as I'd gotten out of the car in Star Valley, my lungs had been assaulted by pollen and whatever else had been aggravating my allergies that summer. Thank God for fancy cars with air filters.

I fitted the squishy headphone foam to my ears and clicked play on my book. I was well into the spicy romance part of the book, and the main characters had already made love once. They were ramping up to a second part, and their witty dialogue brought a smile to my face as I stared out the window at the passing foliage and broken-down barns.

He knelt before her trembling thighs, his gaze fixed on the crease between her legs and his fingers gentle with their rising exploration. "What was that about kneeling, Valerie? You don't like it?"

I flicked a gaze to Amos, hoping he couldn't hear what was happening in the book.

Valerie sighed, letting her head fall back as he pressed a kiss to the top of her thigh. "I don't kneel. But I'll accept worship."

I swallowed hard, feeling heat climb up my cheeks. *This might not be the best book to listen to with Dr. Brady's strong hands on the wheel a foot from me.* He moved one hand to smooth a finger over his lips like he always did when he was deep in thought. I felt saliva pool in my mouth, following the veins of his toned forearms all the way up to the firm bulge of his biceps that strained under the tight-fitting T-shirt.

Karson's fingers parted her thighs with coaxing control, and she obeyed, leaning against the door for support. His fingers found her heat.

Amos sank his fingers into my hot pussy.

I wrenched the headphones off suddenly. I felt my cheeks flush and I gulped down the sudden moisture in my mouth. I stared ahead at the road to keep from imagining what my traitorous mind had conjured. *What the hell? What was that, June? Amos?*

He glanced over at me, his finger still on his lips. A mischievous grin crept across his chiseled features. "Something wrong with your book?"

"It's boring," I said in a tight voice.

"Oh, boring, huh?" He reached across the console for the headphones, but I threw them to the ground between my feet.

He was quicker, and his long arms reached between my legs like a bear swiping a trout from a river. He yanked the headphones to his lap before I could snatch them back, laughing dispassionately.

I pulled up the Bluetooth settings on my phone, hastily clicking at it to turn off the connection to the headphones. My fat finger pressed the wrong button.

Amos' speaker system chirped, "Bluetooth connected."

I gasped. "No!"

Karson slid his fingers into her heat, deep and sure, and she moaned, head thrown back and hands tangled in his hair. He lowered his mouth to the apex of her pleasure –

I screeched, swiping desperately at my phone to find the audiobook app.

Amos had bent over double laughing, and he barely managed to keep his eyes on the road as he pressed a hand to his chest, like the laugh was tearing his insides apart.

"Yes, there," Valerie pleaded.

"Please, Karson," Amos cackled.

I found the app and hit the pause button.

Weighted silence descended on us, and we both seemed to hold our breath. Then Amos laughed again, sparing me a mocking glance before returning his gaze to the road.

"Oh my God," I moaned. I leaned forward and pressed my face to my lap.

Amos sighed loudly, like it had all been too much for him, and dropped the headphones on the back of my neck. "That is quality literature, Matthews."

I sat up swiftly, my hair escaping its clip to float around my head in a mass of bouncy auburn curls. I gave him a reproving glare. "That was your fault."

He snorted loudly, laughing again.

"You are the *worst*," I growled, letting my anger burn away my embarrassment rather than steeping in it.

"I am," he admitted, putting his hand to his firm, flat chest again. "But if I wasn't, then I wouldn't have gotten to experience that scintillating prose."

I was pretty sure my face looked like a tomato. "It's romance."

He puffed an incredulous laugh. "Is that your idea of a romantic date, June?" He slid a teasing look my way. "You want your date's mouth under your skirt?"

I balled my hands into fists. "I really hate you."

He laughed callously. I pursed my lips, giving him my iciest glare. Then I curled my legs into a ball and put my dirty sneakers up on his dashboard. Amos stopped laughing. He glowered.

I raised my eyebrows, giving him an innocent look. I slid my feet up the dash loudly, and then stretched them out to rest them on the windshield. They left little dirt marks wherever they went.

He tapped a finger on his steering wheel. "Brat."

"Jerk," I shot back.

I flipped through the music playlists on my phone, found ABBA, and started a mix playlist. "*Gimme Gimme Gimme!*" played loudly over the speakers.

Amos looked resigned. "I guess I deserve this."

"You do," I agreed, folding my arms.

He quirked a smile again. "Fine. It was still worth it."

I rolled my eyes and tried to ignore him, but the burn of shame mixed with a strange, swirling desire had settled between my legs, and I found it distracting and disturbing. What was it about Dr. Brady? He made me want to scream, but there was something about his stern demeanor that felt like it could slide into something absolutely irresistible.

I would have to avoid him as much as possible at this retreat thing. *Focus on your hatred*, I said to myself, taking on the gravelly voice from the Emperor Palpatine in Star Wars. *Let the hate flow through you.*

I felt enough hatred to turn my heart to the dark side, but something else gilded the sharp edge of the feeling. Something enticing and erotic.

By the time Amos' SUV pulled up to the retreat venue, dusk had painted the Tetons in hues of pink and purple. I couldn't take my eyes off the dance of colors, which were blending from warm magenta to striking oranges and all the way up the sky to a periwinkle blue that disappeared into violet midnight. It was a breathtaking palette. I wanted to reach up a finger and swipe the colors out of the air so I could smear them on a canvas.

There weren't any signs heralding the name of the retreat space, but I knew from the brochure we'd been emailed that they called it Teton Wild School. As Amos parked in the dirt parking lot several yards from the campus, I noted that all the buildings had been made in the same modern style with cedar wood and black metal finishes. They used lots of glass on their walls and had lined the pathways with tidy, gray paving stones.

The third building down had Edison bulbs strung across an enormous pergola, and that's where the staff had gathered. I heard their chatter and laughter from across the parking lot.

Amos pushed the ignition button to turn off the car, and in the quiet, darkening space, he turned to me with an elbow on the middle console. "Get your feet off my dash."

I pushed away, plunking my feet on the soft carpet under the seat. "Aye, aye captain." I tried to sound plucky, but mostly I was still embarrassed. "I'll find someone to take me to my car on Sunday," I said. Then I pushed open the door and hopped out of his tall SUV. "Okay if I check in first and then come get my stuff?"

He glanced over his shoulder at the pile of my crap in the back. "You might want to bring a friend or two."

"At least I have friends," I parried.

Dr. Brady gave me a cold but amused glare. "Cute."

I shrugged before shutting the door and strutting away. Arrogant, insufferable creature.

The second I walked down the gravel path toward the camp, my lungs seized, and I had another coughing fit. "Jesus," I rasped, choking on a ball of phlegm. I reached into my purse and took out the bottle of allergy pills I'd already taken that morning. They said they worked for twenty-four hours, but I called horseshit. I popped it in my mouth and decided drinks were definitely the best way to get through this whole thing.

It turned out we hadn't missed much. Carla had made an announcement about the retreat, and everyone had gotten "Goal Compass" journals. But then the rest of the evening the staff had eaten tacos at the taco bar and proceeded to get tipsy on as many "Wild School Dirties" as they could handle. I wasn't sure what was in the custom cocktails, but it had local blackberry puree and grenadine to sweeten the burn, and it was way too easy to knock several of them back.

I found Katherine and Maxine already in a giggling mood, and they forced a cocktail into my hand before pushing me away from the gathering and across the campus to where our cabins stretched out in tidy rows leading up to the dark forest beyond. They were cute, log-built structures split in half, with a bed in each room and a shared bathroom between them. Maxine, unsteady on her feet after too many "dirties," tripped up the rustic steps and fished a key out of her linen overall pocket.

"We're cabbies," she sang.

"What—" I started to ask, but Katherine cut me off.

Too loudly, she said, "Like roomie but with a cabin!"

Maxine chortled. Even tipsy, she looked Instagram perfect, with a delightfully fluffy messy bun sending curling blond tendrils around her face. She wore adorable olive green linen overalls over tan-colored high-top sneakers, and pulled the look together with her megawatt smile. She splayed her lithe, dancer body against the wooden door. "Our party room awaits."

"I'm pretty sure I see aspirin in your future, not a party," I shot back, and took a sip of the cocktail.

Katherine guffawed but teetered into me. "I feel amazing. The wilderness is amazing."

I peered at my drink. Did they puree shrooms into these things, or what? Maxine flicked on the porch lights and the interior lights, and after she grandly gestured at the antique-looking, metal-framed, full-size bed swathed in white, she suddenly looked confused. "Wait, where's your stuff?"

"It's in the car," I said, rolling my eyes.

"Oh yeah," Maxine snorted.

"To the car!" Katherine demanded. She wore all black, as she often did, and her wispy tunic floated around her as she careened away, making her look like a bat bride from a bad Sci-Fi movie.

I groaned as they both wobbled their way back down the path. If I let them come to the car with me, they would know I had been rescued by Amos.

Katherine looked over her shoulder, her rich, red-tinted waves glinting in the dull glow of the porch light. "What?"

I sniffed, resting my hands on my hips and looking sheepishly to the side. "My bags are in Dr. Brady's car."

Katherine's mouth popped open. Maxine gasped, and then exhaled with a suggestive, "Ooh!"

"I ran out of gas," I hurried to add, joining them on the well-paved path that was getting darker into the sunset's shadows. "He was behind me, so he saved my butt. Thankfully."

"Oh my God, was that the most awkward car ride of all time?" Maxine asked, her thin hands pressed against her lips like a prayer.

You have no idea, I thought, and the salacious narrative of my audiobook played in my ears with deafening embarrassment. "It was the worst," I admitted, taking another long, bittersweet gulp of the cocktail.

We started back down the walkway, and the chatter and laughter of our colleagues once again drifted over the rapidly chilling air. Maxine threaded her arm through mine, staggering against me. "Tell us! Was he mean? Did he make you pay for the gas?"

Katherine made a choking, gasping sound. "Did he lecture you?"

As we neared the golden glow of the string lights ahead, I told them everything. I told them how surly he was, and how the audiobook had blared over his speakers, followed by his relentless teasing over my choice of literature. I told them about the diary and how he'd scared me from his office with his overbearing grouchiness.

Maxine shook her head a lot, and Katherine led us to the bar to get more drinks, which she downed suspiciously quickly. Her round face had gone red, and her blue eyes sparkled with frenetic energy. "Dr. Brady gets away with too much shit," she said ominously.

I watched her over the rim of my mason jar cocktail. Kathrine didn't usually do more than observe and make cryptic statements like she was actively reading everyone's futures in her head. She wasn't usually so direct. "Oh yeah?"

"Yeah. He thinks he's like… a god or something. It pisses us all off."

Maxine nodded in agreement. She had a slight tinge to her high cheekbones, too. Around us our colleagues chatted and chuckled, but as I stood by the log bar with my fellow receptionists, I felt a kind of chill settle in around us.

"I think he could use a dose of his own medicine," Katherine said, and her gaze slid to Amos.

Across the patio, he stood with Dr. Buchanon and Dr. Andrews, and they seemed to be seriously discussing a topic — most likely work — while they placidly sipped draft beers.

"What kind of medicine?" I asked, taking another drink and letting the buzz lull me into a heady mix of complacency and curiosity. And mischief.

"I have a few ideas," Katherine replied darkly. She held out her mason jar until I clinked mine against hers. "We're at camp, after all. What's summer camp without a few pranks?"

It took a few hours—and several Wild School Dirties—to hammer away at my prefrontal cortex, but eventually, we had a plan. Amos and his buddies had gone to bed early, which was predictably boring, leaving us with plenty of time to scheme. And drink. And then scheme less intelligently.

By the time everyone else had gone to bed, and midnight had long gone, Katherine, Maxine, and I giggled our way across the campus until we found what we'd been looking for—the kitchen. Thankfully, they didn't lock anything at the camp, and even with my vision rocking back and forth like a pirate ship ride, I managed to find a familiar, bear-shaped container of honey.

Katherine fell heavily against the stainless-steel pantry shelf laden with bulk packages of dry and canned goods. "Oh my God," she wheezed, laughing breathlessly. "I can't wait see—to see—to face his see."

I laughed darkly, holding up the honey in the darkened room. "You're so drunk you can't even talk, you dumb bitch."

Maxine folded in on herself, gagging and laughing in equal measures. "I am. I really am."

I was one hundred percent sure I was going to end up spewing blackberry puree and mysterious alcohol before the night was over, but I had a job to do before I lost it.

I had to punish Dr. Brady.

We staggered out of the kitchen, bumping into every goddamn object in our path, and then tumbled out of the doorway and down the steps, our feet crunching on gravel that led to the men's cabins. Before we'd really succumbed to the booze, we'd followed them all surreptitiously to make sure we knew which cabin was his.

Katherine suddenly fell to her knees, retching.

"Oh, come on," I groaned, teetering on my feet. "Babe, really? Oh, come here." Flush with alcohol-induced compassion, I grabbed at strands of her hair and held them away from her dark-colored vomit.

Maxine gagged. Then she spewed.

"Oh, co-come on, guys," I whined. "Seriously?"

Katherine groaned, low and miserable. She tilted onto her side and then turned to stare up at the clear sky. "I'm dead."

Maxine couldn't seem to stop barfing. I went to her and patted her back, too. "Babes, for real, you couldn't even keep it together for the…" I paused, my mind dying like a bulb in a power outage. "The prank," I finished finally. "S'important, you guys."

"I'm so sorry," Katherine whispered, reaching up a hand like the leading lady in a MacBeth performance. "You have to go. Do it. Smear it all."

Maxine nodded, coughing and breathing hard. "*Do it,* June."

I clutched the honey bear between my boobs. "Are you sure?"

"Go," Katherine said, waving a manicured hand. "We'll be fine."

The remaining, sober part of my brain worried that they might get eaten by some kind of wild animal if I left them lying there. I texted Carla from the shadow of a cabin.

June: I think Katherine and Maxine passed out in front of the dining hall.

Three dots blinked on the screen. *Carla: If you three ruin my retreat, I swear to God…*

Okay, I thought, puffing out a sigh, *I did my civic duty. Now, for revenge.*

I sneaked my way through the cabins, plastering my back against the walls like I was Jason Bourne, until I found the one we'd seen Andrews and Brady disappear into, cabin 3C.

My inebriated mind slapped around a few ideas on how to get into the cabin without being detected, but in the end, I figured that with my lack of coordination, I was better off just going through the front door.

Carefully, holding my breath and hunching my shoulders forward, I turned the antique, crystal doorknob.

Unlocked.

Oh, you're fucked now, Dr. Brady, I thought gleefully, and eased the door open. It didn't make so much as a squeak, and schooling my buzzy limbs to stay quiet, I shimmied my body through the door, turning to close it softly. It made a quiet *snap*, and with my heart banging away in my chest, I peered through the darkness for any sign that he'd heard me.

Oh my Hell, this is crazy, I thought, my nerves braiding together tighter than bungee cord.

Dark blue shadows bathed the tiny cabin in darkness, but I could just make out the shape of his full-sized bed and the unmoving, Amos-like shape under the blankets.

My thumb popped open the honey lid.

With shockingly stealthy footsteps, I lunged soundlessly across the wood floors toward Amos' bed. As I neared him, his deep, steady breathing filled me with courage. I silently fist pumped in the air. *Hell yeah.* I'd made it this far. The rest was easy.

I leaned over him, and there he was. Fast asleep, his lips slack and his thick eyelashes fanned out over his rigid cheekbones, Amos Brady lay vulnerable and ripe for attack.

If I hadn't been trying to be stealthy, I would have cackled. I tipped the bear down over his hair and watched the gold liquid slide toward the opening. *Yes, my Ursidae accomplice. Spill your brains all over his perfectly coiffed, silky hair.*

A hand shot out from the blankets, and in a dizzying blur, I felt my body get tugged forward, rolled, and then something soft and springy cradled my back while a very *hard* something else pinned me on top. My arms were wrenched above my head and the honey bear easily plucked from my grasp.

I drew in a startled breath, my world spinning. Then, I realized Dr. Brady had me straddled on his bed, his strong thighs pinning my hips in place and one of his hands clamping down on my wrists above my head.

After clicking on a dim bedside lamp, he held the honey bear at eye level, his hair mussed from sleep and his expression groggily confused. He had slept shirtless, of course, and I really had no choice but to get a perfectly comprehensive view of his toned abs and chest. The man was cut from stone, rippled and deeply etched in all the right places.

I wriggled, trying to escape. Amos pressed my wrists into the mattress. "Don't bother." He glanced from the honey down to me, closing the lid with a snap. "What are you doing in my cabin, Matthews?"

I blinked, fighting hard against the drunken stupor that clogged my thoughts like cotton balls in my ears. *Okay, June. Think. You can talk your way out of this one. Be clever. Be shrewd.* "Thass honey," I slurred.

Amos leaned down, the heady aroma of sleepy male and freshly shampooed hair wafting over me as he angled his mouth toward mine. I inhaled sharply, my stomach contracting.

He sniffed. Then he leaned back slightly. "You're drunk."

"I am," I agreed solemnly.

"And what were you doing with the honey bear?" he asked, his husky voice filled with curiosity.

Well, there wasn't much use in denying it. "I... was gonna put it in your hair," I breathed, struggling again against the tightness of his grip. "So... so the bugs would eat you."

He stared, his face unreadable. I gave him a sheepish smile.

Amos was silent for a few beats, his eyes flicking up and down the length of me, and then he leaned in again, so close, his breath tickled my lips with a cinnamon-scented puff. "Did anyone spank you growing up, June?"

My jaw dropped. *Ohhhhhh shit,* I thought. *I did it. I broke him. He's going to hit me and it's because I broke him.* "No," I said, the word strangled. I pulled away from him as far as the mattress would allow.

"I didn't figure," he mused darkly, his gaze burning my skin with its scrutiny.

A far off, buried voice from the depths of my personal depravity whispered, *let him. Spank me.* I went rigid, staring at him with wide eyes, frozen by the shock of my own thoughts and the fascinating way he was inspecting every inch of my body under his hold. He retreated a fraction again, and the light from the bedside table caught on the scar below his bottom lip. I wondered dimly what had caused the little silver line that slashed through his stubble.

Amos rotated the bear in his free hand, considering it. "And what do you think I should do with you, Matthews? Now that I have you here in my bed."

I gasped audibly, outraged. "What does *that* mean?" I paused, settling my eyes on his strong hand. "What, you're going to spank me?"

"Do you want me to?" he asked, his voice equal parts amusement and something else. Something hot.

"Prob—probably not."

"*Probably* not?" he challenged.

"Definitely not," I lied.

"Hm," he hummed. He returned his attention to the honey still in his hand. "I think it makes more sense to just return the favor. Don't you?"

"What favor?" I asked stupidly.

He popped open the lid with this thumb.

I made a muted shrieking noise before kicking my legs in an attempt to escape. "Fuck, fuck, fuck."

"Language, Matthews," he chided. He tipped the bottle, letting a stream of honey drizzle from the nozzle.

It hit my bare midriff, glazing my skin with cold stickiness. I huffed, my stomach contracting as I fought the manacle-like hold above my head. "I'm sorry, I'm sorry!" I pleaded, ending the word on a screech. "I didn't even get you!"

"Oh, but you would have," he said, moving the stream of honey up my navel toward my ribcage.

I squealed.

With his left hand still holding my wrists, he brought our hands down, pressing my own fingers over my lips to silence me. Amos righted the honey bottle, bending close to our joined hands. Whispering low, he said, "Andrews is dead to the world with a CPAP machine on his face and four months of newborn sleep deprivation to keep him knocked out, but if you wake him up, he's going to make assumptions you can't take back."

I swallowed hard, my chest heaving.

He pinned my arms up again. "Now, where were we?"

SIX
Amos

June Matthews either craved punishment or lacked common sense, and as she lay stretched out underneath me, I had to wonder which combination of the two had convinced her to sneak into my cabin.

I glanced at the honey glistening on her soft belly and the bright flush of her cheeks. Fifty-fifty. Definitely an even dose of both.

She was so short, I barely had to stretch my arm out to keep her pinned beneath me—and I didn't care what kind of man that made me, but I liked it. Laid on display for my perusal, I noted how full her breasts were, how soft her curves dipped in and flared out, rounding out over a stomach just soft enough to be mouth-watering, and then down to generous hips that felt like fitting a puzzle piece between my legs. Her flaming, tightly coiled hair had been spread out underneath her like she was some kind of mythical fire nymph, and her full lips parted with dread as she stared up at me.

If she weren't drunk…

I abandoned that thought. *Eyes on the prize, Amos.* And what was the prize?

The slow, decadent torture of June Matthews.

June turned her head, looking around the room like she might find some means of escape. *Oh no, you don't,* I thought with dark satisfaction. *You're mine, now.*

I tipped the bottle of honey again, marveling at the sheer brilliance of her plan, in actuality. Honey was innocuous but just *annoying* enough that it would have really pissed me off. And the bugs actually might have eaten off my face before I had realized anything.

If she had been stealthy. Which, she hadn't. I'd heard her coming all the way down the path, staggering, tripping up my steps, fumbling with the doorknob, and then shuffling inside. She had probably thought she was a shadow wraith come to life, but that was alcohol for you.

Still, I had given her the chance to retreat. It was only when she had been a hair's breadth from carrying out her evil plan that I had retaliated.

Frankly, I should've felt thankful for the chance she'd given me to dose out some much-needed punishment her way. She'd been driving me absolutely insane these last three weeks.

"Amos," she hissed, her eyes glued to the bead of honey that hovered just shy of dribbling back onto her skin.

"Yes?" I asked innocently.

Thick, amber liquid oozed in a thin stream from the bear's head onto her ribcage.

She groaned, pulling a disgusted face. "Stop! I promise I'll leave you alone!"

I drizzled it back and forth like I was dressing a scone.

She squealed, muted from behind closed lips. "I'll be the best secretary in Utah, I swear."

I moved it up to her breasts, over her shirt, and swirled it in circles all the way up to her cleavage.

She gagged, watching the sticky substance drip down her skin. "Amos, I *hate* honey! It makes me barfy. *Please.*"

I paused, tipping the container back up and giving her an incredulous look. "You're making that up."

"I'm not," she rushed to answer, her chest heaving as she fought futilely against my grip. "I threw up peanut butter honey protein balls when I was a kid," she said quickly, lifting her head as well as she could with her wrists pinned. A tendril of her auburn curls escaped from over her shoulder and fell across the curve of her cheek. She blew it sideways to get it out of her eyes.

"So, what you're saying," I replied slowly, doing my best to keep my features blank, "is that this is ten times more excruciating than I'd hoped it would be."

Her jaw hinged open.

God, she was cute. Too bad she was such a pain in the butt. I lowered the honey bottle to her chest which was well exposed over the deep "V" of her crop top.

She let out a wordless groan of agony, letting her head fall back to my pillows. "I *hate* you, Amos."

I swirled the honey up her neck toward her chin. "Good thing you got—what is this? A bulk honey bear? There's a lot in there." I gave the bottle a hard squeeze, dropping an enormous glob on her chin.

She gagged again.

"Get comfy. We aren't done until this bottle is empty."

She kicked in frustration. "*Fuck* you, Brady."

I filled her mouth with honey before she could close her lips. "Watch your mouth, Matthews."

She coughed, swallowed, and then made a retching sound.

Uh oh.

I managed to scoop her up and get her curled over my arm before she vomited a stream of dark purple liquid all over my cabin floors. Honey from her skin coated my forearm as I supported her, making sure she didn't accidentally turn and aspirate any of the bile. She threw up so violently, it covered us both, splashing up my plaid pajama pants and spraying all the way up her bare legs.

I wrapped her hair around my free hand, doing my best to keep it from getting in the pungent mess as she upchucked what looked like an actual gallon of Wild School Dirties. Well, that was what I deserved, probably. Dirty floors and a guilty conscience.

Muddy, violet puke seeped into a growing puddle on my floor, and I dragged us both away from the bed to keep it from coating my feet any worse than it already had. Her knees buckled, and I lowered her to the floor gingerly. Swallowing a gag, I asked, "How many of those things did you drink?"

Her shoulders shook, and she stayed hunched over with her long, wild hair covering her face.

I considered her warily. "June? Are you okay?" I put a hand between her shoulder blades to make sure she was breathing and not choking.

She trembled, head bowed.

"Are you crying?" I asked, horrified. The only thing that could make this situation worse was a hysterical, weeping female.

A low sound escaped her, and for a heart-rending second, I thought I really had made her cry. But then it deepened, and her torso shook with silent laughter that only grew in volume.

"You're *laughing*?"

She laughed, cackled really, low and long, and then sucked in a loud breath before letting loose another unbroken, unbridled laugh that filled the quiet cabin.

I slapped a hand over her mouth to keep her from waking up Andrews. "You're *laughing?*" I hissed in her ear.

She gulped, nodded, and between breathy laughs muffled by my hand, she rasped, "You have to clean up my puke."

I made a disgusted sound and pinned her hands to her sides, squeezing her like an anaconda from behind. "You little —"

A knock sounded on the adjoining door that connected my cabin to Andrews'. "Yo, Brady," he said from the other side, "you alright, man?"

I ground my teeth together. Of course, things would backfire on me. Served me right for messing with a tornado like June Matthews. "I'm good!" I called back, silencing June's drunken giggles with my hand again. "I think I ate something bad from a gas station on the way up here."

Andrews made a sympathetic sound. "You need anything?"

June kicked one of her heels, which were both tucked between my knees as we crouched on the floor. She connected with my balls.

Pain lanced through me from my groin, up to my teeth, and all the way down to my toes. I wheezed, bowing forward and covering June in a crushing hold. Coughing, I managed to eke out, "No, man. I'm good."

"Well, you sound terrible. Let me know if I can help."

"Yep," I croaked.

June snorted out another laugh, coating my hand in snot.

"Oh my God," I groaned, removing my hand and wiping it on her shorts.

She cackled from underneath me.

"Okay, that's it," I growled, ignoring the pain still lancing through my dick, and stood, taking her with me.

She stayed curled over my arm and picked up her feet in an attempt to drag me down.

I pulled her up against me hard, knocking the wind out of her. She coughed, and I dragged us both backwards, pausing at the door to grab two towels from a wicker basket and my duffel bag. I shoved my feet in my hiking shoes, grateful they were well used and loose, and then hauled the wriggling woman on my arm over to my nightstand so I could swipe up my phone from the bedside table. I turned off the bedside light, hoping Andrews would assume I had fallen asleep again.

June literally dug her heels in. "What — are — you — doing?" she gritted out, fighting my hold.

She was so pathetically weak, it was almost amusing.

Almost.

I shifted my grip on her, taking hold of her left wrist, and then twirled her around, bending at the waist as I did so I could hitch my shoulder against her ribs and fold her over my back. I wrapped my arm around her butt, ignoring her protesting kicks, and bundled her out of the cabin before she could wake anyone else.

"Amos," she hissed. "Put me down. Where are we going?"

"Shower."

She bucked, fighting me in earnest. Apparently, puking most of the alcohol out of her system had sobered her enough to fight back. "Amos, I swear to God, I'll scream."

"You do that," I said, my voice low and as threatening as I could make it at that volume, "and I'll make sure everyone knows we've been sleeping together."

"We aren't sleeping together," she shot back acidly.

"Prove it."

"Prove…? Goddamn it, Brady."

I swatted her rear end. "Language."

She kicked at me, but I was prepared this time. I pinned her legs against my belly as I headed to the communal showers a good ways away from the main cabins. Each one of our cabins had its own shared bathroom, but I didn't dare try to keep her quiet while I hosed us both off in mine. The communal showers away from the main camp had two logical benefits: They were out of hearing distance of everyone else, and there was no risk of anyone using them when they had their own bathrooms.

Gravel crunched under my shoes, and the cool night air prickled at the moisture on my skin as I navigated the darkness with the flashlight on my phone. Eerie shadows danced at my feet as the flashlight hit leaves and branches.

"Brady, get your hands off me. This is assault." She paused, as if thinking about her words. "I think."

"You sneaked into my cabin and then covered me in honey, puke, and snot," I countered. "We're well past professional boundaries, Matthews. At most, we've entered domestic dispute territory."

"I will *never* be a domestic *anything* with you, you moldering, reeking heap of dog shi—" She squeaked as I slapped her cheeks again. *"Will you stop that?"*

"You'll learn eventually," I grinned.

"I'm reporting you to the…" she paused, and I could practically hear the drunken confusion clouding her thoughts. "BBB," she said finally.

"The Better Business Bureau?" I asked with incredulous amusement. The dim exterior light of the shower building came into view then, so I turned off my phone light, slipped it into the pocket of my soiled pajama pants, and adjusted my hold on June, juggling the duffel bag draped with towels while trying to keep her inebriated self from slumping off my shoulder.

"You watch, I'll do it," she grumbled, slapping my bare back. I winced. That was going to leave a mark. "I'll send a whole fucking manifesto about your crimes."

I slapped her ass. Hard. She growled like a mountain cat. Laughing caustically, I bent slightly and angled my body to reach the door to the showers. "I would love to read that report. 'Dear sirs, my boss drizzled me in honey and spanked me for my filthy mouth.'"

"Brady, you d—" she paused, reconsidering. "Doody head."

I smirked. With my heel, I eased the thick, wooden door open, and as it creaked in the silence, I reached over with my left hand to switch on the lights. Flickering fluorescent bulbs crackled and illuminated the space with blinding light. Blinking against the glare, I carried June into the long, generously sized building slatted with waxed planks made of knotty pine and faded blue tile. There were two sides to the communal showers, and I'd taken her into the men's side where four shower stalls, all made with cheap plastic and thick vinyl shower curtains, lined the left wall. Behind us, three sinks below reflective metal panels rounded out the utilities available in the older building.

Hardly anyone used these anymore unless they were a substantially large group like a student body or youth camp. But lately, Wild School made most of its money from corporate retreats like ours anyway—a far cry from the adventure camp I'd attended here every summer from sixth grade through tenth.

I felt June's panic in the way she clenched her stomach and pushed against my back to right herself. "What are you doing?"

I dropped my bag in front of the sinks, pulled my phone from my pocket to set it on the chipped porcelain, and then walked toward the showers.

"Amos, I am *not* kidding. You put me down right now."

I deposited her unceremoniously in one of the shower stalls, making sure she fell safely onto the wood slatted bench.

Curly hair disheveled and falling around her face, she snarled and tried to push past me, but I hooked my left arm around her waist and slammed on the shower button with my right. Icy water cascaded over both of us. The outdated showers only had one button, which heated to whatever temperature they had it set to, and that was it.

She gasped loudly, her mouth dropping open and her body stiffening. It was my turn to laugh spitefully at her expense. "Sit down, Matthews."

She turned in the circle of my arm, glaring up at me. Water dropped from a bouncy curl at her forehead down to her full lips. She licked the drop unconsciously, biting her lip in frustration.

Oh, boy. I might not have thought this all the way through. Angry June I could handle, but soaking wet, sullen June with her big, emerald eyes and pouty lips was not on my list of safe situations to find myself in.

The water sprayed us in a freezing stream, gradually warming to a lukewarm temperature. Shaking against my body, June pulled her arms against her chest. Her teeth chattered.

As the water heated up, I reached up to grab the shower head, which was attached to a long hose for particularly messy cleanups after long days in the outdoors.

Or party girl puke.

June folded her arms under her breasts, shoving herself in the far corner of the shower stall and glaring at me. Her cream T-shirt had gone completely transparent, and, if I was honest, I couldn't help but note the outline of her white bra beneath. Or rather, the uselessness of it. The defined shadow of her nipples pebbled as she narrowed her eyes at me, shivering and dripping wet.

I clenched my jaw as I felt my traitorous dick start to harden. Then I turned the nozzle and sprayed her directly, washing away the honey and puke all over the front of her.

She spluttered, holding out her hands and stomping her soggy shoes. "Stop, oh my God I'm going to fucking *kill* you, Brady."

I splashed her face. "Language."

She coughed, blocking the stream with her hand and screwing her eyes shut. "Amos," she whined, that time sounding truly desperate.

Taking some pity on her, I hooked the shower head back in its cradle, and then left her with a stern point. "Stay," I commanded.

She slumped to the bench, drawing her knees up and resting her head on her knees. "I'm gonna be sick again," she groaned.

I squelched across the tile floor to my duffel bag, crouched down in front of it, and unzipped it. After sifting through the contents and depositing the ones I needed in the sink above me, I stood and glanced over my shoulder toward the shower stall. June still sat with her forehead against her knees, eyes closed, and her arms went slack. She was falling asleep in the shower—actually sleeping.

I hurried to shuck off my sodden pajama pants, and then I pulled on my swimming trunks. I grabbed my toiletries bag, fished shampoo and soap from it, and returned to Sleeping Barfy.

She moaned, rocking her forehead against her knees. The shower, steaming now, only hit her shins from where she sat. She looked miserable. And vulnerable. And every part of her tugged on my heartstrings in that moment, causing me to pause. I had taken an immense amount of vindictive pleasure in teasing her, but I realized an abruptly sobering fact:

Right now, I was the one being tortured.

My groin tightened and my fingers gripped the soap bottle too tightly, causing it to creak. The undeniable truth of how attracted I was to June slammed into me with sudden, staggering force. I wanted her.

I wanted her badly.

But I couldn't have her for a whole *manifesto* of reasons, not the least of which because I had made her life a living hell for no particularly good reason other than it satisfied my need to control her. *But why do you want to control her, Amos?* I asked myself with grim acceptance.

Because you want her.

I angled into the shower stall, suddenly desperate to have her washed off and a significant distance away from me. Those feelings were not something I could indulge. I crouched in front of her and gently removed her white sneakers, followed by her soaking socks.

June protested, pushing at me with her feet, but I caught her ankle and lathered soap along her feet and up her shins where her vomit had stained her pale skin with huckleberry puree. June picked up her head, green eyes hooded and little droplets of water falling from her lashes. Her mouth opened a fraction in surprise.

I swallowed hard, trying to ignore how touching her body made me feel, but it was impossible. If I got through this without ripping off her clothes and pinning her against the shower wall, I deserved some kind of medal. "Gentlemanly conduct in the face of a soaped up, soaking wet goddess. First place."

I pulled her to her feet, turning her body so the warm water cascaded over her breasts and down her belly. Sucking in a breath, ignoring her glassy doe eyes, I lathered more soap between my hands and smoothed my palms over her stomach where I washed off the sticky residue from our honey war.

June's breath hitched.

I ground my teeth together. *Don't you dare, June. Stop looking at me like that.*

I moved up to her ribs, and she let out a little sound, barely noticeable, but its source was undeniably lusty. As I worked around her ribs to her back, over her shirt and to her collarbone, she leaned into me, gusting out a low moan.

Crap.

SEVEN
June

I smacked a dry mouth around my tongue, waking groggily to the sound of a phone alarm somewhere in my room. My head pulsed with a painful beat that slammed in rhythm with the grating alarm tone.

I hated that alarm sound. I never used it.

I flopped a hand around, searching for my phone. My hand connected with someone's face. "Nnrg," a male voice groaned, vibrating into my chest through the mattress. Someone grabbed my wrist and shoved it back down to my side.

I peeled my eyes open with hazy confusion. "What?" I croaked.

Still holding my hand against my hip, Amos Brady lifted his head from a downy white pillow and peered at me, squinting his eyes against the daylight. "Stop hitting me, Matthews."

I gasped, sitting up so fast, I banged my head against the wrought iron headboard.

"Christ, June," Amos grated out, pressing his hands to my skull as stars danced in my vision. He massaged the place I had whacked. "Chill."

I pushed his hands away from my head, my jaw slack. "What the fuck? What are you doing in my room?" I looked around, disoriented.

"Language," he mumbled, but for once, he didn't really sound like he meant it, and rolled over in *my* bed to inhale deeply, stretch, and pull one of *my* pillows over his face.

I yanked the pillow back. "Get out of my room, you perv."

He glared, his hair perfectly disorderly and a dark five o'clock shadow sweeping along his sharp jaw. He wasn't wearing a shirt, and as he propped himself up on his elbow, I watched in dazed fascination as his pecs and arms did a tasty ripple thing. His smug smile told me he had noticed me ogling.

I blinked hard and pressed the heels of my palms against my temples. "I'm so confused."

"How much do you remember, Monet?" he asked, pulling his earlier nickname for me out of a top hat.

Horror drained the blood from my face. "No," I breathed, drawing my knees to my chest and angling away from him. "No, we didn't."

He raised two perfectly straight, dark eyebrows. "Didn't *what?*"

"Oh no," I said, shaking my head and starting to back out of the bed. "No way. No. Absolutely not."

He watched me with a placid smile.

There is no way I lost my virginity to Amos Brady and forgot about it. "Fuck no. Brady, stop messing with me. I'm not kidding."

He grabbed my ankle and dragged me across the bed back to him. I ended up on my back, laid out along his side while he towered over me, still holding his weight on one elbow. He squished my cheeks together. "Stop. Cursing."

"Fuck you," I said through scrunched lips.

His eyes traveled over my features, one brow twitching up, and then he sighed, as if in resignation. "No, Matthews, we didn't sleep together. Well," he amended with a tilt of his head. "We *slept* together, but I didn't steal your virtue or whatever."

"Okay, Mr. Darcy," I snorted.

"I repeat," he said, as if drawing on every ounce of patience he possessed, "how much do you remember?"

I let my eyes slide to the side, scrunching my forehead as I tried to remember. There had been a lot of drinks with my receptionist posse, some scheming to get revenge on Adonis over there, something to do with honey… then Amos had caught me honey handed.

I hiccupped, tensing. Amos chuckled, low and sharpened with a razor's edge. "Keep thinking." I screwed my eyes shut as memories of me barfing all over his floors flashed right before the memories of the shower.

Oh, God, the shower.

I rolled suddenly, grabbing all the blankets and sheets to cocoon myself in a blanket fort of shame. I kept rolling until I would inevitably fall to the floor and hopefully die of a freak aneurysm from the impact.

Strong arms caught me before I tipped off the edge, and then Amos plopped me onto the middle of the bed. "You are so weird, you know that?"

"Yeah," I said from the claustrophobic darkness of my nest.

He peeled back a few layers to unearth my face. "I just want you to know that you've given me a lifetime of blackmail. You're basically my indentured servant, now."

I wriggled angrily in my cocoon. "Screw you, Brady. You illegally detained me and tortured me with honey."

"The audacity," he intoned with shuttered lids.

I kicked at him. "Get out of my room."

Amos gave another low, sensual chuckle, and then the bed dipped as he pushed himself off the mattress. "You've got a lot of nerve telling me what to do, peasant."

I shimmied my body until my head poked out of the blankets, veiled by my unruly hair. "What are you even doing in *my* bed, *Doctor* Brady?"

"You puked on mine," he replied, hands low on his hips.

"Oh."

"Plus, you begged me to," he grinned wickedly.

"*I what?*"

Amos grabbed a shirt from the foot of the bed, slipped it over his head, and gave me an irritatingly cheerful wave. "Don't be late for breakfast."

"Or what?" I shouted after him as he opened my cabin door. He glanced over his shoulder, his eyes darkening. I swallowed hard.

Then he was gone, and the room suddenly felt huge and empty. I buried my head back in my sheets and screamed.

I found Maxine and Katherine folded limply over one of the mess hall tables, each of them with a cup of coffee in their hands and their eyes as sunken as mine. "Mess hall" was a bit of a misnomer if you asked me. The building, the largest on the property, had been built out of black metal trim and enormous panes of glass that gave the whole thing the feel of a fancy airplane hangar instead of a dining hall. The style could best be described as "luxury wilderness retreat with a hint of industrial farmhouse."

I'd managed to get myself out of bed and had braided my hair, combing through the tangles with my fingers and trying to ignore the fact that I smelled like Dr. Brady's shampoo.

I couldn't remember anything past arriving at the shower stall. The world had spun on its axis like I'd done one too many loopty-loos on a roller coaster, and after that... nothing. Just nothing.

Maxine glanced up at me as I approached, her satin blond hair, for once, a tangled mess she had gathered in a low ponytail down her back. She still wore a designer athleticwear set she'd probably received in exchange for a few well-thought-out Instagram pictures, so she had one up on me at least. I had donned a pair of black leggings and because I'd been feeling *spunky* when I'd packed my bag, I had only packed crop tops and revealing tank tops. So, I wore a tan and brown ribbed crop top with a mushroom print smack between my boobs and a zipped up hoodie over it.

"Hey, Maxie," I said, sliding onto the bench next to her.

She rolled a look up to me, her thin face stretched as she leaned heavily against the heel of her palm. "'Sup."

Katherine rotated a stirring stick in her (most likely compostable) coffee cup. "I feel like death."

"You look like death," Maxine agreed.

Katherine glanced at me, and then as if snapping back to reality, sat up straight with a jerk. "Oh my God. Wait. Did you do it?"

I moaned, letting myself fall forward so I could cover my head with my arms. "I really love working with you guys, but I'm going to have to find a new job. Actually, I need to leave the country. I'll get a fake passport and find a job as a fishmonger in Barbados."

"The fuck is a fishmonger?" Maxine asked, scrunching one side of her nose.

"Wait," Katherine seemed to be the only one with half her brain cells left that morning. "You… Shit, June. He caught you, didn't he?"

I nodded into my arms.

Maxine gasped, looking around the mess hall like she might find the despicable villain himself.

"Did he yell at you?" Katherine hissed. She was wearing all black again, although the sheen of her leggings and T-shirt told me it was breathable workout gear of some kind. An unusual look for her, in all honesty, but she had been smarter than I had. I would probably get a perfect ring of sunburn around my belly and my back. She shook my arm. "June, tell me. Are we screwed? Are we all going to lose our jobs?"

I sat up with a sigh, looking down at the pine table and tracing a tree knot with my finger. "No, he doesn't know you guys were involved."

"Are *you* getting fired?" Maxine whisper-screeched, still looking around the room.

I thought about the way Amos had smiled at me, almost indulgently, and the fact that he had happily climbed into my bed to sleep after he'd showered me off. But, then again, I had puked purple all over his bedroom. And kicked him in the balls. I rubbed my eyes hard. "I don't know," I admitted.

"We'll defend you," Maxine said with sudden intensity. I imagined her standing up to Amos, her hands on her narrow hips and her pretty, pink lips all pouty with indignation. *It's giving… Peach v. Bowser,* I thought with a twinge of amusement.

I gave her a half-lidded glance of amusement. "Thanks, but no. Trust me, you don't want to mess with Brady. He spanked me, you guys." Katherine's red-tinted lips popped open. Maxine gasped again, bringing her hands to her mouth. "Yeah." I continued, "and then he hosed me off in the showers after I'd puked on his floors."

Maxine covered her eyes and Katherine shook her head, mouth still agape.

"The whole night was an unprecedented disaster," I cringed. "He caught me before I could even get a drop on him, and not only did he just," I paused, pulling a face and mimicking the squeezing of a bottle with both hands, "all over me. All over. But he literally kidnapped me. I'm telling you —"

Katherine's mouth snapped shut and Maxine went rigid, her hands in her lap. But I didn't notice because I was too desperate to spew my story like I was giving myself an exorcism.

" — he fucking enjoyed it, too. Like, maybe not the part where I puked on him or the part where I kicked him in the balls —"

Both girls gasped audibly.

" — but the man is psychotically interested in tormenting me."

Two large hands landed on the table on either side of me, and a warm, familiar presence caged me in from behind. Amos bent down near my ear and whispered, "Psychotic?" I jumped, my body stiffening. I gripped the edge of the table, wondering if it would be too violent if I slammed the back of my head into his chin. Amos put a heavy hand on top of my head like he expected me to do just that. "Good morning, ladies," he said.

"Morning," Katherine said, her eyes dancing between the two of us. Maxine made a squeaking noise that wasn't actually a word.

"It's been good to get to know my employees better," Amos said, straightening away from me. "Enlightening."

I caught Katherine's gaze, widened my eyes, and mouthed, "Psycho."

Amos patted my face obnoxiously. "I'm excited for the activities. Team building, right?"

I swatted him away, but he was already gone. Flustered, I pushed escaped curls away from my face and tried to wipe my cheek like I could get his warm, masculine scent off me.

Katherine's blue eyes tracked Amos's retreat, and then her attention sucked back to me. She splayed her hands out on the table, and I noticed that she was already missing one of her glossy, black acrylics. She gave me a meaningful look. "What in the sexual chemistry, June?"

"Excuse me?" I asked in outrage.

"No, no," Maxine said from beside me, unfolding like a pill bug. "That," she said, gesturing with her hand in my general direction, "was definitely a thing."

"There's no 'thing,'" I argued.

They both snorted in unison. "Bully romance," Maxine said, as if she'd received an epiphany.

"Enemies to lovers," Katherine added with a serious nod.

"Stop that," I snapped. I got up from the bench. "I'm getting breakfast. No more insinuations. I just got over my nausea—I don't need another round."

"Grumpy/sunshine!" they both exclaimed, pointing at each other.

Which one of us is supposed to be the sunshine? I thought with a roll of my eyes. *I am definitively grumpy this morning.*

As I got in line for breakfast, Carla stood at the head of one of the tables and motioned to gain everyone's attention. "Good morning, OCC Campers!" she said with deafening positivity. I grabbed a muffin from a basket, listening with half an ear. "I know we went over most of the itinerary last night, but I just wanted to remind you all that this is an *opportunity* to foster relationships and develop meaningful progress as a united team."

I wonder how late she stayed up writing this speech, I thought, heading for the coffee machine. *Ooh, they have a cappuccino maker.*

"So, here's the plan, people," Carla continued. "We're going to push ourselves to the limits. We'll scale those towering cliffs together, showing each other that we trust and rely on one another. We'll navigate the wilderness together and overcome the odds as a united front."

I pushed the caramel cappuccino button, starting to feel an inkling of dread about the speech. What did she mean "odds?"

"To that end," she went on, clapping her hands together and sweeping a look across the room that had a definite *glint* to it, "we're starting off strong. You'll each be paired with an employee I hand-picked for you to really break down those walls…"

I paused, my hand frozen around the coffee cup. *Oh no.*

"… and stitch any wounds that might have opened up. Our job is stressful, people. It's hard work. But it's not as hard as a five-mile hike through the wilderness. And I think you'll find that if you work together, you'll realize that interpersonal communication is a cakewalk in comparison."

I looked around desperately. There was only one person Carla knew I didn't get along with. In fact, he was the one person who had been responsible for this cursed Wild School gathering in the first place. *Maybe if I sneak out the back, they won't notice I'm gone.*

Moving slowly, like the hungry eyes of a T-Rex were trained on my back, I lifted a lid from the stack next to the cappuccino machine, quietly fitted it around the mouth of the cup, and then clutching it between my hands, I backed away slowly. Slowly. Past the omelet bar. Around the juice machine. The kitchen doors were only a few steps behind me.

I bumped into something solid.

Two hands clamped around my upper arms like manacles.

I squeaked, and craning my head to confirm my worst fears, I stared up at the perfect jawline of towering Dr. Brady.

He flicked a glance down at me. "Going somewhere?"

EIGHT
June

I swallowed, turning my attention to Carla just in time to hear her read off the pairs. "Andrews and Black, Rhodes and Nayar, Vasquez and Collins." Little ripples of unhappy noises had already started to fill the gaps between each set of names. "Brady and Matthews…"

"Fuck," I hissed.

Brady squeezed my arm painfully. "What was that?"

I stomped my heel down, intending to mash his toes, but he was quicker, and sidestepped me easily.

"Alright, everyone got their assignments? Come on up here and grab your maps! One of you will use the compass and the other will use the map, and together, you *will not come back* without the scavenger hunt items." That last part Carla said like a bloodthirsty Spartan warlord.

Amos pushed me forward. "Map or compass, Matthews?"

"Neither," I ground out. But I couldn't exactly make a scene. Not when my colleagues, who seemed just as displeased as I was about the pairings, were obligingly standing from their tables, coffee cups in hand, and heading over to the folding table at the front that held laminated maps and sporty-looking compasses on lanyards.

"I feel like`you're less likely to screw up the compass part, so I'll take the map," he said.

"Gee, thanks," I muttered.

Amos gave me another push at the small of my back, and then we were walking amongst our colleagues, shuffling along toward the table. Because we'd been in the back of the room, we ended up with the last map, and I got a grumbly feeling in my stomach about that.

Amos picked up the laminated map, examining it. His brows pinched together.

Carla came up beside us and glanced at the map in Amos's hands. "Honestly, you two deserve that route," she said with an enormous amount of sass. "Good luck. We'll see you for dinner."

"Dinner?" I asked in horror. "As in... this is an all-day thing?"

Amos blew out a sigh, and still examining the map, leaned over to snatch up the compass and hand it to me.

"I don't know how to use these," I warned him.

"You'll figure it out." He folded the map, causing the plastic to squeak and crinkle, and then shoved it into the back pocket of his gray pants. They looked like a cross between joggers that cinched in at his ankles and athletic wear with swishy material and pockets in smart places. His army green T-shirt looked so soft, you could wrap a newborn in it. He had also put a dark gray baseball cap over his thick hair, and it had an embroidered logo that indicated that the hat likely cost more than my virtue.

Amos glanced down at my feet. He frowned. "What are you wearing?"

I bent over to look at my strappy, gladiator-style sandals, and wiggled my toes before turning a reproachful glare on him. "My sneakers are wet."

He pursed his lips guiltily. "Oh."

"Yeah, 'oh,'" I said, mocking his tone.

"Don't forget your backpacks!" Carla shouted above the noise the partners made as they conversed about their routes. Most of the pairs were bent over their maps, discussing the trails and making a plan. I gave Amos an expectant look, raising my eyebrows and folding my arms.

"What?" he asked. He walked around me to swipe up two backpacks from the pile near the door, one dark green like his shirt and the other black.

I snatched the black one away from him. "Aren't we going to make a plan or something?" I unzipped my hoodie, already starting to overheat in it, and slid it down my arms so I could tie it around my hips.

"I have a plan." He looped the backpack over his enormous biceps, and he looked like the Rock wearing a kindergartener's backpack.

"Care to share?" I pushed.

He shouldered open the glass door. "No. Let's go."

"What? Are you for real?"

He motioned with his head for me to exit ahead of him.

"Unbelievable," I groused. Pushing past him, I stomped across the porch and down the steps. I looped the compass around my neck and inspected it. The orange and black compass had been mounted on a white plastic plaque inscribed with numbers and geometric lines I had zero understanding about. It also had a plastic case that hinged up when I clicked it open, revealing a mirror like a makeup compact. There were a lot more numbers and measurements than the cheap compass I'd gotten in a cereal box as a kid.

Amos caught up to me easily, his hands on the straps of his backpack. "You want me to show you how to use that?"

I pulled it away from him like I was hiding a toy I didn't want to share. "No." There weren't even letters to indicate the direction. Just numbers and lines embedded in other measurements around the outside. I clicked the outside ring, turning it experimentally.

"Well, as long as you adjusted the declination correctly, we should be fine," he said.

I slid a look his way. His eyebrows lifted in challenge. I sighed in disgust, pulled off the compass from around my neck, and threw it at him. "Fine, you do it."

He caught it, mouth lifting to one side. "I said I'll show you. You can do it once you know how."

"I don't want to," I sniffed. Amos lassoed the compass back around my neck and let it fall down my back. I growled, reaching behind me and doing a spin like a dog chasing its tail.

"I know where our first point is, anyway. We won't need it until after lunch."

I gave him a dubious look as I twisted the compass back around to my chest. "How? You're telling me you're some kind of expert map… reader?"

"You mean an orienteer?" he clarified cooly.

"You are *such* an as—"

Gravel crunched as his feet slid, and faster than a viper strike, he pulled me up hard against his chest and pressed his hand over my mouth. I stared up at him, eyes flaring with outrage. His left hand was wrapped around my bare, lower back, and his hold nearly brought me off my feet.

"Let me give you a few useful words, Matthews," he said, his voice deadly quiet and his eyes sharp as steel. "Jerk. Toad. Moron. Dingbat. Blockhead. I'll even accept 'dick' on occasion because I do have a tendency to act like one."

I breathed heavily through my nose, glaring at him.

"But I don't like cursing. So, stop." He slowly lowered his hand from my mouth, but he didn't release his hold around my waist.

The contrast of his warm forearm pressed against my cold skin sent goosebumps down my arms. I was grateful he'd trapped them to my sides, so he didn't see. If he knew that being pinned to the length of him sent a trill of excitement through me, he'd never let me live it down. But how was I supposed to react when my labored breaths pushed against granite hard abs, and his thigh had been wedged between my legs? I wasn't a robot. He was hot. And I realized, as my dumb brain chugged back to life after I'd been staring at him for several seconds too long, he knew it.

He fucking knew it.

I pushed against him, furious that he'd taken on a smug, amused expression, and I stumbled backward in my haste to put some distance between us. *Goddamn it, June*, I thought, mentally slapping myself. *Stop that. Bad June. Bad. You may not lust after your boss. He's the enemy.*

Amos chuckled, low and full of sexy potential.

I fast-walked ahead of him, but a squeezing tickle clenched in my chest and up to my throat, and I coughed hard, bending over. Wilderness. I hated the wilderness. My body hated the wilderness. I felt a wheeze constrict my air as I inhaled hard, and then coughed again, angling my mouth into the crook of my arm and bracing myself on my knee with the other hand.

Amos tilted his head. "Hey, you okay?"

I nodded through the coughing fit and croaked out, "Allergies."

"Doesn't sound like allergies," he stated.

I shook my head as I righted myself, wiping tears from my eyes and willing my lungs to even out. "It is," I said thickly. "Just bad this year. I always get it."

"Hm," he said, unconvinced.

We entered the thick foliage on a hiking path. The trees cast cool shadows overhead, and we moved up an incline as the path headed toward the base of the mountains. It wasn't the easiest hike. Rocks and roots conspired to twist my ankle with every other step, and the further we walked, the steeper the path sloped.

It didn't take long for the straps of my shoes to dig into my skin, either, and I cursed Amos for *that*, too.

After a few moments of silence, in which my lungs burst into flames, I asked, "So, what's the deal? You're a clergyman or something?"

"A what?" he asked, almost offended.

"Like, a Mormon bishop or something?" He gave me a confused eye squint. "My dad is the first counselor in the fifteenth ward." I swallowed, trying valiantly to hide how out of breath I was. "So, you don't have to like… hide it or anything. He doesn't like cursing, either."

"First of all, what Mormon do you know who hides their religion? They talk about it incessantly. Secondly, I think you have me confused with Andrews," Amos said, smiling slightly and moving gracefully up the path. "He's the bishop in one of the LDS churches. Not sure which. It's why he looks like he's had twenty years drained from his lifespan. That and seven kids. Why would you think I'm Mormon? Lots of people don't like cursing."

I gave a shrug. "I don't know… You're the only dude I've ever known who didn't have condoms in your gym bag or desk."

He blinked. "Why on earth would I bring condoms to work?"

"Uh," I faltered. He had me there. I liked to play it cool, but the truth was, I didn't have the first idea what sexually active people did, having never been "active" myself.

"So, when you snooped in my office," Amos said, stopping to put his hands low on his hips, "you found a lack of condoms, paired it with my distaste for cursing, and came up with 'clergyman?'"

I halted on the path, one foot on a raised root and sweat already gathering along my hairline. "Uh," I panted, trying to catch my breath, "yeah. Pretty much."

"Matthews," he shook his head and moved forward again. "You are something else."

I hurried after him. "Well, fine, then you tell me why you don't like cursing. What's the deal with that?"

Amos looked away in thought and then finally answered, "Usually, I tell people it's unintelligent and crass, and I don't like it."

"What a charmer."

"But really," he pressed on with an annoyed glance, "it's because my dad cursed at me. A lot. And… I hated the way it made me feel. When people curse at me, it brings back those feelings."

Guilt punctured my heart with a dozen stab wounds. Wow. I was a dick. I had unfairly assumed that he didn't like cursing because he was overbearing and annoying, and I hadn't thought to give him one charitable assumption that, if I had stopped to think about it, made perfect sense. Even if he had been an LDS clergyman, I should have respected that.

I floundered for a few seconds, wondering how I could adequately respond to such a vulnerable confession. Finally, I reached out my hand and touched his arm, stopping in the middle of the path. Amos stopped, looking me up and down with a silent question. "Amos, I'm really sorry," I said. "That was insensitive of me. I should have asked earlier."

He sighed through his nose, took a step closer, and hooked a finger under my chin with a playful bump. "You're fine, June. I cuss in my head often enough, and I don't care if it's said in jest, but being cursed *at* isn't my favorite. Maybe if I were more honest with people about it, I could avoid the whole grouchy bear reputation."

"Doubt that," I teased with a smile.

He bobbed his head back and forth, his lips pressed into a smile. "Yeah, maybe not."

As we started again, I gasped. "Oh my God!"

"Wha--?" he started to ask.

"Wait, sorry, back up. Can I say that? Is 'Oh my God' okay?" I babbled.

Amos gave a long-suffering sigh. "Yes, June, I'm not religious, for the second time. What?"

"Carla's evil plan is working," I pointed out.

"What evil plan?"

I gave him a meaningful eyebrow raise. "We're stitching stuff."

About twenty minutes into our hike, it became abundantly clear to me that I was beyond out of shape. I wasn't any shape at all. I was an amorphous blob made of primordial goo and cappuccinos. I looked over at Dr. Brady and wondered what kind of dedication it had taken on his end to whittle that six-foot-something body into this toned, fluid-moving machine that navigated the uneven terrain with perfect grace. He even managed to shoot a hand out here and there to steady me when my sandals slipped in the dirt.

I peered at him as my lungs wheezed, and I tried to ignore the burning in my chest. "How tall are you?"

He flicked a glance to me. "Six-four."

"I knew it," I gusted. "You're a giant."

"To a house elf like you, I'm sure I'm a Goliath."

I laughed, squeezing out the last of my labored breath as I stopped and put my hands on my waist. Amos Brady, the closet nerd? "Oh, my God. House elf?" I put a hand to my chest in mocking offense, coughing slightly. "That's an ignorant assumption. What if I'm a Christmas elf?" Amos stopped, but instead of laughing with me, his eyebrows took on a concerned tilt. "What?" I panted, wiping sweat off my forehead on my sleeve.

"Maybe we should take a break," he suggested, already sliding his shoulder strap down his arm. "We can take a drink and I'll try to figure out where we're at on the map."

"Yeah, alright." Grateful for the break, I meandered off the path a bit to where a fallen log called to me with its concave middle padded with moss. Velvet fern fronds tickled my ankles as I threaded through pine saplings and rough grass. I swung my backpack to my side and plopped down on the log with a grateful sigh. Oh, yeah. That felt amazing.

As I unzipped the bag and dug around for my water bottle, a rustle to my right caught my attention. I leaned forward, peering around the log, and then gasped.

Lying partially obscured by a cluster of bluebells and ferns, a baby moose lifted its head. Its ears twitched in question, and it blinked at me with large, black eyes under long eyelashes like dandelion wisps.

I scrambled to find my phone in the side pocket of my leggings.

"What is it?" Amos asked, looking up from the map.

"Shh!" I waved him away frantically. I pulled up my camera app and leaned forward, pinching the screen to zoom in and get a picture.

"June, what are you doing?" he asked, his voice wary. He took long strides through the brush toward me.

"Stop!" I hissed, waving at him again. "You'll scare her."

"Scare *whom*?" He halted with a scowl.

I scrunched my shoulders, overcome by the calf's cuteness. "Baby moose," I grinned.

Amos didn't share my enthusiasm. He looked around, as if alarmed. "June, get away from there. Come here."

"No, this is perfect," I said, leaning forward again to get a few more pictures. The soft contrast of the baby blue flowers against the muted browns and blacks on the moose made for a stunning tableau. I had to use this as inspiration in my magical woodland mural. I clicked another picture, but then a strong hand yanked me up. Amos dragged me away from the log.

"Brady," I hissed, planting my feet and pulling against his hold. "What are you doing? Get *off* me."

Undeterred, he practically lifted my feet off the ground as he steered me back to the trail. "If there's a baby," he explained slowly through gritted teeth, "then what else do you think is here?"

I swiveled my head around the forest. "A mom?" I gasped again. "That would be so cool! I've never seen a moose."

"June," he groaned, as if I caused him physical pain. "You don't *want* to see a moose in the wild. They're dangerous."

"Pfft," I scoffed, and when we reached the trail, I wiggled loose from his grip. "They're just deer."

"They're not deer," he said, pinching the bridge of his nose. "Come on, we need to get away from here before the mom comes back."

A loud, low grunt sounded from behind us.

Amos whipped around, his arm shoving me behind him and his steps forcing me backward.

Coming up the hill with her head lowered and nostrils flaring, an enormous moose crashed through the underbrush toward her calf. She was gigantic. *Huge.* Her legs were so long, she could easily step on the hood of an average-sized sedan, and her sides heaved with anger directed straight at us. She let out a braying sound, her throat vibrating as she stretched it toward us.

Fear leaped into my throat and pounded through my veins.

"Go," Amos said, not bothering to be quiet. "Go, June. Up the hill."

I backed away as fast as I dared, and Amos followed, his eyes trained on the cow as she grunted again, darting toward us. Amos grabbed my arm and forced me to a run. A feral kind of bray followed our motion, and in that moment, I was absolutely certain my death certificate would read, "Moose mauling."

Amos tugged me hard to the right, off the trail and toward a thicket of trees.

Branches cracked and plants rustled as the moose chased after us. I looked over my shoulder and wished I hadn't. Her long legs carried her so fast, she'd be on us in seconds.

"Up here," Amos said suddenly, taking hold of my waist and pulling us to a halt. "Up the tree. Ready? One, two…" He lifted me off the ground and then vaulted me into the air and straight up to a thick branch jutting out from a cottonwood tree. He pulled himself up behind me, and as my hands scrabbled for purchase on the tree, knowing we weren't nearly high enough to escape the tall animal, Amos reached up and did the world's most impressive, one-armed pull-up and folded his body over the next highest branch. He reached down and latched onto my wrists. Then he heaved.

My feet left the branch and I kicked against the trunk to give him some leverage. Blowing out a breath, he finished pulling me up the tree and managed to drape me across the same branch, facing the opposite way.

The moose crashed into the trunk.

I screamed, hanging onto the branch as the whole tree shook. She was only maybe a foot below my dangling sandals. I looked up between the pale green leaves to see if we had anywhere else we could go. It was an older tree, thick around the base and full along the top. Maybe three feet above my head, a "Y" in the trunk cradled a decent-sized space like a banana chair.

Amos must have chosen the tree for that reason because as the moose grunted, shaking its head and swaying side to side, he lifted himself onto our branch and curled his feet underneath him, planted firmly on the bark. I shrieked as the branch dipped low and shook under his weight.

"Hang on," he said, his voice strained. He angled his body with his back rested against the trunk and his feet dug into the junction where the branch grew out from the main body. Then, he held out his arms to me. "Come on, we can make it up to that trunk collar."

Still hanging with my feet dangling and my hands balancing my weight so I didn't teeter back or forward, I stared at the space between us. "How?" I asked, breathless. I felt like I couldn't suck in a good breath. My chest heaved, but the air wasn't going down.

His eyes danced over me. "June, hurry. Come on, just reach for me. I won't drop you."

The moose brayed, charging for the tree again. When it made impact, I swore my heart stopped from the fear. Our branch bounced with me on it, dipping me down close to the moose and back up again, and I heard a broken scream escape my throat as I turned and straddled the branch, wrapping my limbs around it like an octopus securing its prey.

"Scoot forward," Amos said, reaching his hands for me.

I pressed my cheek against the branch, fighting for air and seeing little spots dance in my vision. "I ca-I ca—" I stuttered.

"June," Amos snapped, his voice stern and frightening in its intensity. "Come here. Now."

My breath wheezed as I sucked in, but his tone broke through my paralyzing fear. I inched forward, pulling my stomach across the branch and wincing as it scraped my flesh. I only had to move two feet before Amos' long arms could reach me, and then he pulled me to him, fitting me between his knees as he crouched on the branch with balance like a tightrope walker.

"Step on my knee and I'll lift you to that juncture up there. Do you see it?"

I think I'm hyperventilating, I thought with another jolt of fear. *I can't breathe. Why can't I breathe?*

"Matthews," he barked. My chest sucking in harshly, ribs concaving with each labored breath, I nodded.

He put his hands under my arms, holding me steady. Weirdly, my vision had gone wavy and thick, like I had been dunked under water. With heavy limbs, I balanced one foot on the branch, bracing my hands on the trunk, and then lifted my foot to his knee. He wrapped his hands around my ankle. "Ready?"

I looked up to the juncture, prepping myself to grab for it. I nodded.

He heaved, and I stepped hard, and then I went weightless for one terrifying second before my left knee crashed onto the surface. I pulled myself forward to the safety of the curve. Amos followed almost immediately after and scooped me up, fitting his back against the trunk again and settling me between his legs with my back to his belly.

Stars prickled at the edges of my vision. I fought for air and my lungs made a terrifying sound like a clogged vacuum hose. "Wha-wha—" I struggled to ask.

"You're having an asthma attack," Amos said. And just like that, he was Dr. Brady. He sat us upright, pushed my arms out to the side, and laid his hand on my chest from behind. "You have to calm down. We're safe here, so you need to relax so you can breathe."

I looked down through the branches and leaves where the moose, further away now, still snuffed and grunted, swaying back and forth with agitation. But she was down there, and we were up here, sitting on solid wood and in no danger of falling. I tried to draw in a calming breath. Panic gripped me when I realized I couldn't.

"Breathe," Amos whispered in my ear, drawing in a deep breath and lifting my torso as he did. "If you panic, it'll get worse.

Relax your shoulders. Relax your jaw." He inhaled deeply again. "And breathe."

I tried. I forced my shoulders down and opened my mouth, but the wheeze my lungs made when I tried to draw a breath sounded just as painful as it felt. Amos kept us upright, and his hand tapped my chest. "Again. Deep breath in."

I sucked in, feeling like I was being forced to breathe through a straw the size of a needle.

"Purse your lips and blow out."

I let out a little gust of air, desperately sucking in for more.

"Slower. Come on, June. Breathe in." As he talked, Amos kept one arm wrapped around me and the other shucked his bag off his shoulder and onto the bit of space to our left. He unzipped it and yanked out the first aid kit. I forced air down my lungs, my hands shaking. "And out, *slowly*." Amos unscrewed the lid to his insulated water bottle.

I tried, pushing out the little bit of oxygen I'd managed to snag through pursed lips.

"In," he encouraged, his voice low and reassuring. He opened the first aid kit and pulled out packages, which he threw onto his lap behind me. I pulled in a breath, and it was a little easier that time. "Out," he whispered.

I blew it out through pursed lips.

"Do you have an inhaler back at the camp?" Amos asked. He tugged the thick, plastic straw off the water bottle cap, brought that to his lap with the first aid supplies, and then dug back into the bag. I shook my head, fighting to draw in another breath. He inhaled deeply, and I sensed him trying to stay calm. He pulled something else out of the bag, but I couldn't see what it was. With his right hand still on my chest, he rubbed in soothing circles. "Okay, that's alright. We'll get you through this one and then I'll get you some medicine that will help. Have you had an attack like this before?"

I shook my head, wishing desperately for my airways to just open and let me take a full breath. It was like drowning. Like being buried alive. I wanted to scream and freak out.

"Just stay calm," he murmured, pressing his face against mine.

I closed my eyes, grateful for the contact. It helped. I forced another breath into my lungs, but it was so much work. It was exhausting. I'd never appreciated the automated action of breathing day in and day out more than I did in that moment.

Amos held me, sturdy and warm. "I've got you. Keep going. In and out. Slow it down. Your lungs are balloons. Expand them as much as you can before exhaling." I tried, pushing my ribs out as far as I could. "Relax your jaw. Relax your throat. Open your airways," he said. His voice was so calming, so low and full of compassion. It hummed through my back to my bones.

I closed my eyes, visualizing what he'd suggested. Each breath got better. Like the swirl in a snow globe gradually settling, my fear eased, and the attack retreated. When I had taken several deeper breaths, still wheezing slightly but beginning to feel some relief, I sagged in his arms.

Amos hugged me close, and whatever medical supplies he'd placed between us crinkled. "Thank God," he sighed. He craned his neck to look down through the branches again. "I think she left. Hopefully she took her calf elsewhere." I nodded

"Let's give you a few more minutes," he suggested, and leaned back, pulling me with him.

I settled against him, my raw lungs working hard and exhaustion slamming into me. "Stupid," I gasped out, "moose." Every syllable got sucked out of my mouth with a painful hiccup.

He laughed softly, and his hands ran up and down my arms, still soothing me, still encouraging me to relax. "I did tell you."

"Don't be a…" I sucked in a labored breath, "… dick, Brady."

"Wow, using the one humdinger I gave you," he teased. "Rude, June. Just rude."

I felt like I'd run ten miles uphill. Both ways. My eyes drooped closed, and I melted into Amos's firm body. Memory foam had nothing on Amos Brady's body. Sleep clawed at my consciousness, and I welcomed it. As I fell into murky dreams, the faraway sound of running water tugged at my memories. I could almost feel it, the steam from the shower and the way my clothing stuck to my body. Soap slid all over my skin. Amos slid all over my skin…

NINE
Amos

As June relaxed into my chest, her head lolling to the side, I lifted a hand from her body and watched in shock as it trembled.

My hands never trembled. I never wavered, and I certainly never panicked in a medical emergency. But watching June's lips go blue while she clung weakly to a tree branch, only a failed breath away from falling and being trampled by a *moose*? I'd never been more terrified in my life.

I looked down at my lap where I'd moved the water bottle straw, alcohol pads, gauze, and pocketknife within reach and thanked God that she'd managed to get the asthma attack under control. A tracheostomy with a pocketknife and a water bottle straw in a tree would have been almost impossible.

I mentally kicked myself for not preventing this in the first place. I'd seen her cough and I'd heard her wheeze. I'd known she had some form of asthma, but I hadn't dreamed that she had no idea she suffered from it. I should have made sure she had an inhaler before leaving on a hike, but I'd been too distracted by my own revelations the night before to think clearly.

Namely, the revelation that curly-haired, filthy-mouthed June was likely to feature in every erotic dream I had for the foreseeable future. And it wasn't just her body. It was everything about her. The way she took on everything with feisty indifference, the way she found awe in the ordinary, the way she cracked comebacks like the end of a whip—all of it had been embedded in my brain. And it felt permanent.

June inhaled laboriously, letting the breath out with a painful squeeze. Although she was breathing deeper, each inhale crackled and wheezed.

I now had the impossible task of getting her to medical care without triggering another—possibly fatal—asthma attack. My phone had no service, naturally.

I stared down at her, slack in the circle of my arms and restless as she gasped and coughed in her sleep. Her braid had loosened in the commotion, springing auburn curls all down her long neck and shoulders. She had a round face peppered with freckles, and the contrast to her willowy neck and shoulders honestly did something to me. It made me want to kiss her cheeks and then lead her in a dance.

A dance. Seriously? I shook my head, drawing some oxygen into my lungs and considering the situation from a rational point of view. *Take June out of it. What would I do if she was just a patient?*

I had to leave her, I realized. The safest thing would be to climb down the tree and run back along the trail until my cell got service. Then I could call for medical transport. June would stay safe, and she'd get medical attention fastest that way.

But the thought of leaving her tore me apart. I rubbed my eyes. *Okay. Buck up, Brady. This is the best course of action, so detach and let's go.*

I sat up, shuffling June and trying to wake her gently. "Hey, June," I said, my voice just above a whisper. She let out a harsh gust of air, and then her spine stiffened. "Hey," I said again. "You're safe. Relax."

She cleared her throat, looking around the tree and getting her bearings. "So-orry," she gasped out.

I rubbed her arms to ward off the chilled air under the shade of the tree. "Listen, you need to get to a hospital." She opened her mouth to protest, twisting in my lap. "Which," I added before she could get anything out, "is not negotiable."

She scowled.

"And listen, the only way to do that safely is if I go back down the trail until I can find cell service."

June twisted all the way around, her knees scrunching up. She looked absolutely stricken. "Take me," she wheezed. "With you," she struggled to force out between increasingly shallow respirations. "Take me... with you."

I placed my hands on both her arms. "Stop that. Breathe."

Her breath shuddered as she struggled to draw it into her lungs.

"This is exactly the reason I have to leave you. You aren't stable enough to go hiking down a mountain, and you need help." I pointed to her chest to punctuate my point. "You need oxygen and medicine. The fastest way is if I leave to get help. You're safe here *as long as you stay calm.*" She shook her head, her eyes reflecting the vibrant greenery around us. I moved my hands to frame her face. She was going to seriously shatter my heart with that look. "This is not a good time for you to wilt, Matthews. You're strong. You've got this."

Her lips pressed together, trembling. I traced my thumb under her full lower lip, wondering what her mouth would feel like if I bent down a few inches.

Her breath hitched.

I tweaked her nose instead, trying to lighten the mood. "I didn't take you for a delicate, fainting maiden, Matthews." A scowl slammed down over her verdant gaze. I loved that her eyebrows were a darker, duskier auburn than her hair. It gave her an intractable edge. I pinched her chin between my crooked forefinger and thumb. "You got this?"

Her throat bobbed. Finally, she nodded. "Okay," she mouthed.

"Okay." I gathered the things I had dumped out of my bag, stuffing them all in the main pocket, and then handed her the backpack. She had left hers back on the trail. "I'll run, and as soon as I get a hold of someone and give them the coordinates, I'll come right back for you." I gave her a mocking grin. "We barely made it a mile, anyway. I'll be gone twenty minutes tops."

She clicked her tongue, rolling her eyes. "Buh… blockhead," she growled before coughing hard, her lungs vibrating with mucus.

I patted her back, smiling at her use of insults I had provided earlier. "Deep breaths, June. You got this."

She nodded, wiping her mouth on her shoulder. "Got it."

I adjusted our positions so she sat with her back in the curve of the tree trunk. Then I gave her one last look over my shoulder before I lowered myself to the branch below. "Time me," I grinned to hide my fear.

She grabbed her phone, swiped twice, and then held up a stopwatch. With her eyes holding a challenge, she tapped the start button.

I booked it.

Running downhill went blessedly faster than it would have been the opposite way, and with six miles under my belt every morning, and a clocked time of 6.23 a mile, I knew I could make short work of the distance. I ran carefully, watching my feet to make sure I didn't crack an ankle, and every hundred yards or so, I slowed to check the bars on my phone.

No luck.

My mind wandered back a few months earlier to when I'd been making dinner at home. I'd been trying a new recipe—beer can chicken—and I'd forgotten to grab the roasting pan after I'd already precariously balanced the whole chicken over an open can of beer. I'd dashed away, only to leave it teetering on the counter while I scrambled to grab the pan before it could fall over.

Multiply that by fifty times in intensity, and that was exactly how I felt leaving June in that tree. If I didn't hurry, she was going to tip over some edge, and I'd lose her.

I skidded down a steep part of the trail, my heart pumping and sweat slithering down the middle of my back. My phone read 11:22 AM, but no bars. At that rate, I'd make it back to camp entirely before I managed to get service. Then a bar appeared in the top right-hand corner.

I dug in my feet, not wanting to mess with whatever invisible mojo cell phone service required, and I dialed Carla. She answered on the third ring. "If you quit on this thing, you're fired," she said.

"June had an asthma attack," I panted, getting straight to it. "She needs EMS."

"Where are you?"

"About one point four miles up the arrowhead trail," I said. "Severe restriction of airways, cyanosis, and tachypnea, but I managed to get her calm and stable for now. She doesn't have an inhaler at camp."

"I'm sending EMS to you now," she said. She hung up, and I turned back around, jogging up the trail with my heart beating painfully against my ribs.

It seemed like the run back to her tree took forever, but I knew that logically it was less than a mile. Finally, I recognized the landmarks. I turned left first, finding the log June had been sitting on, snatched up her bag, and then dropped it in the middle of the road for the EMS to find. Then I veered right and sprinted back to the cottonwood. Breathless and covered in a sheen of sweat, I smacked the tree trunk. "June!"

A choking sound came from overhead. Panic lanced through me like lightning in my veins. "June!""

Suddenly, she leaned her head over, smiling mischievously. She held up her phone with a paused stopwatch. 15:24.

I gusted out a breath, relieved that she hadn't succumbed to another attack… and then absolutely furious with her. I glared. "Don't move. I'll come get you."

It took some finessing, and I had to admit that I was overly paranoid about taxing her strength, but I managed to get her seated on a low-lying branch before I jumped down and held out my arms.

June put her hands on my shoulders, and I lowered her carefully to the ground. Her small frame slid down mine, and she looped her forearms behind my neck, supporting her weight as I guided her feet to the ground. Her chest pulsed against mine with her short, staccato breaths. Despite her condition, she leaned into me, smiling like she wanted to crack a joke.

I settled her feet on the ground and pressed my thumb against her lips. "No jokes," I glowered, my voice barely audible. "Not funny, Matthews." She bit her lower lip, lashes flitting up to give me a puckish eye squint. I pinched her bare midriff. "When you're better, you're going to pay for that. I almost had a heart attack."

Sucking in short breaths, her lips still alarmingly blue, June swayed on her feet. "For," a sharp breath in, "ho-ney."

Her tachypnea was getting worse again. I scrambled around in my brain for a way to keep her calm. "I thought the puke was payback for that," I teased. I guided her down to the ground and braced my back against the trunk of the tree so she could lean against my side. I hated how her lungs struggled for air, bronchitic with every inhalation.

"Tha-tha-h," she tensed, her hand digging into the dirt as she battled to keep her composure while her body resisted all her efforts.

"Stop," I chided, pulling her head down to rest on my chest. I wrapped one arm around her soft body. "I get it. I'm the worst."

She nodded. "You're about to really hate me. EMS is on its way."

She sat up again, green eyes darting side to side. "N—" wheeze, "nuh-oh."

"What else did you expect, June? You thought they'd send an ATV and give you an antacid tablet back at the mess hall?"

"Fuhhck."

"I'll give you a pass on that one," I said, rolling my eyes. "Stop talking."

"Ha-hah-hate," she ground out, her auburn brows pinched together.

"I never understand people who hate hospitals," I mused, forcefully guiding her back to my side. When she had settled against me again, I pressed my fingers to her wrist. *One, two, three, four, five, six, seven, eight…* "I like them," I continued, glancing at my watch while I counted silently in my head. "I know bad things happen there, but a lot of miraculous things happen, too."

She made a derisive sound.

Fifty-five, fifty-six, fifty-seven, fifty-eight… "Babies are born in hospitals," I pointed out. "Cancer patients ring bells when their treatments have ended. Loved ones wake up from comas."

"Hm," she mused, as if considering my words.

Ninety-one, ninety-two, ninety-three, ninety-four. My watch hit the thirty second mark. *188. Way too high.* I gathered her closer to me, scanning the quiet forest for any signs of EMS.

"'Mos?" she breathed.

"Hm?" I asked. My brain danced around all the worst-case scenarios and what I'd need to do to keep this girl alive until EMS arrived.

"You," she fought against her swollen airways. "Kissed. Me." I went rigid. She made a little "kuh," sound like a weak laugh followed by a painful coughing fit that sounded wet and raw.

So, she does remember. I rubbed her back until her coughing fit eased and she fell back against me, exhausted. "If you want to get technical about it," I replied slowly, still not sure how she felt about that fact, "*you* kissed *me.*"

"Lies," she said with a wave of her hand.

I smiled to myself. Ridiculous. Who held onto that much sass with their life on the line?

The distant roar of off-road vehicles filled the silence. June sat up again, and a little line creased her forehead as she looked from the trail and back to me.

"I'll stay with you," I promised. I wasn't sure why I promised that or why I thought she would want it, but it was all I had to offer to make things easier.

"Prom-uh-ise?"

"Are you questioning my integrity, Matthews?" I joked and pushed a curl away from her cheekbone.

"Ye-uh-s," she glared.

The engines grew louder as what sounded like several off-road vehicles closed the distance between us. "Just do what the EMTs say, okay?"

"'Kay."

The cavalry arrived in a cacophony of revving engines, dust clouds, and screeching brakes as the EMS skid, which was a glorified golf cart with a gurney-sized bed on the back, arrived, followed by several ATVs carrying EMTs and a couple park rangers. June shrank back against me, clearly not liking the chaos. The EMTs jumped from the skid and ATVs, bags in hand, and ran through the thick undergrowth to make their way over to us.

They worked quickly, administering steroids and bronchodilators, and I tried to stay out of their way. Although I was able to give them pertinent information about her condition, I knew there were boundaries in our professions, and in this case, I trusted them to get her to the hospital safely.

They got her loaded on a stretcher, and she gave me a look like a cat wrapped in a bath towel. I walked with them toward the skid, smiling slightly to myself over the image of June trapped on a stretcher. I took a mental picture to chuckle over later.

One of the EMTs leaned her mouth toward a receiver on her shoulder, relaying information to the hospital to expect June, and gave a quick rundown of her condition. Someone on the other end replied in a muffled voice, and then the EMT said, "Ten-four. They have Dr. Schuler on standby."

June coughed. "I have a doctor." The EMTs looked down at her in confusion. She jerked her head my way. "Dr. Brady is my doctor."

The EMTs all looked at me in surprise. My chest constricted painfully. She might as well have shoved her hand through my chest Indiana Jones style and ripped out my heart.

Uh oh.

TEN
June

It took forever, and I mean *forever*, to get discharged from the damn hospital bed. Amos was an absolute, overbearing ass, and he made me sit there for hours with a blood pressure cuff that squeezed the guts out of my arm every ten minutes, and then he made me keep the nasal cannula in my nose even after my oxygen levels had returned to normal. I wanted to rip everything off and scream like a banshee.

Even worse, they had wanted to keep me overnight for observation. At that point, I had actually grabbed Amos by the shirt and threatened to put his entire schedule into pig Latin when we got back to the city if he didn't do something about it.

And *that* was how I knew for sure that Amos Brady wanted to sleep with me. Because as he had discussed my discharge with the on-call, Dr. Schuler, Amos had offered to stay with me for the night and monitor my vitals, so I didn't have to stay in the hospital. And then a slow smile had crept up my face because no man would voluntarily sleep with a woman for a second night in a row if he didn't want to *sleep* with her.

If we were going to sleep in one bed, then I had no choice but to initiate my plan:

The slow, decadent seduction of Amos Brady.

Because here was the thing; I was very much a virgin. I hadn't intended to be, but life had panned out that way, and regrettably, my moment had never presented itself. Men were generally douchebags, I'd found. And, yes, okay, I'd assumed that Amos Brady was also a douchebag, but I might have been the teensiest bit wrong about that. Or, he was so sexy, I was willing to overlook it. Regardless, I had plans.

It still took an entire Biblical lifetime to get paperwork filled out and my IV removed, but with my lungs clearer than they'd felt since I could even remember, and a prescription bag containing my necessary meds, I finally walked through the sliding double doors of St. John's to a pitch-black summer night. I inhaled deeply in satisfaction. Brady followed behind me at a slow pace, his attention on a phone call with one of his colleagues about some kind of research project.

I called my parents and told them what happened, and my mom said she'd always sworn I had asthma. My dad wisely agreed with her excellent foresight and told me to come visit for dinner, which I… made a face at. My siblings had a lot of kids. Loud kids. I penciled in a date I would force myself to go to Chaos Dinner as we got to the car.

A notification from Instagram caught my attention and I opened it.

Archer: Hey, just checking in! Would it be too last minute to ask if you could schedule the mural next week?

I kicked myself for not finding time to make that sketch. I'd been a bit distracted. I texted him back.

June: Hey Archer! Let's plan on that. I'll get the sketch done in the next few days and send it your way. That gives me some time to tweak it before I come and get started.

Surprisingly, although it was eleven o' clock at night, he answered immediately.

Archer: Looking forward to it.

I rubbed my forehead and implanted a reminder in my brain to work on that tomorrow.

A notification came through for a text from Liz.

Liz: Look up "jellyfish shot." You're welcome.

I smiled to myself, wondering how much to tell her. It felt like so much had happened in two days.

June: I might need a few of those. I'm going to try and get laid tonight.

I chewed on my lip, wondering if I shouldn't have told her that. There was no guarantee Amos would actually act on his attraction to me, but the way he had touched me all day told me otherwise. And the panic in his voice, my God. I'd been fooling around by pretending to choke in the tree, but the way he had screamed my name made me instantly remorseful. Whether it was a doctor thing or a "you're not so bad after all, June" thing, he did seem to care about me. And that was something, right?

Liz: STFU for real???

June: We'll see. IDK how to seduce a guy, but imma try.

Liz: Show him your tits.

I snickered, looking down at my filthy, mushroom print shirt. I needed a shower first.

June: Long story, but he's staying in my cabin tonight.

Liz: Show him your tits.

I laughed out loud, and Amos gave me a sideways glance, still listening to someone on the phone. I covered my mouth, slowly making my way across the dark parking lot.

June: Tits. Check. Anything else?

Liz: Don't tell him you have your v card obv.

June: Obviously.

Liz: Ur hot. Just get some. Whos the guy?

I sent her a zipped mouth emoji.

Liz: Ok ok u keep ur secrets. Have fun!

Still grinning, I slipped my phone into my legging pocket as we reached Amos's car. He was still going on about brain imaging, and he didn't even think twice about coming around to the passenger side and opening the door for me. I gave him a raised eyebrow look. *Oh yeah. Come on, he totally likes me.* Amos didn't even notice my expression, and he shut the door after I'd climbed in.

As he talked with his colleague on our drive back to the cabin, I let my mind wander into forbidden places. Fun places. Places I'd never really been able to go myself, but for once, felt within reach. And with fucking *Amos Brady*, the hottest tall-dark-and-handsome specimen I had ever seen. He didn't strike me as a long-term relationship guy—why else would someone that hot have avoided getting a ring on some woman's finger?—but I didn't need one of those. I just needed someone with experience and amazing chemistry, and unless I was massively mistaken, I might have found that.

I tapped my hands together as I thought.

What if I was wrong, though? What if I was reading the situation all wonky and he really was just… a… benevolent guy?

No way.

My short nap in the tree had brought back the memory of our kiss in the shower, and he'd confirmed it for me. I half thought I had dreamed it. But, no, it had really happened. Dr. Brady had kissed me. Well, actually, I had kissed him, but he sure as hell had kissed me back.

I remembered how his hands had lathered soap all over my body, and the fire he had ignited in my core was such a scorching memory, it was no wonder my mind had brought it back to the surface. I had leaned into him, lust roaring in my blood, and with no inhibitions to keep me back, I had caught him off-guard and pushed him against the shower wall like I was some kind of male lead in a K-drama.

He could have shoved me away, but he hadn't. And I'd grabbed his shoulders, lifted myself on my tip toes, and pulled him down to me. He'd only hesitated a moment before his thick lashes had fanned out across his cheeks, and he'd closed the distance between our lips. I'd probably tasted like puke, honestly, but oh, he had tasted so good. His toothpaste had an interesting cinnamony aromatic flavor that went perfectly with his tan skin and moody personality.

He hadn't let it last long, but it was enough. I squeezed my legs together at the memory. God, he was hot.

And what an absolute flex that would be — my first time with someone like stern, sulky, sizzling Dr. Brady. If there was any time to be brave, it had to be this moment.

I chewed on my bottom lip and sneaked a glance at him sitting in the driver's seat and leaning his elbow on the window as he listened and nodded while someone talked his ear off. I was grateful for whoever was on the other line. I needed time to scheme.

By the time we pulled into the Camp Wilderness parking lot, I had a plan. It was a shoddy plan based on romance novels and a desperate prayer, but it was a plan nonetheless.

"Okay, I'll touch base with Melanie about the finance section and get back to you next week. Yeah, I'm still at the retreat thing." Amos paused, listening. Then he chuckled, and his eyes strayed to mine. "Uh, no." Another pause. "I'm hanging up now, Cade."

"Everything okay with the… research thing?" I asked politely. Amos gave me a look like I'd confessed to leading a drug cartel ring. "You saved my life," I said primly, sniffing. "I'm just being nice."

"It's freaking me out."

I pursed my lips. "Rude."

Amos turned in his seat, leaning his left forearm on the steering wheel and giving me a speculative look. "If you're trying to get out of our deal by being the Sugar Plum Fairy, then you can forget about it. You're going straight to bed, and you have to let me take your vitals every half an hour."

I bristled. "I keep my word, you know."

"Hm," he said, unconvinced. "You're up to something."

You have no idea, Amos Brady. I gave him a bright, sparkly smile, and then exited the car with a bounce. "Go ahead to the cabin. I have to grab something first."

"June," he warned, and shoved open his car door.

I pointed finger guns, walking backwards. "I'm fine. Go to the cabin, and I'll be there in like five minutes."

"June," he said again, his suspicion nearly coming out as a growl.

"BRB," I waved. Thankfully, he respected my request, and I was able to sneak through the dark buildings toward the mess hall. I wondered who had managed to find their scavenger hunt items that afternoon. Did anyone else get attacked by a moose? Probably not.

I tiptoed into the kitchen, found what I was looking for, and then hurried back across the campus. My lungs were sore, and even though I'd slept most of the day in the hospital, fatigue hammered behind my eyes. But I didn't have time to indulge in silly things like sleep. This felt like one of those chances — one of those things where if I didn't at least try, I would not only regret it forever, but I likely wouldn't get another shot at it.

I didn't want to be a virgin. Truthfully, it pissed me right off. I wasn't scared of having sex, and I loved how being turned on felt. I loved how orgasms felt. I'd been more than willing with the handful of "boyfriends" I'd had in the past, but I had spent the first eighteen years of my life with — understandably — chaste men from my religion. And then, when I'd veered away and gone on my own path, it seemed like my "newer" options were just assholes, in the end.

Brady was an asshole, but he was a good kind of asshole. The kind that annoyed the fuck out of me, but also, not very deep down, cared a whole lot more than his pride wanted to admit. It gave him an edge that called to me. I would bet my left butt cheek that Dr. Brady was a gentleman in the streets and a freak in the sheets.

Yes, he was perfect. *You got this, June. Make it happen, Cap'n.*

Even in early summer, Jackson Hole plummeted to icy temperatures at night, and as I made my way slowly through the empty campus, my path illuminated by the Edison bulb-strewn patio to my right, I blew out a foggy breath in wonder. Tilting my head back, I let the blanket of stars overhead drape me in courage. In an endless universe like that, teeming with undiscovered life and shimmering with mystical, faraway fairy lights, I realized how magical the little moments could be. This moment had magic written in it like runes, and only time would tell if I was casting a curse or a charm.

I padded up the stairs, wincing a little as my sandals pulled against raw spots on my ankles. They had left little rub wounds from the running and tree climbing debacle, and I'd be glad to never wear the damn things again.

As I entered, closing the door softly, I found Amos unpacking my medications from the crackly pharmacy bag and setting them up in a tidy row on my bedside table. The cabin, while simple, had an elegant charm about it. An antique, wrought iron full bed had been placed against the right wall, and two log end tables sandwiched it neatly. Each table had a shaded table lamp which provided most of the light in the small space. A woven, indigenous-style rug took up the empty space between the door and bed, and a vanity and sink had been built on the left wall. There were plenty of windows, all of them draped with homey, country-style curtains, and extra blankets and pillows had been piled on a table and in wicker baskets by the front door.

I hid my extracurricular activity behind my back. Amos glanced up, back down at the medications, and then swiftly back to me. "What's behind your back?"

"Nothing." I backed up a few steps toward the bathroom. "I'm going to shower."

"What is your middle name?" he asked, advancing on me with annoyance written all over his handsome features. "I need it if I'm going to constantly redirect all your bad choices."

"It's Ella," I said innocently, still backing up toward the bathroom. "But only people who like me get to use my middle name."

"I like you," he said quickly. The way his face froze told me he slightly regretted blurting that out. My lips twitched up. Amos folded his arms gruffly. "Do you need your bag?"

"Yes, please," I smiled. I crossed the bathroom threshold and closed the door all but a sliver, which I poked one eye out of. "Just toss it in after I'm in the shower." I took the chocolate syrup into the shower with me just in case he remained suspicious and tried to do some snooping.

While I showered, I tried to scrub away some of my nerves. It was one thing to feel unshakable confidence at the *idea* that Dr. Delicious might want to fool around in my bed. It was another thing entirely to maintain that confidence while I shaved every surface of my body and went over the possible outcomes.

Outcome one, he comes onto me first and my job gets five hundred times easier. Outcome two, I come onto him, and he uses his smart brains to oblige that request.

Outcome three, I come onto him, and he outright rejects me. Ouch, but I emotionally steeled myself for this possibility. If it was a no, then it wasn't meant to be. No biggie.

Outcome four, I chicken out and go to sleep without so much as touching him.

The only one I didn't think likely was outcome one, because Amos seemed like one of those morally steadfast types with enormous amounts of self-control. He'd be all, "But you just had an asthma attack." And his brain would talk him out of making a move. Not that I was going to let him get away with that stupidity.

I did my best to keep my boisterous hair out of the shower water because, although I knew literally nothing about actually having sex, I didn't think a wet mop of hair would make it enjoyable for either of us.

When I'd finished, I stepped out of the clawfoot tub, sliding aside the white vinyl shower curtain, and saw that Amos had placed my bag on the pedestal sink. As I dried off, I rummaged through my bag for the strategic "please take me" outfit that would give me some confidence. I hadn't packed lingerie obviously, but I had a better idea.

Deodorant on, teeth brushed, moisturizer slapped on my cheeks, and a spritz of chai perfume prefaced the tossing of the chocolate syrup in my gym bag to hide it. I left my hair down, slightly damp from the foggy bathroom, and surveyed my appearance. Not bad. Not great, either. I was nowhere near Amos's league.

Shoving aside that insecurity, I took a deep breath, wrapped myself in false confidence, and sashayed out of the bathroom. I went for cool indifference, toweling off the base of my curls that had gotten wet, and padded across the cold wood floors to my bedside table. I felt Amos's eyes follow me from his spot on the bed where he sat with a book. Ignoring him, I bent down to plug my phone charger into the wall.

Amos snapped his book closed. I jumped, straightening. Well, so much for indifference. He stared at me with dark chocolate eyes that burned with intensity. "*What* are you wearing?"

I glanced down at myself. I'd chosen a white spaghetti strap crop top with ribbed fabric and three buttons that strained against my breasts as they practically spilled out of the top. And if that didn't get him, then the outline of my nipples would. I normally wore this under my other tops to keep my bra colors from showing through, but on its own, it made my tits look fantastic. My pajama shorts were practically boy cut underwear with lace along the bottoms.

I gave him a blank look. "What?" He folded his arms, scowling. Uncertainty plucked at the fraying edges of my plan. "What?" I asked again, plugging in my phone and pretending to scroll through it.

"That's—you're not even wearing anything."

I gave him a derisive look. "They're pajamas, and anyway, you sleep topless. I could sleep topless if you'd rather."

His Adam's apple bobbed.

I plopped myself on the bed, arranging the down pillows behind me, and stretched my body out so I lay propped up on one elbow and facing him. I scrolled through my phone with my left hand, only half paying attention to what my artist friends had posted on their social media profiles. The other half of my brain was screaming that I was an absolute idiot, and that I should run back into the bathroom and put on my nightgown.

Amos watched me so intently, I could have sworn I felt scorch marks on my skin. He started to turn back to his book, and then paused. "What happened to your legs?"

I looked down. Welts and angry red crisscross marks from my sandals streaked down to my feet where blisters and cuts marred the skin. *Ah, hell.* I'd forgotten about them entirely. I shrugged, "I wore sandals on a hiking trip, remember?" *Ignore them,* I pleaded silently. *That is not part of the seduction plan, dammit.*

"Do you still have that antibiotic ointment I gave you?" he asked.

I flitted my attention to the scab on my right shin I'd completely neglected. I searched around in my head for where I might have put it. "Uhh…"

Amos sat up, giving me a reproachful glare. "You didn't even use it, did you?"

"I got drunk and then a moose attacked me!" I retorted defensively.

With a sound of disgust, Amos stood and went to the bathroom where my bag still sat on the sink. "Is it in your bag?"

I racked my brain, wondering if I'd stuck it in my purse. Or maybe I'd left it in his car. The sound of Amos unzipping my bag ripped through my senses. I gasped, flying off the bed. "Wait!"

But it was too late. Amos turned in a half circle with a bottle of chocolate syrup in his hand. He inspected it, turning it like he had with the honey, and then cocked an eyebrow. "Why do you have chocolate syrup in your bag?" My mouth opened, but no words came out. His gaze raked me from toe to hairline.

"I like chocolate," I said weakly. The cogs whirred behind his eyes. Oh my Hell, that was what I got for trying to "sneaky seduce" a smart doctor. I could practically see all the gears lining up perfectly in his brain before the conclusion whirred to life.

"June Ella Matthews," Amos said, his voice deepening into a hum as he took slow steps toward me. He'd put on a pair of white joggers and a long-sleeve gray Henley. He looked mouthwateringly menacing with his mouth curved into a "gotcha" smile. "What's the syrup for?"

Abort. Abort. Engine failure. "N-nothing."

His eyes took in my outfit, and then bounced back to the syrup. Incredulously, and almost as if he were wondering out loud, he asked, "Are you trying to seduce me?"

Mayday, mayday! Evacuate! Eject!

Amos glanced at the chocolate syrup with a hint of curiosity. "With syrup?"

"No," I huffed unconvincingly. I backed up a few steps until my legs hit the edge of the bed. "I was… I was going to get revenge. You know… for the honey."

"I might have believed that if you weren't the worst liar in the last century," he said, his advance toward me unhurried.

I swallowed against a dry throat. "Well, it's not exactly what it looks like?"

He tilted his head. "Was that a question?"

"It's, uh…" My brain erupted into a frenzied panic like a room full of stockbrokers during a crashing stock market.

He took lazy, long-legged strides until he stood a foot from me. He plunked the dark brown bottle onto my nightstand. My heart went zero to sixty in two seconds. Amos looked like he might be fighting a smile. "I'm dying of curiosity, Matthews. What, exactly was the plan here?"

Shame slithered over my disappointment, a gooey earthworm writhing and defenseless. "Well, I don't like honey, so I thought—it made sense in the moment."

He closed the remaining distance between us until the heat from his body sizzled against my frozen skin. He bent down to close the considerable gap in our heights and tilted his head, his breath caressing my jawline. "Do you want me to lick chocolate off your body, June?"

I hiccupped with a sharp intake of breath. I stared at his chest and wanted so badly to lay my palm on the firm dip and rise of his muscles. "Yeah," I admitted.

Amos pushed my chin up with his knuckles, forcing me to look him in his molten dark eyes. "I want to hear you say it, then." He inched forward and hovered his lips above mine. "What do you want, June?"

My stomach swooped and bottomed out. My eyes danced all over his features, so close to mine I could see each rough dot of stubble on his smooth jaw and the scar below his full lower lip. With my eyes transfixed on his, I whispered, "I want you."

He pulled my chin higher, bringing me so close to his lips, I could practically feel their softness. "Want me how?" he asked roughly.

"I want you to fuck me, Amos."

White flashed from his brief grin, and then his lips slid over mine. And, oh God. They were everything I remembered. Full and warm, and then commanding as he fit his lower lip to the seam between mine before moving languorously with deep, insistent strokes. Slowly, he coaxed my lips open until he could run his tongue along the inside of my lower lip. His left hand cupped my face while his right reached around and grabbed my ass, pressing me hard against his erection. A sighing moan escaped me.

I felt his smile against my lips. "I really should have better self-control than to do this."

"No," I breathed, rising on tiptoes and wrapping my arms around the back of his neck. "You really, really shouldn't."

"You pretty much doomed me to failure when you came out with your ass hanging out of your shorts."

I gasped, pulling back with a teasing reprimand. "Language."

Amos lifted me at the waist, gently, and then laid me back on the bed, hovering over me with his knee between my legs and his forearms on either side of my head. He dipped a kiss to my neck that sent a flutter straight to my nipples. "I forgot to mention," he murmured, his breath hot against my throat as he dragged his nose up to my jaw where he whispered another kiss. "I only curse when I fuck. And June," he brought his mouth back to mine with a scorching kiss. "I'm going to fuck you."

ELEVEN
June

I shivered with anticipation at the promise of his words. *Yes!* I thought with elation that threatened to steal my breath with its intensity. *Yes, yes, yes!*

Amos kissed me again, this time hot and needy, and his tongue delved deep in my mouth, flicking, sliding, and then retreating as he sucked my bottom lip between his teeth. It hurt, and at the same time, nothing had ever felt so good.

When he lifted his head, I followed, desperate for more. He bit my lip lightly and nuzzled a sensitive spot beneath my jaw with his nose. "June, I don't know what type of men you've been with…"

None.

"… but I might be a little *more* than you're used to."

Breathless and drunk on lust, I blinked at him with glazed eyes. "More what?"

He tilted his face to the side and scratched one cheek. "I wouldn't call my proclivities banal." I twisted my face into a, "huh?" look. He huffed a laugh, running his tongue along my upper lip before kissing me deeply again. Against my mouth he murmured, "I'm a far cry from vanilla."

"Oh," I wisped out. *I literally don't know what that means, but it sounds so fucking yummy.* Not wanting to outright lie, I said, "I have no interest in vanilla men."

He raised his head, searching my expression.

"Dark chocolate cupcake with chili powder and bourbon frosting," I said with raised eyebrows.

"Sure," he replied, his lips pressed in amusement. "If the cupcake is chained and begging for mercy."

Heat pooled between my legs. "Oh," I smiled.

Amos groaned, raising himself slightly and wincing. "June, I don't know about this."

I yanked him back down, putting us nose-to-nose. "If you leave me with blue balls, Brady, I'm going to sleep naked and pleasure myself in front of you until your dick explodes." Amos made a sound like he might be genuinely in pain. "Show me, Amos."

He growled, ducking down to nip my neck then replacing it with a kiss as his hand skimmed up the side of my waist. "You want to be my kind of cupcake, June?"

"Only if you eat me."

"Fuck," he whispered. Amos hitched me higher on the bed and his knee spread my left leg wide. One arm supported his weight while the other slid up my abdomen toward the hem of my shirt. "Okay, gorgeous. But I have two rules."

Rules. Hot. "Okay," I said, my back arching as his hand traveled slowly, tickling under my crop top.

"One, and I don't care if it's not sexy or you think it kills the mood — we share lists and safe words."

Lists? I thought with a jolt of panic. *What the hell is a list?*

"Two," he bit my earlobe. "I don't let my personal life leak into work. So, keep this on the down low."

I nodded, barely breathing. "Fair."

His hand skimmed the underside of my breast from beneath my shirt. "List, June. Let's hear it."

I screamed internally. "I, uh… What's yours first?"

He lifted his head again, giving me a suspicious look. "It's a list of what you are okay with and not okay with, sexually. You've never talked about that with your partners?"

My features stretched apologetically. "No, I don't think I have a list."

"Safe word?" he asked with a tilt of his head.

My brain did a slapstick comedy routine falling all over itself. "Syrup."

His eyes hooded. "You just made that up."

"Yes, I did."

Amos gusted out a sigh. "Oh boy."

"Fine, so I'm a blank cupcake," I admitted. "But I'm still… tasty."

His eyes went gooey warm again. "Cupcake, I know you're delicious, and I haven't even tasted you yet. That is not where my reservations come from."

I groaned in frustration, trying to shift so his fingers would inch closer to my nipple, which ached for his touch. "Amos, please."

"God help me," he muttered, caressing the underside of my breast and skimming ever closer to my nipple. "You're driving me crazy, June. The things I want to do to you."

"Do them," I whispered. "That's what safe words are for anyway, right?"

He sighed, ending it with a growl. His attention stayed glued away from me, and I could practically see the zeros and ones computing best- and worst-case scenarios. Finally, when he returned his focus to me, it simmered with promises of unspeakable things. "Okay, Cupcake. Let's play a game."

I gave a happy squeal, but he pinched my nipple, and it ended in a moan. "Oh, fuck."

Amos lifted himself on his knees above me and then he smoothed both hands up my ribs and under my shirt, lifting it away from my breasts slowly so it grazed the very tips of my nipples.

I let out a soft gasp and my eyes unfocused. I'd never felt a sensation like that. Like it tickled but it had also pressed a button that ignited an ache between my thighs.

He freed my breasts from the tank top, and then he raised my hands above my head, sliding the shirt over my face and all the way to my wrists. With a deft movement I couldn't begin to understand, he twisted the shirt and it tightened almost to the point of pain.

I craned my neck up to see what he'd done, but I didn't get a good look because he lifted me suddenly, sliding me so my head rested on pillows and my hands met cold wrought iron. With another practiced tug, he secured them to the bars. I gaped at him, equal parts thrilled and nervous as fuck.

"I seem to remember," he said, sitting back on his heels and drinking in the image of my naked torso displayed on the bed, "that I had promised to torture you." Amos leaned forward, arms on either side of my breasts, and he whispered a kiss just under the curve of one. "Isn't that right?"

"Yes," I said, my voice husky with desire.

"And you desperately want me to finish that, don't you, June?" he asked, kissing just outside my nipple.

I nodded, too overwhelmed to speak.

"Close your eyes and keep them closed until I say."

I obeyed, shutting out the dim light from the bedside tables. The bed dipped as he moved off it, and then a squeak of the mattress accompanied his return. I felt his knees straddle me like he had when he'd trapped me with the honey. The pop of a chocolate syrup cap made me jump. "How did you do during spelling bees, Cupcake?" he asked.

"Uh… not great."

"Oh dear," he clicked his tongue. "You really are in for torture, then."

A cold droplet of syrup landed on my nipple, and I let out a little gasp. When his tongue lapped it up, the electric current of desire went straight to my clit. I moaned again.

"Did you like that?" he asked.

"Yes," I breathed. Having my arms tied above my head and Amos straddling my hips recalled all the forbidden, dirty thoughts I'd had after our honey episode. It was almost more than I could take.

"That's your prize if you win. I'm going to spell a word all over your luscious body. It might be on your tits. It might be going straight down to your clit. It might be on your thigh or your stomach. If you guess the word, I clean you with my tongue."

"Oh my God," I groaned. So hot. He was so, *so* hot.

"If you lose," he added with a hard edge. "My cock gets to clean up the mess. And who do you think is going to lick off my cock, Cupcake?"

"Me?" I squeaked out.

"You," he agreed. "Best of three is the winner. Do you agree to the rules?"

I'd never seen a penis, let alone put one in my mouth. But this was no time to cry uncle. Or "syrup." I wanted to know what it felt like to have a dick fill my mouth. Would it be hard? Soft? Would it taste like his skin smelled? I wanted desperately to find out. "I agree."

"Good. Here's your first word." Cold syrup surprised me as it looped over my breasts and nipples, and I was so shocked by the sensation, I forgot to pay attention to the letters. The cap snapped closed. "Well?" Amos prompted.

Oh my God. I'm about to suck a dick. This is crazy. "I-I didn't catch it."

He tutted. "Pity. I like the way you taste, June. Do better next time." His hands covered my breasts, kneading them together deliciously. Every time he touched me, I wanted to burst into flames. Then something hard and straight—*his* something hard and straight— slipped between my breasts, rubbing and dipping in and out of the cleft. "Open your mouth."

Heart hammering, I opened my mouth, making sure to cover my teeth with my tongue. I knew that much, at least, from what I'd read.

Amos shifted on the bed to my right side. He turned my head to face him with his fingers in my hair, then pried my mouth open wider with a thumb to my chin. His cock, harder than I imagined it would be, probed at the entrance of my mouth. Desire roared in my ears. Shit, this was amazing. He tasted like chocolate syrup and salt, and as he pushed further into my mouth, I tilted my head to take him easier.

Amos groaned, his fingers gripping my hair tightly. He pulsed further down my throat, and I swirled my tongue to lap up the chocolate. "All of it," he said roughly. I sucked and licked, pulling chocolate and droplets of cum down my throat. He pulled out with a pop, and even with my eyes closed, I could tell he was breathing heavily. "Fuck, June," he growled.

I grinned, cleaning chocolate off my lips with my tongue. *I think I can take that to mean I did that right.*

Slightly breathless, then, he said, "Okay, minx. Next word."

I braced myself, trying to clear my head to guess correctly. But before he poured the syrup, Amos slipped his strong fingers beneath the waistband of my bottoms and tugged them down my legs until they were all the way off. He pried my legs apart. "Here it comes," he warned. Chocolate drizzled from my navel and heading down to my pussy.

H-O-?-E-Y

I let out a puff of a laugh. "Honey?"

"Good girl," he purred. Then his tongue was on me, sliding over my stomach, dipping into my belly button where he inserted his tongue in and out provocatively, making me wish desperately that his tongue — his cock — would do that to my throbbing pussy. He moved further down, carving a path through chocolate straight to where the liquid had dripped down into my slit. I vibrated with need and nerves.

When he reached the end of his path, Amos shifted so he sat between my knees, and his warm palms spread my legs wide apart. I was suddenly incredibly grateful that my eyes were closed because I didn't think my self-confidence could take seeing Amos Brady hovering just above my pussy.

The flick of his tongue along the outside of my labia caused me to gasp again. He moved deeper, far more thorough than I had been with him, and his tongue circled the entrance of my vagina, rising straight to the cluster of nerves that screamed with need. When his tongue pressed against my clit, I almost lost it completely. My legs shook and I gripped my shirt helplessly.

Then he was gone, and I was left gasping for air.

Amos covered me with his body and dropped a chocolate-covered kiss to my lips. "June, relax. If you feel like you can't breathe, we can stop. Okay?"

"I'm fine," I assured him quickly.

His tongue lashed out to lick the seam of my lips. "Alright. One more word. You ready?"

"I'm dying," I admitted. "I want… God I don't know. You're killing me."

"Good," he whispered savagely. Then he rose again, and the lid snapped open. "Here it comes." He dropped letters on my neck, smaller than the other ones, and leading down to my breasts.

?-O-O-?-E

I shook my head, not sure. "Uhm, God. Loop?"

Amos tweaked my nipple. "Does loop end in 'e,' Matthews?"

I scrunched my face. "Shit."

"It's moose."

I laughed. "I should have known."

He grabbed my face, and not gently, turned my head to the left where he rubbed his cock along my neck and down to my breasts. I panted. Why was that so hot? I wanted to reach out and grab him. "Open."

I turned my head back to the right and opened my mouth wider now that I knew how big he really was. His cock dipped into the warm moisture above my tongue, and surer than before, he pumped it straight to my throat, his fingers tangling in my hair again. I moaned in pure rapture, loving the taste of him and the feel of his firm length filling me so fully. The idea that I was giving him pleasure in the same way he had driven me crazy with his tongue was the best kind of power trip. I swirled my tongue around the underside of his dick as he dipped in and out, and I did my best to suck as he moved, keeping my teeth tucked away.

"Christ," he gritted out.

I smiled around him.

He pulled out again, and then my T-shirt was loosened from the bedframe. He wiped my mouth with his thumb and kissed me again, stoking the fires already burning me up from the inside. When he left, it was like stepping into a February morning. Foil crinkled, and then seconds later, Amos said, "Open your eyes, June."

I did, fluttering them open and squinting against the relative brightness in the room. Amos hovered over me, and rubbing my wrists tenderly, he lowered my arms back to my sides. He licked his lips.

I mimicked him, tasting salt and chocolate.

"You never asked what the winner got," Amos said, quirking one dark eyebrow.

"Oh," I gusted. My body was wound up so tight, I was going to break. I didn't know what I wanted, but I wanted it badly. In theory, I knew what I wanted, but I fairly vibrated with anticipation at really experiencing it. Just taking him in my mouth had been more intense than I could have ever hoped for.

Amos had stripped off his clothes while my eyes had been closed, but I only got a brief look before he pulled me into a sitting position. Then he leaned back, guiding me forward. His hands, strong and confident, took hold of my hips and settled me on top of him so I straddled him with his cock nestled between my legs. I stared down at his bare torso, marveling at the hard, muscular shapes engraved in his caramel tanned skin.

"Winner picks position," he said with a sideways grin.

Thank God he won. I wouldn't have known what to tell him, anyway. I looked between us, and using what brain cells still fired away in the inferno that consumed every part of my mind, I assumed he wanted me to ride him. I balanced my palms on his chest, lifted my ass off his perfectly toned body, and peeked between my legs.

Mother of God, I thought. *How the hell did that fit in my mouth?* I realized he couldn't have gotten even half of it to the back of my throat. I'd have to be a sword swallower to take that cock all the way down my throat. And my vagina? Fuckity fuck. I was going to die of embarrassment if, for some reason, his overly generous dick didn't fit in my decidedly inexperienced vagina. He'd already fitted a condom over it, and I thanked my luck once again that he hadn't asked me to help. I definitely would have botched that operation.

His cock pulsed, echoing the clenching need I felt at my center.

Drawing an inconspicuous, steadying breath, I leaned forward on Amos, craning my neck to catch his lidded, hungry gaze. I fitted the head of his cock against the wet entrance of my pussy. He let out a harsh breath and steadied my hips with his hands. I lowered myself over him and an instant, electric shock of pleasure shot all the way to my toes. I gritted my teeth, letting my head fall. "Ah, Jesus, God."

Amos pressed me further down his length.

It stretched and burned, and I curled my fingers, trying not to panic at the sensation. It was normal. I knew it was normal. I just had to move past it.

Amos made a strangled sound of pleasure. "Shit, you're tight."

"No, you're huge," I gritted out.

He let out a strained laugh. "Come on, baby. You can take me."

His words caused my pussy to clench deliciously, and I lowered myself further on his cock, lower, lower, pushing past the burning and stretching that made my thighs tremble. Finally, he filled me to the point of discomfort, and I pressed my ass on him hard. Pain and pleasure had never been so tangible.

Amos groaned, his teeth gritting. "Fuck, you feel good."

I moved up, testing my tolerance for it. *Agh, this hurts,* I thought with a twinge of despair. But there would be no "syrup." Not when I was so close.

Amos guided my hips up, then down, slowly at first, and then faster. I balanced myself on his solid chest and braced my knees on the bed as I began to find a rhythm. As I moved on my own, Amos let his hand wander to my breast, sticky with chocolate, and he lifted my breast and let it fall. Then he squeezed, and I threw back my head from the distracting rapture of it. "Don't stop," I begged.

He squeezed my nipple, and I felt a gush of fluid cover my pussy from my own arousal. I made short, staccato sounds as I moved faster, pushing past the burning sensation and letting the toe-curling arousal take over my mind again. Amos thrust his pelvis in tempo with me, and I sensed his orgasm climbing with mine.

And then, to my utter dismay, my insecurities slammed into me like a right hook to my pleasure. *I'm jiggling a lot,* I thought, looking down at my soft body as it wobbled with every thrust. *And I'm not close enough yet. He's going to get there first. Fuck, how do I fake an orgasm?*

I didn't know if Amos had read my mind, or maybe it was normal to switch positions mid-sex, but he suddenly gripped my waist, lifted me like I weighed nothing more than an oversized teddy bear, and flipped our positions so I lay under him. Then, he pumped into me with relentless, exquisite strokes.

I let my head fall back again. I'd known from my own explorations that I had a sensitive G-spot, and he was hitting it just *fucking* perfectly with his cock as he thrust in and out in fluid, rapid motions. I felt the coil starting to tighten. My legs tensed, and I clenched my teeth and screwed my eyes closed. *Come on, June, you have to get there. You can't let your first time be fake. You can do it. Just like you do at home.*

I reached between us and found my clit, rubbing in tempo with his thrusts.

"Good girl," he said, low and breathless. "Fuck, you're gorgeous."

I let out a little, strangled cry, straining hard to get myself there. Amos grunted, tensing.

I pinched my clit, and legs rigid, toes pointed, I forced myself over the edge. I groaned as the orgasm clenched around him, squeezing tight and releasing some of the pressure he'd built up inside of me. It wasn't exactly the same as I was used to in the quiet of my room and having all the time in the world to get myself there. But he'd cranked me up so tightly, the release—any release—was euphoric.

Bending his head down to my shoulder, Amos tensed, thrusting in short, fast strokes, and then went still, breathing steadily and softly.

I let my body relax, amazed that I'd managed to do it. I'd actually had sex, and not only had it—mostly—felt good, but it had also been fun. Really fun. And I'd managed to give myself an orgasm along with him, so all in all, that felt like a success to me.

And with that, I thought with a cat-like smile, *I give you my V-card, Amos Brady.*

TWELVE
Amos

June went limp beneath me, her chest heaving and a sheen of sweat covering her luscious body. I cradled her against me, letting the aftershocks of the best orgasm of my life subside in excruciatingly satisfying pulses.

Respectfully, June... what the actual fuck? Where have you been?

I glanced between us, still in awe at the goddess who had so innocently, so sweetly pulled me into bed with her. She had the body the classic artists salivated for. She had a sensual, playful nature that couldn't be replicated or faked by the best actresses. June was, quite simply, perfection. I couldn't get a read on her sexual experience, but I was leaning towards "not much." I'd tested her a little, pushing the usual "first sex" norms (barely), but she hadn't balked for one second. Actually, she'd been eager. And just the thought of it was making me hard again.

She clutched my neck, her arms shaking. "Oh my God," she breathed.

I couldn't have said it better myself. I dropped a kiss on the curve between her neck and shoulder. "You okay?"

She laughed, one heavy gust of air that ended on a slight wheeze. "Okay? Brady, you're a sex wizard."

I nuzzled under her chin with my nose before kissing her cheek. "I mean your lungs."

"Oh," she laughed again, nervously. "I think I'm alright."

I lifted myself off her, sitting back and putting my hands around her ribcage to help her into a sitting position. Her wild, red hair looked like a lion's mane, and her eyes had a soft, sedated droop to them. She bit her lip, drawing up her knees and smiling uncertainly.

I almost passed out from cuteness overload.

"How-how was that?" she asked hesitantly. "I mean, I've never, you know," she searched for words.

My stomach lurched. *You've never* what *June?*

"… played games like that," she finished, lifting one side of her mouth and resting her chin on her knees. "Was that the kind of cupcake you like?"

I liked cupcakes strapped down, moaning for mercy, and panting for my cock in every orifice in their bodies. Usually. But I was starting to think I would like any cupcake that had "June" written in sunshine yellow frosting over the top. I reached over and caressed her lips gently. "You are stunning, Cupcake. Literal perfection."

Her eyes sparkled.

I looked down at my stomach covered in sticky syrup. "Shower?" I suggested.

She leaped out of bed. "Okay, but you have to soap me up again."

"Touch you? The inhumanity."

While we showered, June peppered me with questions about my personal life. Yes, I had a dad. He lived in California. My mom had passed away several years before, and no, June didn't have to look at me with her pitying puppy dog eyes. Yes, I had siblings. My brother Zev and sister Azura were hot-shot lawyers in Denver. Apparently, June had four older brothers. Yes, I liked being a neurosurgeon. No, I didn't have any pets. My favorite color was green. Why? I liked nature—forests, gardens, meadows… I didn't tell her that my favorite shade might be her eyes, which reminded me of rustic earth tones and supple moss. My favorite food? Sushi.

I helped her dry off her hair, stealing kisses when I could because the luster of her pale skin, sloping and curving in all the right places, had me working myself back into a frenzy. I wanted to hold her. I wanted to wrap her tight and squeeze every inch of her until she gasped my name.

Which, I had noticed, she hadn't. Yet.

June donned a simple, cap-sleeve babydoll nightdress that stopped mid-thigh and had tiny blue flowers printed on it. I rested my hands on my hips. "You had that thing this whole time?"

She shrugged innocently, brushing her hair. "I had to seduce you."

"I hate to break it to you, June Bug, but I've wanted to screw you since you plopped your ass in my office chair the other day. I doubt your clothing would have influenced it that much." Her mouth made a little "O." I winked before pulling my shirt over my head.

"You gave me a nickname," she sang.

I could give her a hundred nicknames that would never convey how adorable I found her. Sunshine, sugarbug, honeybunch. She personified every cavity-inducing, sweet nickname all rolled into one spunky package. "I've been calling you 'Cupcake' all night," I pointed out.

"I like that one, too." She plopped onto the bed and crossed her legs. "I suck at coming up with nicknames, though. I don't even know any that would fit you."

"Don't," I suggested wryly. I sat on the bed next to her. "Plus, it's time to pay up, buttercup. You promised to let me take your vitals."

She schooled her features into a serious expression. "Of course, Dr. Brady."

Uh oh. I was in *so* much trouble with this girl. Dopamine overload. I slid my medi bag between my feet and zipped it open. Then, I pressed the button on the pulse ox monitor first, slid it over her pointer finger, and fished out the blood pressure cuff and stethoscope.

"So… you cuss when you fuck, huh?" June asked.

I rolled my eyes over to her. "Yes. I do."

"Why?" she asked, drawing out the word with a tilt of her head.

I fitted the cuff around her arm. "I guess because it's something good. Something fun. It's not curse words themselves I hate. But most of the time, people use them when they're talking to or about other people, and that feels uncomfortable for me."

She nodded thoughtfully, her rosy lips pursed. "So, if you didn't curse *at* anyone, or about another person, would it really be so bad to let a salty one slip sometimes?"

I searched for her brachial vein, palpating the inside of her elbow. "I guess I could probably ease up a bit," I admitted. "Outside of work, that is."

I clenched the bulb rapidly, and she wiggled angrily. "Could you ease that up a bit, dude?"

"No," I said callously, and fitted the bell of my stethoscope to the inside of her elbow as I watched the needle rise. I released the pressure slowly, listening for the systolic sound.

"I think you all do that on purpose because patients are annoying."

"Shh," I chided, paying close attention to make sure I got the reading right. Her blood pressure had been the thing I worried about the most. If it dipped too low, then the risk of her organs not receiving enough oxygen could put her in serious danger.

"So, are you going to spank me if I say them outside the bedroom?"

I lost focus like a waiter dropping a tray of iced teas, and the cuff deflated too rapidly. I blinked down at her. "What?"

"You know," she gave me a coy smile. "If I slip up. What if I stub my toe and let out an F-bomb? Are you going to spank me?"

My cock got a painful shot of desire and went half hard in an instant. "Jesus, June." She shrugged, knowing full well what she'd done. I narrowed my eyes and clenched the bulb again. I didn't *have* to tighten it past 140, but I may have let it squeeze a little harder than necessary.

"Ow," she growled.

"Shut up, Matthews." I listened as the needle fell. Eighty-nine systolic. It kept falling until I finally heard the diastolic low tone. Sixty-two. Not terrible, but I didn't know what her base reading usually was. I let the cuff release the rest of the air and ripped it off. "Do you know your usual blood pressure reading?"

She frowned, thinking. "No. The last time I went to the doctor was five years ago to stitch up my finger." She held it up so I could see the little silver scar running across the pad of her left pointer finger. "Utility knife slipped off my charcoal pencil."

I glared. "Are you telling me that you work in a surgical clinic, and you don't get your yearly exam?"

"I thought only kids did that," she mused.

"June," I groaned.

"I don't get sick!" she protested. "I'm the healthiest person alive." I rotated a meaningful look at the orange pill bottles and shiny new inhaler on her bedside table. "That doesn't count," she sniffed. "Are you done?"

I glanced at her pulse ox, which looked fine. "Your blood pressure is low, so if you feel dizzy, don't be a hero. Just say something."

"I will, fine. Are we done?"

I fitted the earpieces of my stethoscope to my ears again. "No, and you have to shut up again while I do this part. Can you manage that?"

"For King and Country, I will try," she said somberly.

I wanted to pick her up, drop her on the bed, and punish her in every filthy way imaginable. Drawing on my dwindling patience reserves, I fitted the diaphragm of the stethoscope just above her breast. "Just breathe normally."

"Yeah right," she said, her voice strained. "You're making me nervous."

"I don't know why this would make you nervous. I'm just listening to you breathe."

"You're touching me and doing hot doctor shi—stuff," she said.

I rolled my eyes. "June."

She squirmed. "Okay, okay. I'm chilling. Zen mode activated." She took a deep breath, pulling in air like a helium balloon on a nozzle.

"June," I barked. "I said normally."

She blew it out fast. "Right. Normally." She took in a breath, paused, and then released it. "I can't remember how to breathe normally."

"Christ," I muttered.

"Can we just go to sleep? I'm tired."

I sighed, put the stethoscope around my neck, and pinched her cheeks together so she looked up at me. "You're a pain, Matthews."

"Thank you."

Reluctantly, I returned everything to my bag, turned off both lights, and slid under the blankets of the absurdly small bed. Who used full-sized beds anymore? I'd had a bigger bed as a kid. My feet practically hung off the end of this one.

June settled in, letting loose a contended sigh, and curled up into a ball on her edge, which was more like the middle anyway. I reached over and dragged her across the sliver of space, fitting her against my stomach.

She snuggled closer. "You smell good."

"Mm," I said, sleep already settling over my tired mind. Keeping June alive had me more exhausted than my medical residency days.

A few seconds ticked by and then June said, "Thank you, Amos. That was really everything I hoped it would be."

"Mm," I said again, although my brain plucked at that, setting it aside to inspect later because it was a strange way to thank someone for sex. But then June's breathing settled into a deep, restful rhythm, and I sank into dreams with her.

I sat beside June, watching her paintbrush as it dappled magic highlights and shadows on a spring tree, turning it from a random blob of colors to a hyper-detailed birch. Behind the tree, majestic mountains like the ones she'd stopped to sketch on our drive up here, had been dropped in perfect proportion to the trees and flowers in the foreground.

Everything had started out darker, and as she moved closer in perspective, the colors grew lighter. I didn't know how she had done it, but she'd taken elements from our surroundings and fashioned them into a "sketch" of a fairytale forest. The fact that she considered this a sketch boggled my mind, but she'd insisted it was the crucial first step to painting a large mural for one of her clients.

While June sat in her camp chair and stroked away at the canvas on an easel, I jotted down words and phrases that drifted through my mind as I watched her. We'd set up on the edge of campus facing a wall of trees that bordered towering mountains like natural wainscoting. Stray, puffy clouds floated over the dazzling blue sky overhead, and it finally felt like summer with the sun warming my shoulders and the back of my neck.

Miracle of miracles, Carla had planned the "Imagination Oasis" this morning to help us find our "calm center" when dealing with conflict resolution in the future. I didn't know how writing poetry now would help me stay calm when June inevitably mashed every last button on my patience control panel in the future, but sure. Oasis. Nice. At least it kept June from pushing her already taxed lungs and might give her a chance to recover.

June looked over at me with a bit of green paint smudged on her chin. "How long have you been writing poetry?"

I shrugged, scratching out a phrase. "Since I could legibly put two words together. It's my 'Imagination Oasis' if you will."

She snickered and then cocked her head, examining her painting. "I kind of hate it."

"Stop," I intoned. "It's a commission for a kid. It's fine."

"Yes, but it still represents who I am as an artist," she said defensively.

"Well, it represents you as an artist who is clearly skilled at what she does. I wouldn't worry," I said simply.

She turned a soft smile on me, which quickly puckered with mischief. "Aww, Brady. You *like* me." I rolled my eyes. "Brady and Matthews, hiding in a tree," she sang. Then, veering off course from the song, she continued, "to run from a psycho moose, hee, hee, hee."

"Wow. That was beautiful," I said sarcastically, not looking up from my book.

"It did rhyme," she said with a lofty tilt of her chin.

"'Hee' is not a word, June."

"It's an onomatopoeia. Spell *that* in chocolate, mister. I dare you."

I leaned over in my camp chair so my lips hovered inches from her surprised face. "Careful what you ask for, Cupcake."

June's cheeks flushed and an imp-like gleam entered her forest green eyes. She had one dimple on her right cheek that peeked out as she smiled and asked, "Please?"

I released a breathy laugh, leaning away and shaking my head.

"So that's a no, then? That's okay." She turned back to her painting and sketched out shapes along the forest floor with dark paint. "We can use something else next time. Ooh, caramel."

I smoothed away a smile. Honestly, I'd expected June to do the whole "let's define this" bit when we'd woken this morning. But no, she had popped out of bed and danced her way through her morning routine like a daffodil in a breeze. She didn't seem phased by the fact that she'd almost died or that she'd had sex with her boss, which could potentially complicate both our lives.

No, she seemed wholly unconcerned about what to label our relationship as, and for some reason, that needled me. I usually hated it when women did that. But something feral inside of me wanted her to nail me down and force me to declare my exclusivity with her.

I used to think that men who became besotted with a woman were overly tame. Sedate. Boring. But the urge to grab onto June and make sure I never had to share her with anyone else felt like the exact opposite of that. It felt wild and uncontrolled. It was a gnashing, slavering thing that lusted after every part of her, and it barked at anything that might get between that.

My phone buzzed in my pocket, so I closed my book and looked at the caller ID. It said it was Lachlan and I answered immediately. "Cade," I said.

"Brady, what's up man? How's the wilderness?"

"If you have a development, what is it?" I asked, irritated that Cade always wanted to engage in small talk before getting to his point. The guy was way too nice and was basically rural Idaho's own Steve Rogers.

"You're so charming, Brady. It's what I like about you. Okay, I wanted to draw this out and make your whole year, but whatever. We got the green light from U of U to use their new 3T. Carte blanche."

I stood, my heart thumping. "Seriously?"

"Right in our backyard. Our initial research caught the eye of Dr. Fontel and he wants to peer review when we finish, so now it's in their best interest to collab."

"You're joking."

"You know I wouldn't joke, Brady. Full access."

This was so much better than getting a machine in Colorado. I'd known that the University of Utah had purchased their own MRI 3T machine, but it cost money to use it by the hour, and our funding hadn't justified that cost, yet. "That's amazing."

"Well, you can thank my girlfriend for that. She searched 'MRI 3T,' and when it came up with the U, she literally emailed Dr. Fontel our preprint and straight up asked if we could finish our research in their facility."

That stunned me into momentary silence. "Your *girlfriend* cold-called a renowned research facility?"

"She's smarter than I am. Anyway, we need to go over scheduling. You available tomorrow? I'm already clearing half my schedule to get over there."

"Yeah, I can meet you," I said, glancing down at June who stared up at me with unabashed interest. "Tomorrow, nine AM? My office?"

"I'll be there."

I hung up, hardly believing our luck. The problem with our preliminary research report was its lack of concrete imaging data. The MRI 3T technology was finally catching up, and now we had the chance to utilize it properly.

"What happened?" June asked, setting her paintbrush on the edge of her easel.

"We just made a huge break in our research. We've needed specific facilities to get the data we need to," I hedged, trying to find the right words, "basically to back up our claims. Cade just called and said we've been given full access to the equipment."

She beamed, standing. "That's amazing!"

"Yeah," I breathed. I tugged on one of her curls gently, watching it spring back up around her temple. "I'm sorry to leave."

She waved a hand. "Are you kidding? Of course you have to go! I'm so happy for you."

"Don't forget your meds and take it easy for the rest of the day," I reminded her.

"I know," she said, rolling her eyes.

A terrifying string of possible "June episodes" that could happen while she was still at the camp suddenly clicked through my head like an arcade game spitting out a full roll of tickets. She could get drunk again and do something stupid. She could get lost hiking. She could *go* hiking, period, and that had its own subcategory of horrifying possibilities. I stared at her, not sure what to do with my traitorous mind that had gone from calm and uncompromisingly logical to batshit crazy.

"What?" she blinked.

"I, uh… your car is still stranded. Do you want to come back to the city with me? I can drop you off at home and we can send a tow—"

"Amos," she frowned, turning to plop back in her camp chair. "Don't look at me like that. I'm fine. We're leaving tomorrow morning, anyway. Use the extra day off to work on your research."

She was right, of course. I had to go. And she would be fine. Totally fine. She was a full-grown woman. I sighed through pursed lips, letting my cheeks billow out. "Yeah, I hear you. Okay, I'll get my stuff. See you on Wednesday?"

"Good luck!" she smiled.

Ignoring my misgivings, I folded up my camp chair and then hurried back to my cabin. As I did, my mind rolled over into research mode, and the process took over my thoughts.

THIRTEEN
June

"Honey," Katherine said, watching my car lift off the asphalt, "your Mercury is in retrograde or something."

I frowned as the tow truck winched my sad sedan onto its flatbed. My shoulders slumped forward in defeat. "What do you mean *my* Mercury? Everyone has the same Mercury."

"Uh, uh," she stuck a lollipop in her mouth, shaking her head. "Yours is on a different plane of reality. It's messing with your chi."

"You're mixing up metaphysical concepts, now," I muttered.

Katherine leaned her plump hip against the hood of her compact car. "You get your own category."

We watched in silence as my deader than dead car rode the dolly up the incline of the tow flatbed. My inner June screamed in tune with the metal-on-metal screech the flatbed made as it leveled out and finally came to a stop. Katherine had offered to take me to my car, and even though we had filled it with gas from a red gas can, it had started and then immediately smoked before bursting into actual flames. I knew what the car was worth. It was totaled.

My bottom lip wobbled. Katherine looked over at me, and with an indulgent sigh, pushed herself off her car and put her arm around me, wrapping most of my torso in her black, lacy shawl. The pungent aroma of roses and lavender plumed around me. "Aw, come on. It… it was kind of an ugly car."

"I just paid it off," I whimpered.

"Yeah," she patted my arm. "That's unfortunate."

I swallowed a lump of tears, cursing my rotten luck. "I think this might be karma."

"Now who's mixing metaphysical concepts?" Katherine teased, sticking her sucker back in her mouth. "But why? Did you sleep with your head facing north?"

"No, but I slept *with* someone," I moaned. "I gave away my virginity and now God is punishing me. My mom was right. God saw me *doing things* and now he's going to bankrupt me."

Katherine tucked her chin down and popped the lollipop out of her lips as she gave me a dubious look. "I don't think God punishes people with bankruptcy."

"How do you know?" I squinted as tears stung my eyes, mingling with the dust and pollen that had coated everything in Idaho's sweaty armpit. "It's 2023. Maybe a bottomed-out credit score is the new locust plague."

"Maybe you should take a drink of water or something," Katherine suggested.

I sniffled again.

"Who did you sleep with, anyway? There wasn't anyone up there." She paused, and I let her fill in a couple of blanks. "Oh my fucking God."

"I mean, he was god-like," I mused.

Katherine pulled away from me, her features accusatory. She pointed her lollipop at me. "You slept with Amos Brady."

"*You* said we had chemistry," I pointed out. "But yeah, I think the whole rescue bit did it. He made a really hot knight in shining… athletic wear. And don't worry, I didn't mention the whole 'V-word' inexperience, so he was just *fun* about it. It was awesome."

She nibbled on the corner of her lip, suddenly uncertain.

I frowned. "What's that look? I mean, I know he's my boss, technically, but it's nothing serious."

"Well, maybe not, but," she looked around, her heavily-lined eyes blinking hard like she was looking for an apparition to appear and scare us both. "You did lie to him."

"What do you mean?"

Katherine used a long, acrylic nail to delicately scratch the side of her nose. She had a diamond nose ring that sparkled in the bright noon sun. "You know. The virgin thing?"

"Of course I lied to him," I scoffed. "If I'd told him, he would have been all 'oh, no, I have to protect her delicate flower' or whatever, and he wouldn't have done half the sexy shit we did."

"Right," she agreed slowly, cautiously. "But don't you think *he* should have been allowed to decide if that was okay, too? What if he finds out?"

"He won't," I said with confidence I didn't feel.

"All I'm saying is he might not be very happy with you if he does find out."

"And?" I prompted.

"*And* he's still your boss? A relationship that he very much would need to trust you with?"

I blinked, staring at her. She blinked back pointedly. "Shit," I breathed.

"Retrograde," she said firmly. "Definitely retrograde."

I tried not to think about the unlikely possibility that Amos would find out about the V-card thing. I tried to pretend, on the outside, that her words hadn't affected me. I listened to music and let my hand soar on the wind outside my window as we passed through Star Valley. I chatted and listened to details about Katherine's upcoming fair appearances for her palm reading.

On the inside, I panicked. I should have known better. Brady had said he didn't like to mix his personal life and his work life, but we had thrown the two together in a blender, and it might as well have been poison for me to down. Even if Brady didn't find out that I'd lied to him, what if things went south? What if things were awkward now? Why hadn't I even considered the possibility that this was going to ruin my whole job?

I had to get my mind off it. I had to find something to distract myself. I pulled up my mural client's number, which he'd given me so I could text him, and asked if he would mind if I started the mural tonight. I had my pencils, charcoal, and chalk. I could start the sketch, at least, and that might take my mind off the litany of bad outcomes my brain was producing.

Archer texted me back and said that he'd love to have me start early. He gave me his address, and I copied it into my map app after asking Katherine if she'd drop me off there. I could probably afford a rideshare from an app to take me home if it wasn't too far away.

Archer's house ended up being a fair distance from mine—Salt Lake City was a vast, sprawling metropolis with suburbs carved into the mountains and trailing down the valley. Archer lived in one of the mountain homes amongst multi-million-dollar estates and glittering mansions.

As we drove up to his address, Katherine and I stared in mute wonder before she stopped just outside the black metal gate. The house had been made, most likely custom, to resemble storybook architecture. On either side, rounded mini turrets bracketed steeply pitched roofs and alcoves, arched, diamond-paned windows, and curving balconies. The lawn was expertly manicured and dotted with natural stone features like a curving staircase up to the front door and fairy circles lined with bright flowers.

"Holy sheep," Katherine whispered. "Who do you think their contractor was? The Seven Dwarves?"

More like a fairy godmother. Only magic could have conjured an estate that enchanting. I texted Archer to let him know I was there, and then I gathered my art supplies in my beat-up tote bag that had seen better days. I was only sketching, so thankfully, I wouldn't need to worry about paint just yet.

The gates opened, and Katherine gave me an exaggerated bounce of her eyebrows. "Good luck, I guess. Do you need a ride back home?"

"No, I'll call a ride," I said, opening the door and trying not to look as gobsmacked as I felt. "Thanks for the ride. Oh," I reached a hand around the front seat to grab the blue daypack I'd tossed on her back seat. "Almost forgot my meds. Can I get the rest of my stuff out of your car tomorrow after work?"

"Sure thing," she said, shooing me from the car.

I waved, walking briskly through the double gates, and then followed a river stone path to the slab stairway that curved gently up to the alcove above their front door. When I knocked on the rustic, thick-slatted front door, it only took two raps before Archer opened it for me.

Middle-aged and attractive in a Toby McGuire way-past-his-prime kind of way, Archer stood aside to let me into the foyer. He was wearing a pair of crisp, white tennis shoes with socks that reached his calves, and he had tucked a striped polo into khaki shorts. Forrest Gump couldn't have chosen a better ensemble. "Hi, June!" he said brightly. "I'm so glad you could make it."

I held out a hand as I stepped over his threshold. "Hey, Archer. It's my pleasure. I'm just glad you liked my work."

He shook my hand firmly, his too-large, blue eyes crinkling with his smile. "Oh man, are you kidding me? We're in love with your work. My wife had to have you."

Thank God there was a wife. Katherine knew where I was, but part of me had balked at going to some guy's house on my own. A larger part of me should probably have balked harder, but hey, he had a wife. Something about that put me at ease.

I hooked my thumbs in the open sides of my overall shorts and looked around the foyer. It had a rustic, French country feel that used creams, muted golds, and opulent fixtures to decorate the space. A little settee that had probably never held a single butt in its life had been placed to my right, and to the left, an arched alcove curved over a distressed white vanity table with meaningless, decorative knickknacks on its surface.

As Archer left the foyer, explaining that his daughter was staying at a friend's house, I took in their main living space with enormous eyes. If a castle courtyard could have been made into an open-concept main floor, then this would be it. There were pillars that circled a middle area, which was huge and filled with over-stuffed sofas, polished wood end tables and coffee tables, and a gigantic double-sided hearth. The kitchen, which was Gordon Ramsey-worthy, had been built to the left, and a second living space that looked more like a media room had been built to the right. We passed a dining area as Archer took me down a hallway toward the bedrooms.

"Meg, my wife, loves fairytales," Archer explained as we went down a storybook hallway decorated with twigs, vines, and fairy lights. "So, of course, we had to make my daughter an enchanted forest bedroom."

I silently wondered what the daughter liked. Maybe she was into steampunk or weirdcore. I hadn't even asked how old she was.

"And Bridget loves fairytales too, of course," Archer said, as if that were a given. Bridget, I assumed, was the daughter in question. I took a new look at this man with speculative eyes. Even if his wife liked fairytales, did he also like them? Why was everything—and I mean everything—in her style?

We reached the bedroom Archer wanted me to paint, and I had to touch my chin to make sure my jaw hadn't hit the floor. If there was a romantic, renaissance era detail you could add to a room, this one had it. Fireplace? Check. Gabled ceiling? Check. Lush, intricately woven and definitely custom carpet? Check. The windows were diamond-patterned and Gothic style, and although it was devoid of furniture, the light fixtures and wall decor were enough to fill the space with claustrophobic decadence.

Archer pointed to a free wall that adjoined the Gothic-style windows. "Here's where we were thinking of putting her mural. This will be her art and reading nook.

"Nook," was a loose term. The space was palatial, and the wall where they wanted me to paint the mural was massive. I took it in with fear clutching my heart. Then I slapped it away because this was an amazing opportunity. Taking a breath and approaching the wall, I asked, "Well, do you have a ladder?"

Archer laughed. "We definitely do. What do you think? Can you make it work?"

"Of course," I said automatically. "I'll have to modify the sketch I sent you."

"We trust you," he said easily.

He kept saying "we." Where was this wife who had spun herself a web of fantasy? As I surveyed the wall, my mind already mapping out where each element would go, Archer asked from behind me, "Do you need anything? Water? Food?"

"Just a ladder would be great," I said, turning to smile at him.

He smiled back. A little too long. I turned back to the wall, but I felt his eyes on my back, and then he said, "Sure thing. I'll be right back."

I pulled my phone out of my overall pocket and stared at the screen. I wasn't sure why I had done that. To call someone? To text someone? I chewed uncertainly on the inside of my cheek. *Grow up*, I chided myself. I slid the phone back in my pocket and turned my mind to my work. Everything was fine. I simply didn't love social situations with new people. And really, who did?

Archer brought me the ladder, and even though I hadn't asked for it, a bottle of water. I set it to the side, and as I pulled out my chalk and pencils, my eyes danced over the wall already filming over with a picture of what I wanted to sketch. Starting in the middle, I got to work on my proportions with my headphones on my ears and an ABBA playlist blaring. It wasn't because of Amos and our conversation about his music tastes. Unrelated.

I lost myself in the process. Time had no meaning when I felt inspired to create, and the more I worked on the initial background sketch, the more excited I became over the possibilities. Cotton candy sky. Jewel-tone mountains. Darkened forest with glowing orbs and fairy lights amongst baby forest critters. I could see the palette in my mind's eye, and I knew when it was done, it would be truly magical.

After getting the rough sketch done, mostly focusing on proportion and background to foreground perspective, I pulled out my phone to check the time. It read nine at night. I hadn't meant to stay at their house so long, and suddenly felt guilty that I might have kept them awake or intruded on their time.

As I descended the ladder, I caught a shape in my peripheral vision. Archer was lounging against the doorframe, watching me with keen interest in his eyes. I jumped almost imperceptibly, but there was a weird moment where Archer seemed to notice that he'd scared me. There was a pause—not long, and barely something I registered—but he watched me with sharp eyes in that fraction of a second that held an emotion I didn't recognize. But then he waved apologetically. "Sorry, I didn't mean to scare you. I'm just amazed at how quickly you did that."

I glanced at the sketch, and truthfully, he was right. I had done a lot in four hours. "Thanks," I said, slightly breathless. My fingers itched to pull up the rideshare app and get home, and my inward breaths had taken on a slight wheeze again. I tried to remember if I'd taken my meds that morning.

"Meg will love this," Archer said, advancing across the room with his arms crossed. He still had on his tennis shoes, khakis, and polo. "Do you need a ride home? I noticed that you had someone drop you off."

"No, it's fine," I replied, grateful for the excuse to pull up the app. "I'll grab a driver. Oh," I looked up, catching his too-bright eyes. "I forgot to go over the particulars of payment. Sorry. I got so excited about getting started. This wall *is* a little bigger than I first anticipated."

"Of course," he replied nonchalantly. "Just let us know what you're charging. No problem."

Looking at their house, I didn't doubt his ability to pay. "I'll send it to your email if you'll text that to me," I said, bending down to drop my ruler, tape measure, and pencils in my bag.

"Sure," he said, hands in his pockets while he watched me.

I typed out a message to the driver with my fingers shaking. I could feel his eyes on me. He didn't move. He just stood there, watching me. I couldn't tell if this was a generational thing, a bizarre personality thing, or a red flag thing. All I knew was that I desperately wanted to get out of the house, so I bent down to scoop up my art bag. "I'll be back this weekend to start painting," I said with a smile.

Archer nodded, his body strangely still. "Sounds good, June."

I resisted the urge to duck my head. I gave him a friendly wave instead and walked around him. He twisted, watching me leave. A shiver skittered over my skin, but as soon as I was back into the warm night, it eased away.

It took the driver less than seven minutes to get to the house, and I waited for them outside. I looked over my shoulder a few times while I stood outside the gates, but the lights had been turned off and the half-moon cast a silver film over the fairytale house, limning the edges like gilded pages. Shucking off another twinge of unease, I greeted the black sedan as it pulled up.

It wasn't until I was in my empty home that I realized I'd left my day bag with my medicine at Archer's house. I refused to face the real reason I didn't want to go back to get it. I could grab it on Saturday, I decided.

FOURTEEN
Amos

Sweat clung to my back in a sticky film, sucking my white button-down shirt to my skin. Some of it trickled down the valley of my spine like an insect that skittered down to my waistband. I adjusted my position, punched the cool air flow button for my seat, and leaned my head back on the headrest of my car. As I crawled through traffic, Cade talked nonstop on the other end of the line about our imaging protocol overview.

"If we shoot for four—six? Six sessions, say an hour each, with resting-state and task-fMRI data, then we can ensure that we have structural, dMRI, and fMRI data," he said. I could hear him typing while he talked, which was a skill I shared. It was why I had been able to count June's pulse while still babbling away about hospitals.

I cleared my throat, my mind mostly on our research, but a tiny bit on June now that I'd remembered that. "Are we sticking with our original task protocols for the tfMRI scans?"

"I don't see why not," Cade said. "Unless you think they need to be updated."

A text came through on my phone, which lit up on the screen on my dashboard. It was our inter-office communication system.

June: Mr. Larsey is back. He wants a word. Should I tell him to wait in your office?

It was the patient with shoulder arthritis who was convinced he needed his spine fused because a search engine had said so. I sighed deeply and typed a quick response back.

Brady: No, he needs to make an appt with Andrews or shove off.

June: …I'll paraphrase that.

Cade paused, "Something wrong?"

"Day job," I intoned.

"Your receptionist still giving you hell?" he teased.

Not for the reasons you'd think, I thought grimly. It wasn't that I had expected June to text me, but… okay, I kind of figured she would text me. And I could have texted her too, but something told me that if happy, lemon-drop June hadn't sent me a funny text or an offer to hang out, then her brain was doing something very different than what my brain was doing.

Or my brain was overthinking that.

"Brady?" Cade prompted.

I cleared my throat again. "She's a pain in the ass, but no. We're… working through our differences."

"Weird," Cade said.

I flicked my blinker, getting into the turning lane that would take me into the medical district. "I was bound to get along with someone eventually."

"Yeah, except you said you'd trade her for the Tasmanian Devil like three weeks ago."

Fair point. "I was wrong."

Silence crackled over the line. It stretched on and on, and I tapped the screen to make sure his call hadn't dropped. Finally, Cade said, "What the fuck?"

"Language," I intoned.

"Did you just say *you were wrong?*"

"I'm hanging up," I droned, hovering my finger over the red button. "I'll touch base at four."

"Wait a second, who is this gir—"

I tapped the end call button and blew out another breath.

He had a good question, though. Who was June to me? I'd been able to lose myself in research protocols for a solid day and a half, but I found my thoughts wandering to June more often than they should. It was hard to ignore how differently she made me feel than other women I'd been with. Hell, I felt different about her than the long-term relationships I'd had and let go. It wasn't just that I wanted to be in her company, because I was no stranger to that feeling. No, it was different than that. It was magnetic. It was gravity. It was some kind of science I didn't fully understand.

Actually, it was a lot like connectomics. When I studied a slide of inhibitory axons, the main cells were presented in rainbow colors. Each cell looked like a large, bright dot on the slide, and they could be seen easily. But behind those cells, like a fine web or loose tapestry, the microscopic nerves that meshed around those cells were a mystery to us. At least, at the moment, they were.

June was like those neurons. She had somehow tangled herself in the background of my thoughts, always there and necessary for my brain to function, but a complete enigma to me.

As I parked and exited my car, heading for the air-conditioned surgical center, I wondered if, for once, I'd gotten in over my head with a girl. As I opened the front door to the lobby, I knew immediately that my assumption was right.

I wasn't in control. Because I suddenly wanted to beat an old man to within an inch of his life.

Mr. Larsey's voice rang loudly through the lobby, which at this hour, only had two other patients in chairs by the window. They were glaring at him with undisguised annoyance, but it wasn't for their sake I wanted to shuck off "do no harm" and pull the old man's arthritic arm out of its socket. It was because he was bent over the desk and yelling loudly in June's face.

My June.

"... if you're telling me you can't punch my name into that schedule," Larsey said, hammering his finger on the top of June's monitor and causing her to flinch, "then you're a dumber bitch than you look."

I saw red. The tendons in my arm pulled painfully as I gripped my fingers into a fist. Then my better judgment went tumbling out a back door as my rage took over and propelled me across the room.

But before I could take more than two steps, June, who hadn't even seen me enter, stood suddenly and flung the contents of her boba tea all over the front of Mr. Larsey. The old man spluttered, coughing and hacking as he took several steps away from her desk. "This is a surgical center," June said, her small frame visibly trembling. "And I don't care who you are, you will *not* speak to me that way."

Larsey gasped, looking down at his tea-stained plaid shirt and blue slacks. A couple boba beads rolled off his hair and plopped to the ground. He wiped a shaking hand across his face. "You crazy bitch. You—you—where is your—"

"Boss?" I asked darkly.

All eyes swiveled to me. June went milk-tea white, and the other two receptionists, Maxine and Katherine, stood from their chairs with horror on their faces. Larsey turned last, his aged skin drooping and dripping with iced tea like the sugar was actively melting him. Anger pinched his large lips, and completely misreading my thunderous expression, he rounded his outrage on me.

"Dr. Brady, is this *your* employee? Did you witness what just happened here?"

"Oh, I saw it," I said softly.

June, still holding the plastic cup in front of her, looked stricken with fear. The idea that she was afraid of *me* made me want to go on a Godzilla-style rampage. I didn't ever want to see that look on her face again. I'd saved her life two days ago, for God's sake. *A little credit here, Cupcake?*

"This is unacceptable," Larsey continued, clearly convinced that my ire was directed at June and not at him. "I've never been so—"

"Mr. Larsey," I clipped.

The man had some sense, after all, because his soft jowls quivered as he snapped his dentures together. I saw the slow awareness creep over his features—the dawning realization that my scowl was directed at him. His pose shifted and he angled away from me.

"Ms. Matthews represents my practice. She is an extension of myself, and I believe you called her a bitch. Do you feel that I, too, am a bitch, Mr. Larsey?"

He said nothing, quivering.

"I will be transferring your care immediately," I said, and moved through the lobby, dismissing him. "Remove yourself from this surgical center or I will do it for you."

"You'll be hearing from my lawyer," Larsey said at last. With one more glare at June, he limped out of the foyer.

The two patients in padded waiting chairs gawked. June crunched the empty cup to her breasts with her green eyes wide like jade stones. I pulled my keys from my pocket and gestured toward the hallway, my gaze on June. "Come with me, Matthews."

Katherine and Maxine swiveled their astonished expressions from me to June, and I could tell they wanted to protect her from whatever wrath they expected me to rain down on her head. But June obeyed immediately. She set the cup down on the counter and walked briskly around the front desk. You could have knocked me over with a boba tea straw—she'd actually done what I'd asked.

As she emerged from the cover of the desk, I had to make a concerted effort not to stumble into the door. She looked downright edible. She was wearing a puffy, babydoll-style dress with pastel, rainbow-hued colors splashed over the fabric like an abstract watercolor painting. The sleeves curved just off her shoulders and puffed out like two cotton candy swirls. The skirt flared out from her generous bust and ended mid-thigh. She put her hands in two pockets on the skirt of her dress and chewed the inside of her lip as she approached me.

I wasn't going to make more of a scene in front of patients and other staff, so I opened the door to our back rooms and gestured mutely for her to walk through. She did, her back pencil-straight and her soft, auburn curls trembling slightly. She didn't even wait for me to lead. She went right for my office, and then I opened the door with my key.

She paused at the threshold, her wide eyes bouncing between mine like she could read her future in my gaze. With my arm holding the door for her, I bobbed my head in the direction of my office again. June breezed past me, smelling like cherry blossom lotion, and then plunked herself down on one of the chairs across from my desk.

I shut the door, leaned against my desk, and gave her a once-over. "Are you okay?"

She looked up from her lap like I'd asked for directions to Mars. "What?"

"Are you," I repeated slowly, folding my arms, "okay? He didn't touch you, did he?"

"No," she said, her brows contracted in confusion. "You... aren't you mad?"

"Why would I be mad with you?" I asked softly.

June mimicked the splashing of the boba tea thing. "That. I did that." She did it again, tossing an invisible cup of boba tea at me. "All over a patient."

"He was threatening you," I said, pushing off from the desk and unfolding my arms. "You beat me to it. And," I admitted with a guilty stretch of my mouth, "probably saved me from battery charges."

She gaped up at me.

"Cupcake," I said, and leaned down, resting my hands on the arms of her chair so my face was angled down a hair's breadth from hers. "The benefit of winning over the bad guy is being on his good side. I will pulverize anyone who talks to you like that again."

"Holy sheep," she whispered.

"Now," I said, straightening again and holding out a hand. "The real reason I asked you back here was to ask you out for dinner. Are you free?"

She took my hand, standing, and her slack-jawed amazement turned glittery. "For real?"

"June." My eyes hooded to half-mast with derision. "I hate repeating myself." I tugged her to me, sliding a hand around the small of her back and holding back the urge to take a huge bite out of her. She *looked* like a cupcake. A sherbet cupcake that smelled like flowers. "Send me a list of the places you like."

Uncertainty suddenly clouded her features. She chewed on her lip so hard, I half expect to see blood. "Yeah, okay."

"What?" I asked.

"Nothing," she smiled, banishing the cloud and replacing it with Sunshine June. "I'll send you a list. Can I ride with you? My car got towed."

I gave her a suspicious squint. "Why? What did you do?"

"What did *I* do?" she asked, offended. "*I* didn't do anything but have the misfortune of being a starving artist with a crappy car."

"You chose to be a starving artist," I pointed out. "You could have been a neurosurgeon." She gave me a look like she might actually translate my files to pig Latin. When she tried to push away from my hold, I tightened it, pinning her length to mine. It took massive concentration on my part to keep from getting an immediate hard on. I leaned down so our lips were nearly touching. "I'm joking, Matthews. You make a perfect artist." I kissed her softly, and then released her.

She looked surprised again, her cheeks flushed and her tongue darting out to lick where I'd kissed. "Thanks."

Something was off with her. I wasn't sure what—the car? Me? But something had definitely gotten under her skin. Good thing she was the world's worst liar. I could weasel it out of her over dinner. But not before because I needed her to focus on her job.

I really didn't want to have to yell at her before I took her out to dinner.

FIFTEEN
June

I had to tell him. I had to. I couldn't take the guilt anymore. Not since Katherine had worded it in a way that made me sound like an absolute asshole. I hadn't really thought about *my* virginity affecting someone else, but the more I thought about it, the more I realized Amos would be super angry if he knew. It hadn't felt like a big deal at the time, but my lie had been outrageous enough that he thought I was sexually experienced... he thought I liked "dark chocolate" sex. I didn't even know what the hell the difference was.

He had been really insistent that we be open about each other's preferences. He had been kind and careful and had wanted to make sure that boundaries stayed in place. And I'd taken all his boundaries and thrown them around like a drunk rodeo clown with a lasso. *Yeehaw! No one cares what* you *want, Amos!*

I let out a self-pitying sound and dropped my forehead on my desk. Maxine looked over as she shouldered her Hermes Kelly handbag. "You okay? You still freaked out over the old guy who yelled at you?"

"No," I groaned, and I bounced my forehead lightly against the wrist cushion in front of my keyboard. "Something else."

She leaned down and whispered, "Is it because you slept with Dr. Brady?"

My eyes snapped up to hers. Her fake lashes fluttered innocently. "Maxine," I growled, "where did you hear that?"

"Kat," she said, as if it were obvious.

My spine straightened. "Who else did she tell?"

Maxine shrugged.

"You can't tell *anyone* else," I insisted. "I don't think he's the 'declare your relationship' type, you know?"

She nodded seriously. "I get that. I've never seen him with a girlfriend."

"Exactly," I muttered, looking around. The lobby was empty because we'd already seen our last patient out and locked the doors. Brady was all the way down in the surgical wing performing a laminectomy, and he'd said it would take him an hour or so to finish. I wasn't sure who I was looking around for—everyone was gone. But I *so* didn't want to add "told everyone we're having sex" to my list of sins.

Maxine sat down again and rolled Katherine's chair closer to mine. "Is it good? The sex?"

I sucked in my lips, looking around one more time for good measure to make sure we were alone. Dead quiet. Leaning forward, I said, "Amazing."

She laughed and encouraged me to go on. "Like how? I've been dying of curiosity."

I had no idea what the etiquette of "don't play games with chocolate syrup and tell" were, so, haltingly, I admitted, "Well, he's got that whole 'I'm in charge' kind of thing going on."

Maxine groaned, tilting her eyes to the ceiling. "I knew it. He's all surly and sexy."

"Exactly," I grinned.

Maxine held her two pointer fingers together and varied the width between them questioningly. "Bigger, smaller than other guys?"

I grimaced, lowering my voice. "I wouldn't know."

Her jaw hinged open. "June, no way."

"Yeah… he was my first."

"Hoooooly shit," she drawled. "*June,* your first guy was *Amos Brady?*"

I shushed her, looking around the deserted lobby again. "He doesn't know. I didn't want him to like… coddle me or something. I knew he'd be all dark and broody and it was *so* good."

She brought a hand to her mouth. "*You didn't tell him?*" she squeaked.

"That's why I'm trying to bang a dent in the desk with my forehead," I admitted. "I need to tell him. I thought it was no big deal, but the more I think about it…"

"You can't start a relationship with a lie," Maxine said seriously. "Especially not with guys like Brady. I don't think his DNA will let him lie."

I made a pained face. "So, you think I messed up, too?"

She scrunched one side of her nose like she always did when she was thinking. "I mean, it's your virginity and all but… yeah. I'd still tell him."

I sighed heavily. "I don't want to."

"Don't blame you," she replied honestly. "Glad it's not me."

I suddenly wondered if my first time with him might have been *better* and not worse if I'd told him. And once the idea took hold, it wouldn't let go. I blinked, staring off into space as the truth of that smacked me between the eyes. He probably would have been extra patient with me. And I wouldn't have had to rush anything.

Maxine watched me think with her eyes bouncing all over my features. "What?"

I swallowed against a dry throat. "I, uh... this might be TMI."

She waved a hand. "No, it's not. You have to talk to someone about these things, right?" She mimicked sealing her lips and throwing away the key. "I won't say a word."

I released another breath and pushed away from the desk with my feet, letting my chair roll and turn slowly. I stared at my new sandals, which crisscrossed over the red weals from my previous (now banished) pair. "So, I'm not sure I had a typical orgasm. I mean I had one, and the actual *sex* was so fun. But I got in my head at the end, and it was kind of hard to get there. I had to force it."

Maxine shook her head, flicking a piece of lint off her navy blazer. "Tension orgasm. I get it."

I stopped the chair's momentum and planted my feet. "That's exactly what it was."

"Happens," she shrugged. "I mean you had one, right?"

"True," I said slowly. "It did feel different than my normal ones I've had on my own."

"Well, yeah," she laughed. "It's going to. No worries. Practice makes perfect," she grinned.

I gusted out a laugh. "Yeah. That would be nice."

"Hey, upside is," she said, "if you tell him, then he can show you all the stuff he knows *and* be patient with you at the same time. Although," she screwed up her face dubiously, "I can't really imagine Dr. Brady being patient about anything."

"He's patient," I said, still thinking. "I don't know, Maxie. On the one hand, I get your point. On the other hand, what if it makes it awkward? I don't need him to show me anything. I've read romance novels. I get the gist."

Maxine snorted. "Don't let him hear you say that."

"True," I muttered, looking around one last time. "He's going to be insufferable about this whole thing. I can feel it. He's going to freak out over getting handed my V-card, and I won't even have a good excuse for him."

Maxine winced, standing. "Good luck?"

"Thanks."

She bumped my chair with her hip before leaving. "You got this, babe."

"You better not put this on Instagram," I called after her. She waved without making any promises. I slumped in my chair and spun myself again, hoping the centrifugal force would squeeze a solution into my brain. It was all well and good to decide I needed to tell Amos, but it was another thing entirely to figure out *how* without fully pissing him off.

Earlier, when he'd taken me back to his office, I'd nearly fainted from shock at how gentle he was. Angry, towering Amos was starting to look more like protective bouncer Brady. If he was on my side, then I had a big, scary shadow that could make me feel safe.

And I really liked that idea.

SIXTEEN
Amos

I leaned against the wall, my heart banging around in my chest like a ricocheting tennis ball. June *mother clucking* Matthews.

Just when I thought I had found my footing with that red-haired imp, she sent me careening off-kilter the other way.

She had been a virgin?

I pinched the bridge of my nose as she continued her conversation with Maxine, oblivious to the fact that I was on the other side of the door that separated the lobby from the nurse's station. *News flash, June. The doors aren't soundproof, you doofus.*

"… not sure I had a typical orgasm," June's voice admitted. "I had to force it."

My eyes bulged open. *What?*

Maxine commiserated with her, but all I could think was that I'd had the best sex of my life and June *the virgin* had gotten in her own head and hadn't had a decent orgasm.

I gritted my teeth and forced myself to stay still. Forget the honey prank. Forget the puke I'd had to clean up on my own. Forget the moose and the stupid stunt in the tree that had bottomed my heart out of my stomach. This was so much worse, and if she thought I'd been punishing before, then she had no idea what she was in for. That cupcake was toast, now.

I was supposed to be in surgery, but the patient had gotten a case of COVID, and at the last minute, needed to cancel. Something June would have known if she'd been paying attention to her computer instead of talking about our sex life. I was still in my scrubs and had come down from the surgical wing to let her know I'd be ready early. I looked down at my dark blue pants and tapped my surgical cap soundlessly against my thigh. *I don't want vanilla,* she'd said.

The absolute irony is that I'd gone as vanilla as it got for me because my instincts had warned me that she didn't know what the hell a "dark chocolate and chili powder" fuck would even look like.

"… don't need him to show me anything. I've read romance novels. I get the gist," June said with way more confidence than she ought to have.

I felt my features darken. *Is that right?*

"You'd better not let him hear you say that," Maxine cautioned.

Too late. She's screwed. I looked around as my brain revved up with irresistible ways to teach June a few well-deserved lessons about honesty. There were endless possibilities, but I had a perfect one in mind.

Lesson one: Be careful what you ask for.

SEVENTEEN

June

I went to the staff bathroom to touch up my makeup and get a grip on my nerves before going on an honest-to-God date with Amos Brady. I stared at my reflection with a purposefully goofy face twisting my features. I'd fluffed up my eyelashes with mascara and re-applied blush, wishing for the hundredth time in my adult life that I could use pink and not earth tones. Every time I did, the pink clashed with my hair and freckles, and I looked like a Golden Girl.

I zhuzhed my hair a little, plucking a few curls out from the mass to frame my face, and thanked my lucky stars I'd woken up early enough to shower and use the diffuser. My dress was the best thing in my closet, too. I guess I'd been feeling the need for courage this morning. Even if I'd been able to get over my misgivings with Amos, the interaction with Archer in his house had left me decidedly unsettled. I couldn't say why, though. He hadn't done anything wrong.

Pushing the encounter from my mind, I popped my lips together to spread my lip gloss around, did a little turn in the mirror, and decided that it was as good as it got for me. Amos would be finishing up soon, and while he probably wanted to shower and get dressed, I'd be ready when he was.

A text dinged on my phone, and to my surprise, it was Amos from his personal phone to mine. It was the first real text we'd had.

Amos: Come to exam room 3.

I frowned at the screen. Why was he in the exam room? I checked the time. And early? Weird. Maybe something had gone wrong with his patient.

As I walked out of the bathroom and idly made my way through the nurse's station to the exam room, I scrolled through different text tones I could give Brady instead of the default one. I grinned with an evil chuckle as I found *Toccata and Fugue in D Minor*. Dracula theme song. Still looking at my phone as I tapped on the screen to set the ringtone to his number, I leaned my elbow down on the lever handle to open the heavy door. I pushed it open with my hip and stepped into the dark exam room.

Shadows enveloped me as the door slammed shut. I jumped, looking up from my phone. Amos was leaning against the counter in his navy scrubs, and his arms were folded tighter than his scowl.

I paused, phone still lighting the darkness as I looked around, confused. "What's this?"

He switched on a small task light in the corner before saying, "Give me your phone." He held out a bare, toned arm.

I complied mindlessly, all thoughts wiped clean by his tone. *I don't know what I did,* I thought as I stepped forward and handed over my phone. *But I definitely fucked up.*

He snatched it from my hands and tossed it to a padded chair without looking. His gaze had zeroed in on me, darkened by shadows and silent fury. I took a subconscious step back, but he latched his fingers around my wrist and yanked me against his body. "Change of plans," he said, his voice so low I felt my bones purr.

"Yeah?" I asked. I did an up-down of his smooth but clearly perturbed expression. Wait, was this some kind of role play? Had I missed a message from him?

"We're going to play another game," he said softly.

Excitement bolted through me. "Yeah?" I asked hopefully.

"The game is, I teach you a lesson, and you guess the question."

I blinked. That sounded… ominous. "Okay," I said slowly, drawing it out uncertainly.

"What's your safe word?" he asked, his voice barely above a whisper.

I gulped. "Syrup?"

"Good girl. Get on the table."

My lips parted with uncertainty. I pointed to the exam table. "The… that table?"

He nodded once.

My nerves ratcheted up like the jerky ascent on a belay wall. *Yank, yank, yank* went my nerves like I'd been harnessed up and someone was bodily hefting me to the top of some unknown height. I used the step stool to climb onto the table, and the paper under me crackled like static. I settled myself on it and let my feet swing. "Okay, now what?"

"Lie down," he said, arms folded again and watching me.

I frowned. "You don't look very happy about this game."

"Do you want to play, or not?"

"Okay, okay," I muttered, lying back on the paper so I looked up at the drop ceiling tiles. My nervousness made me lift my head and suddenly ask, "Okay, but if I'm not a fan of whatever you're doing, you'll stop, right?"

"Always," he said seriously. There was a good dollop of earnestness in the promise, too, and I relaxed into the paper.

"Okay. I trust you."

"Actually, you don't," he said, moving finally and kicking his physician's stool over to my knees. "Which is why we're playing. The more trust you have, the more... gratifying it will be."

Giddiness bubbled up and popped like champagne bubbles in my chest. "Okay."

Amos nudged the stool with his foot in front of the table at my feet, but he didn't sit on it. He leaned over me, his large hands forming warm cuffs over my cold wrists. He bent until his lips kissed mine. My eyes fluttered closed as I marveled at the silky-smooth texture of his mouth on mine. I sighed into the kiss, and then he slowly pulled away. "I've been wanting to do that all day," he admitted.

"Me too."

Amos gave me another lingering kiss before he lifted his head and caught my gaze in the semi-darkness. "Okay, here are the rules of the game."

"You really like rules," I drawled. "You should have been a teacher."

"One," he continued, ignoring me, "you keep your body absolutely relaxed. No flexing. No tensing. No curling your toes or closing your knees. If you tense up, I start over."

His words caused an ache to build between my thighs already. "Start over what?"

"Rule two," he barreled on, "I'm ignoring literally everything out of your mouth that isn't your safe word."

I gaped, speechless.

"Rule three, you come when I say you come. No exceptions."

Oh shit, I'm in over my head, I thought with sudden panic. *I should have told him. I should tell him now. But… if I tell him… he'll stop.* And I was dying of curiosity.

Amos reached down between us and with one deft tug, fluffed my skirt off my thighs. I gasped at the sudden rush of cold air, but, true to his word, he was ignoring my reactions. Amos bunched my skirt up so my polka dot, blue panties were exposed, and with barely a glance at them, he hooked his fingers under the waistband and dragged them down my legs. They were dropped unceremoniously next to the table. He carefully removed my sandals, avoiding all the sore streaks that ribboned over my skin. Then he sat on his stool and adjusted the height.

His face was level with my closed knees and crossed ankles, and I suddenly understood what he was about to do. I sat up on my elbows, giving him wide eyes. "Wait, wait, wait, I didn't prepare for this at all. You should have told me. I would have showered or --"

"Lie down," he said with quiet authority. "And spread your legs. As far as you can."

Saliva pooled in my mouth at the sight of him sitting there, his dark eyes full of decadent sex. He had rolled himself right up against the medical table, and I realized he must have adjusted the table in advance. He was at the perfect height for peach eating.

Amos slid both his hands between my thighs, and with gentle pressure, he pried my legs apart. I gusted out a breath, letting my head fall back again. I closed my eyes as my legs were spread wider, wider, *wider*, until my tendons stretched, and cold air hit my pussy. My chest rose and fell as I waited tensely. He put his hands under my ass and dragged me right to the edge of the table and draped my calves over his shoulders. Then he weighed his hand on my stomach, and I clenched under him. "You're starting off pretty bad, Cupcake," he teased. "Relax."

I pulled in a breath and released it, willing all my muscles to melt into the paper. He waited, and the longer he waited, the more I managed to deflate my self-consciousness. After a while, it didn't matter that I was lying like that for him to see. Surprisingly, my brain adjusted.

His chair rolled, and then two fingers slid along the outside of my labia. I jumped, and then his fingers paused. He waited until I relaxed again, and then he did the same thing. I'd anticipated it that time, and he swept his fingers down to my pussy, which was already wet and aching for his touch. He went tortuously slow. He carved a path along the outside edges of every exposed part of me that I wanted him to touch. My breathing picked up, but I willed myself to stay relaxed.

I got this, I thought smugly. *Relax while he pleasures me? Please. He had me all worked up for nothing.*

Amos dipped a finger into my heat, and I groaned, but I kept my stomach slack. My fingers drummed on the table softly as he slid in and out, hooking his finger up to my G-spot and then around in a circle before retreating again. I moaned, and I felt dangerously close to tensing up.

Okay, maybe this is a little harder than I thought.

With his finger still slowly penetrating me, I felt a gust of air over my clit. His tongue slid along the side of it. I gasped, and my back arched. He stopped. I lifted my head with wide eyes. "Wait, when you said 'start over…'"

Amos pulled his finger out from inside of me, and my juices made a sucking sound. Two fingers started on the outside of my labia.

"No," I groaned, letting my head fall back limply. "Are you for real?"

"Rules are rules," he murmured.

"Fuck," I breathed. "Amos, this is going to take forever."

"That's up to you," he reminded me. His finger dragged around the outside of my pussy, and I gritted my teeth at the ache it caused because all I could think about was how good it had felt when he'd had that finger inside of me. And I knew the routine, now. I knew how long it would take.

Okay, June. Eyes on the prize. You got this. Zen orgasm.

He made his way through the sweetest, longest torture with his fingers before plunging them inside of me again. I huffed, eyes closed, and kept my body calm even though my whole being screamed for me to writhe and buck to match the tempo of his finger. A hot breath blew on my clit. I steeled myself, and when his tongue lashed along the edge of my clit, I let out another moan of ecstasy. It was so good and so *awful* at the same time. I wanted to pull down his pants, take out his cock, and slam myself onto it to fill the needy ache inside of me.

His tongue started to do clever things while his fingers pumped. He went around my clit and then over it with pressure, and my legs trembled with the need to arch my back, but I resisted. I'd never imagined it was possible, but even as I tightened on the inside with corkscrew twists of pleasure and agony, I managed to keep my legs and torso slack. And I was getting the hang of it. I focused on my breathing and the tightness at my core, and then on every mind-numbing thrust of his finger and lap of his tongue.

Amos inserted two fingers, and I made a strangled, high-pitched sound. He lifted his head to gust out a laugh, "Something to say?"

"No," I eked out. *Calm, calm, stay calm. You're so close.*

He moved his fingers in and out, slow at first, and then fast. I gasped, bunching my fists and hoping he wouldn't see or care because *dammit* I had kept the rest of me slack and I didn't think I could hold out much longer.

Amos bent his head again, his mouth hovered just over my clit, and then as his tongue lapped a long stroke over the sensitive spot, he sucked.

I screamed, and my back arched off the table again as my legs twitched closed. His fingers stilled and he lifted his head with a smug, molten expression. "No," I breathed. "No, no, no, you can't." He removed his fingers and pried my knees apart again. I gripped my hair by the roots. "Amos, you *fucker*."

His fingers slid along the outside of my labia with mocking slowness. "Damn," he clicked his tongue. "I thought you had it."

I made a growling sound of frustration. My clit pulsed. My center felt empty, hot, and sore. "I can't," I panted as he slid his fingers around again. "I can't. Amos, seriously."

He didn't stop. "Seriously, *what*, June?"

He wanted me to say it. He wanted me to say the safe word and end it if I couldn't take it. I sucked in another breath, grinding my teeth as I did, and forced my body to relax again. I was *not* going to quit. Fuck that.

He chuckled, and from square one, we started again. Twice. Twice, he brought me straight to the top of my pleasure, and as his mouth sucked my clit hard, I lost my composure. And each time he started over, each time he made me climb, I got closer to my orgasm. He probably sensed that because his routine got shorter, and he pulled maddening moans from my body as he pumped his fingers in a steady rhythm. But the third time he lowered his mouth to my clit, I was ready.

He sucked, and I let out a breath, tensing my throat, clenching my fists, but forcing my body to melt as my insides clenched, and pulsed, and clenched again, and then I felt something truly terrifying build inside of me. It was unlike any orgasm I had approached before. It was wild and uncontrolled, and I had a sense that it was going to rip me in half when I got there. Whether I was ready or not, he was going to yank the cord on the pinata and release all the prizes.

"I," I panted, feeling the spring coiled tight and about to release. I let out a garbled, wordless sound.

Amos stopped sucking, but his thumb pressed on my clit as his fingers worked me from the inside. "Use your words, June," Amos said.

"Please," I panted.

"Please, what?"

"I want to come. Please."

He stopped. Suddenly and devastatingly, he stopped. I gasped, my whole body shaking as my orgasm slipped away from me just as quickly as it had climbed. "What?" I panted, lifting my head to look at him in confusion. "*What?*"

Amos wiped a hand over his mouth, and then his fingers stroked the insides of my thighs with excruciating softness. "That's one."

"One *what*?" I screeched, starting to bring my leg off his shoulder so I could… what? Push him away? Kick him until he gave me the orgasm back? *Fuck.*

He tilted his head, regarding me as he put my leg back in place. "I thought you liked dark chocolate, June. It's edging."

"Wha—" my brain felt sluggish. It reeled with confusion. "The fuck is that?"

He kissed the inside of my thigh. "I'm surprised you don't know. It's pretty tame, as far as the darker side of 'dessert' goes. I get to choose how many times I bring you to the brink. And you get to come when I say you can."

I choked. "For how long?"

Amos stood from his stool, his hands pressing onto my wrists again, and he leaned between my legs until his lips hovered over mine. With his voice low and rich like bitter chocolate, he said, "I don't know. How long were you going to wait before you told me you were a virgin?"

Another inarticulate word escaped me. His eyebrows twitched up a fraction. "Oh no," I whispered.

Amos placed a gentle kiss on my lips. "Welcome to the dark side, Cupcake. You know the word to make it stop."

"Stop?" I asked, two octaves too high. "Stop like… like you'll help me finish?"

He shook his head.

"Fuck," I hissed, and let my head slam back onto the table.

"Only good girls get to come, June," he said, lowering himself back to his stool. "If you're a good girl, you'll get what you want."

I made a sound like a metal chair screeching over tile. "Fuck you, Brady. I'm not saying it."

"Good girl," he murmured. His fingers started at the beginning again. "You count the next one. Out loud."

I was already lost in the sensation of his fingers. Then his tongue. Then he was inside of me with two fingers, filling me with punishing strokes, and he sucked my clit so hard, I thought I saw stars. That scary feeling happened again. I'd become used to keeping my body slack, but that inexorable tug pulsed and clenched, sending me straight to a cliff that made me think I'd been jumping into kiddie pools my whole life.

My breath stalled in my lungs, and I briefly considered cheating and not telling him I was close. I considered lying and letting myself give in to the orgasm. And then it hit me. Balanced at the very top of my precipice, the question to accompany his lesson slammed into my brain.

How important is honesty? How can we trust each other without it?

"Stop," I choked. Amos stopped. I wanted to cry, but I forced out, "Two."

Amos dropped a kiss on the sensitive flesh near the apex of my thighs. "Good girl. Keep going."

I hit my fist against the table, but I didn't stop him. He didn't mess around with getting me back to the top, this time. Two of his fingers pistoned in and out of me so fast, he catapulted me straight to my orgasm. "Stop," I screeched. He did, and I swallowed hard as the release waned. "Three," I whimpered.

Amos went slower the next time, circling my clit with a thumb before he hooked his fingers inside of me and dragged them across my G-spot. That was torture. Pure torture, because I didn't get there as fast, but it was deliriously good. He moved his fingers fast again, pressing my clit. "Agh," I garbled. He stopped again, and I covered my eyes. "Four. Please, Amos, I can't. I can't anymore."

He kissed my thighs again, lifting my dress to drop nips and kisses along my heaving stomach. "You win," he murmured. "Good girl, June. You win."

"God," I begged. I wasn't sure how he understood that it was a plea, but he did.

"Come here."

I sat up, hating the feel of it because all I wanted was him between my legs again. But he lifted my dress up my stomach, over my breasts, and then looped it off of me. Every nerve in my body radiated like thrummed strings on a cello. He unhooked my bra, and I realized he was still fully dressed. Hell, no. I lifted the hem of his scrubs, and he obliged, shucking it off his rippled arms and torso before cinching me to the edge of the table so I straddled his erection through his scrub pants.

I tilted my face up to his, desperate for all of him. Any part of him. And it was then I realized he was just as starved for this as I was. His calm demeanor had been replaced by his rapidly rising and falling chest, and his eyes burned with hunger. "Wait here," he said roughly.

I clamped my arms around his middle. "Don't you *dare* leave me, Amos."

He released a rueful laugh. "I need to get a condom."

"Are you clean?" I asked through clenched teeth.

He understood what I meant. "Of course."

I pulled him closer so we were nose to nose and whispered harshly, "Then you'd better bury your cock in my pussy right fucking now because I don't take birth control just for funsies and I am *not* waiting."

He didn't need to be told twice. Amos eased his waistband down until his dick was poised at my wet entrance, long and just as intimidating as I remembered. He looked me in the eyes, his lips pressed together and his breathing ragged. "Do you trust me, June?"

I nodded. I did. I really, really did. He slid inside of me, slowly, so slowly, and I let out a tortured breath as my head fell to his shoulder. That vibrating from my nerve endings increased, and I thought I might shatter from the tension. He inched further in, and I looped my arms behind his neck, panting against his skin.

Amos took his time, even slower than the first time I'd controlled his penetration, and I could have cried, I was so grateful. I should have trusted him the first time because this was Heaven and Hell wrapped up in every delicious sin and miracle known to mankind.

When he moved in and out of me, he whispered, "Stay relaxed."

I did. It was hard, but I did. I let him plunge in and out of me, and as he moved, he coaxed me back onto my elbows. I had a perfect view of his honed body thrusting his cock in and out of my wet heat, and I wanted him to keep going just as desperately as I wanted it to end. The tug I'd become familiar with happened again. It felt bigger this time. The surging climb to my impending release was monumental as he filled me over and over again. It was Everest, and if I didn't let myself fall from the peak, I'd lose my mind.

"Please," I moaned. "Amos."

He reached a hand between us easily, and with his thumb, he pressed coaxing circles over my clit. "Please, what?"

"I think I'm," I struggled to talk. Up, up, up my release climbed and clenched until I was sure I would combust.

"Come for me," he said harshly.

I let go, and it wrenched a cry from my chest as my orgasm crashed and pulsed with such intensity, I half expected something in me to break. I was dimly aware that Amos had sped up his tempo, and then he pulled me to him, keeping me in one piece as we both came down together.

As the coils unfurled and my lungs slowed, I felt like I'd been forced to run the goddamn high school mile again. Each intake of air caused sharp pain near my ribs, and I'd been covered in hot, muggy perspiration. And the satisfaction. Holy mother of God. It was euphoric. It was lighter than air and yet, it dragged my bones to the earth like gravity on another planet. I leaned against Amos, speechless.

He kissed my sweaty temple and wrapped his arms around me. "The last one didn't count," he said gruffly.

"Last what?" I asked drowsily.

"The syrup, Cupcake. It didn't count." He tilted my face up to meet the intensity of his expression. "*Now* you can hand me your V-card."

EIGHTEEN
Amos

As June had astutely pointed out, teaching her a lesson had taken "forever." However, looking at her perpetually half-lidded, content expression, it was safe to assume that she didn't mind how long it had taken. But most of the restaurants I had planned to take her to were closed now, especially because we would have been late leaving the center anyway.

I changed into my button-down and chinos, and by the time I'd locked up and turned off the lights, June was gnawing on her phone case as she waited by my car. I pulled her phone out of her mouth and unlocked the car. "Don't be dramatic."

"I'm not dramatic," she said. "I'm starving. You ate me to death. There's nothing left."

I put a hand against the gunmetal gray panel, sliding my foot between hers and leaning forward so I could trace a finger along the sweetheart neckline of her dress. "Babe, I'd eat you for breakfast, lunch, and dinner. There'd better be plenty left."

She got that stunned look on her face that I was starting to crave in a visceral way. "Wow," she breathed.

I pressed my lips into a smile. "Wow, what?"

"I honestly thought you were a vampire who sucked the blood of sacrificed virgins until like a week ago," she said with a completely straight face. "I thought you were the villain."

"June," I said derisively, "I've *been* sucking on a virgin."

She gasped, like she'd discovered my evil bat lair. "You *are* a vampire."

I nipped her neck. "Yes. Now get in the car before I get snacky."

She gave me a knowing look before ducking under my arm and prancing to the passenger side door. "I like you snacky, Amos."

I liked snacking, so that made two of us. As we fastened our seatbelts, June asked, "Okay, but for real, where are we going?"

"My house," I said simply. She gave me two big, doe eyes, so I reluctantly added, "Unless you'd rather not."

"No, no, I want to," she said quickly. "I'm dying to know what your house is like. In my head," she went on, scrunching her face like she was picturing it, "you have a moat, and when the doorbell rings, it just yells 'go away,' in an old man voice."

I rolled my eyes over to her.

She cleared her throat, and the dash illuminated her green eyes like they were bioluminescent. "Okay, but in all seriousness, I was dreading being alone in my apartment all night. So, thank you."

I frowned. "I thought you have a roommate."

"I do, but she went—" June paused, narrowing her eyes at me. "Wait, how did you know I have a roommate?"

"You have a bad habit of blabbing about your personal life at work."

Her narrowed gaze thinned to slits. "You just ate me out in exam room three, *Doctor* Brady. You're one to talk."

I rubbed a hand over my mouth, smiling. "Fair."

"Anyway," she emphasized wryly, "yes, I have a roommate, but she's in Miami for three months."

I felt my brow crease again. I had a weird feeling about June being alone. It grumbled in my stomach, but I couldn't name the emotion. "When will she be back?"

"She just left last week. I didn't think I would mind because we have our own bedrooms, but it's *creepy* by myself," she said. "You know what I mean?"

"No," I said honestly. I liked being alone. It was my favorite part of being an adult.

"Oh, yeah, I forgot you live with legions of the undead."

"Keep cracking jokes, Cupcake," I said, giving her an eyebrow raise. "I'll introduce you to my dungeon."

She cracked her knuckles with a sly smile. "Why don't the legions of the undead fight each other?"

"Why?" I drawled.

"They don't have the guts."

"That's it." I pulled over on the deserted medical district road and lunged for her.

She cackled, putting her feet between us. "You promised a dungeon! You expect me to ignore that?"

I laughed low, unbuckling her seatbelt, and hauled her over the middle console to my lap. "You made the vampire snacky. Get over here."

We managed to make it through the city with our clothes on, but it was a close call. June was driving me crazy with her smart mouth, and I wanted to shut her up with my tongue. Which I did. On the side of the road. But eventually, I had to gather some of my sense back to my head like reeling in a fishing line, and I plopped her back in her seat before I gave in and took her again in my car.

I clicked on my blinker in front of my building's parking garage, and June made a dramatic gasping sound. "You live at *the Regent*?" She pinned me with a shocked expression that was almost accusatory. "Do you peddle bitcoins on the side or something?"

I rolled my eyes and turned into the garage. The gate opened as it read the pass on my dash. "That doesn't even make sense. No one 'peddles' bitcoins." She watched in mute amazement as I headed for my parking spots, and I resisted the urge to laugh at her expense. "It's a parking garage, June."

"*I* don't get a parking garage," she said, eyes still wide. "I have to scrape snow off my windshield with my dustpan."

I gave her a pained look. "Babe."

"Don't you dare judge me. Those scrapers are pricey."

She continued to look around with round-eyed wonder as we walked across the dirty parking garage and into the painfully conventional elevator where I punched floor nineteen. When the doors opened, she peered out like she might see something interesting, but in all reality, my floor wasn't anything special. The building liked gold and bronze as far as decorative touches went, but they didn't line the walls with celebrities like June seemed to think she'd find.

I punched in my key code for my front door, and she leaned around me, gawking at that, too. I turned to her with a derisive scowl. "Are you going to do that all night?"

"Yes," she said honestly.

With a sigh, I pushed open the door and tapped the digital smart switch on the wall to wake up the apartment. The lights blinked on, the door locked behind us, and the blinds on the eleven-foot windows rose to reveal the city lights beyond.

June looked at me like I'd taken her to an amusement park. I squished her cheeks together—something that was fast becoming my favorite hobby—and gave her a hard look. "Cut it out. You're making this weird."

When I released her, she whispered, "You *are* weird. No one lives like this."

"I live like this. What do you want for dinner?"

"Um," she leaned into me, and I wrapped my arm around her. "Pancakes?"

I made a face. "Pancakes?"

"Yeah, pancakes are easy."

"I didn't ask what was easy. I asked what you wanted," I said.

She pulled away slightly, one auburn eyebrow quirking up in challenge. "Sushi."

"Got it," I said easily, and released her so I could lead her out of the foyer and into the open concept living area. I slid her white purse off her shoulder and placed it on the foyer table.

"You do not have sushi," she accused, following me.

I turned right, pausing to toe-heel my sneakers off at the end of the short hallway, and then went straight for the fridge. I opened one side and plucked a clear container from a neatly organized shelf. I held it out to her. "Sushi."

She gave me a distrustful tilt of her chin. "What would you have said if I'd asked for ramen?"

"No," I smiled blandly, grabbing a container for myself. "Wasabi?"

"Why yes, mister hoity-toity. I'd love some."

"*Doctor* Hoity-Toity," I corrected, tossing a few packets of wasabi on the counter.

She threw them back at me.

While we ate, June played a game of twenty questions… as in, she asked me more than twenty questions about myself and barely took a break long enough to eat. She wanted to know about my sister in Denver, and when I told her we were half-

Israeli, she looked like I'd told her we all had gills on our necks. Which was then quickly replaced with enthusiastic curiosity and wanting to know every minute detail about my childhood and upbringing. I assured her that it wasn't that interesting or different from any other kid. I left out the part where the reason my mom didn't express her Jewish faith and embrace her ethnicity much was because my dad was an ignoramus who thought eagles and light beer were the only cultural elements worth celebrating.

It was a sore spot for my siblings and me. Our mother, Jewish in her heart but fearful of what life would have handed her in the seventies, had chosen to live her life in camouflage. She had been an American-born Israeli, but you wouldn't have known it by looking at us. And then, my mother had died when I was young, and any ties I'd felt to our heritage had died with her.

Cade and I had bonded over that fact in medical school. We'd both watched our fathers destroy our families, and then we'd both lost our mothers in high school. He considered his brother his family and support system, but maybe a bit embarrassingly, I didn't feel the same about my siblings. None of us had taken the train wreck of our upbringing particularly well. I'd mostly shut down and learned to live without relationships. Azura had done the same, but she had gone feral and become a lawyer shark who was more liable to rip out your throat with her teeth than be intimate. At least she was willing to help when the people closest to her needed it.

Zev had buried himself in women and a social life that he'd rather let smother him than try for a life of any true substance.

June curled up her feet on the low-back bar stool, pulling them to her with her arms around her shins, and regarded me with a sharp gaze that seemed to piece me together like a mosaic. "So, you're grumpy because it's easier than trying and failing at relationships."

"I don't fail at relationships," I clarified, leaning my elbow on the counter. "I make necessary ones—like Cade—and I don't bother with anything else." I paused, leaning my cheek on my fist. "And I'm not grumpy."

"Yes, you are," she smiled softly. "But I like you the way you are."

My pulse shot through the roof as her words began a loop in my head. *I like you… I like you…*

"Well, it's not like I can judge much," she admitted, and laid her cheek on her knees. "I only let people get so far. I don't know why—I just hit a wall and don't let them get too close."

That surprised me. She seemed like she had friends coming out of her ears. But quantity and quality weren't necessarily correlative. "I guess the nuclear family isn't always the recipe for success, then," I teased. "Even if they are good Mormons."

"You know *way* too much about my personal life, Brady," she said suspiciously.

"You talk way too loudly in the lobby," I countered, lowering my voice and leaning close to her.

"That's because I'm not a robot," she challenged, mirroring me and bringing her nose close to mine.

"I thought I was a vampire."

"Robot vampire," she said seriously.

I kissed the tip of her nose. "Thank you for clarifying that."

"Anytime." She hopped down from the stool, peering around my living room and then pausing in front of the window wall to take in the glittering city lights. "This is an amazing view." She swished her hand like she had a paintbrush in it. "I want to paint it."

"Bring your paints with you next time," I suggested as I came to stand next to her.

She looked at me in surprise. "Next time?" she echoed.

There is no way in Hell I'm letting you get away, I thought. *Yes, next time. And the time after that.* Out loud, I shrugged and said, "Anytime you want."

"Okay," she smiled. Turning back to the view, she sighed. "Well, as cool as this is, we have work in the morning."

"True," I agreed. "Although, I'm not sure what that has to do with my view."

"I mean, I should get a ride home," she pointed out, like I was stupid. Quickly, she added, "Not that I'm telling you to do that. I was just saying I should go."

I rubbed the side of my nose in annoyance. "Matthews, remind me how many men you've been with before?"

"None, as you know," she groused, folding her arms.

"Right. So, if a man asks you to come to his apartment *very* late at night," I explained, shifting my body so I could pull her against me. "Then it's probably because he wants you to stay the night."

She gave me her best "how dare you" glare. "I'm *aware* of how adults do adulting, Doctor Hoity-Toity."

"Are you sure?" I teased, squeezing her against me. "Because you were about to blow me off, Cupcake."

"And I suppose women simply don't blow off the amazing Amos, do they?" she drawled. The city lights had cast a blue glow on the left side of her delicate features, and the right shone warm with the lights from the kitchen.

I kneaded the muscles along the base of her spine, slowly working my way up and bending down to whisper, "No, they don't. Because guess what spine surgeons are *really* good at?"

"What?" she whispered back, her slight frame already beginning to melt into my arms.

"Back massages."

She groaned, but instead of letting her head fall forward, she tipped it back. "Wait, is that code for some spicy chocolate sex thing?"

I laughed. *"What?"*

She waved her hand between us. "You know, like… doggy-style or something."

"Oh my God," I groaned, laughing still, and then pulling her tightly to me. "Just shut up, June. Please."

"But my mouth is my best feature," she responded, muffled.

I pushed her away from me at arm's length to give her a shrewd, questioning glance.

She winked.

And that was the moment I realized I wasn't getting out of this thing with June intact. Either I was going to unravel myself and attach every nerve ending to her existence, or she was going to leave me in tatters on the floor. The question was—did I let it happen, or did I try to mitigate the damage and back out before the shredding caused permanent damage?

I'd rather triage a room full of hypochondriac Larseys than answer that question.

NINETEEN
June

If there was one thing I could get used to, it was having Amos Brady as a sleepover buddy. For one thing, his apartment looked like an HGTV special, and for another thing, he was nice to look at. Like, seriously, could he get any sexier? I barely remembered falling asleep in his bed after he'd given me the world's best back massage. But when I'd woken up, it was to find Dr. Brady showered, dressed in gray scrubs, and glaring down at me with his huge arms straining against the hems on his short sleeves.

I peered up at him through several coils of my springy hair. "What?"

He checked his watch without unfolding his arms. "Work starts in an hour."

I groaned. "Then why did you wake me up so early?"

"Either you get your butt in the shower, or I'm going to repeat Wild School Dirties night with the water."

I snorted, letting my head fall onto his crisp, downy pillow as I laughed. I ended it on another groan. "Fine. I'm getting up. Wait," I looked down at myself as I realized I was wearing my underwear. I gave him a groggy blink. "I don't have clothes."

"Yes, you do. They're in the bathroom." He unfolded his arms and crossed the wide-plank, walnut floors to the doorway. "You have twenty minutes before I drag you to the car naked."

"Jesus," I muttered. "Hold on, what clothes?"

But he was already gone, and I was left in his minimalistic, modern bedroom by myself. I sat up, stretched, and took a minute to admire how beautiful the view was outside the wall of windows to my right. I had expected there to be windows everywhere—the Regent towered over the city like a solid glass monument. But I hadn't expected Amos to have a sense of artistic flair. The apartment wasn't just immaculate; it was carefully decorated with art pieces I recognized. Greg Copeland, Hunt Slonem, Alex Katz…

I wondered, as I meandered into his open concept bathroom, if he'd found those on his own or if he had hired someone to find them for him. His bathroom was just as ornate as the rest of the house with understated luxury that somehow managed to be minimalistic and still awe-inspiring with its attention to detail. The entire wall behind the porcelain tub had been made of black marble with white veins drizzled through the sparkling texture like icing on a Bundt cake.

On a chair in the corner of the room, Amos had placed a set of new clothing on a padded chair. They still had the tags on them, and my mouth dropped open as I picked them up and studied them. Underwear, bra, and a yellow sundress that were all precisely the right size. I shot him a look over my shoulder like he could see my incredulity. *How did he know my clothing size? What kind of guy pays attention to those details?* But even as I thought it, I knew the answer. Meticulous Dr. Brady did. Naturally.

I glanced at the numberless clock on the wall, and rolling my eyes at the uselessness of it, I still managed to glean that I had maybe fifteen minutes of my twenty left, so I hopped in the shower and tried to wash off fast without gawking too much at everything. The open shower had five heads that each turned on with different handles. I adjusted them each to avoid getting my hair wet—the drying process alone would take an hour if I tried— and pilfered his soap.

When I emerged from the shower feeling like I'd been steamed and pressed in a laundromat, I smelled like Amos, and I found that outrageously delightful. With one minute to spare, I swished out of his bedroom in the floor-length sundress that matched my sandals perfectly. I found Amos in the kitchen pouring coffee into disposable coffee cups. He looked up, his dark features lit by the morning light that filled the room from the wall of windows behind me. The sunlight turned his eyes a sparkling brown like iced cola on a hot day. His gray scrubs pulled against his wide shoulders, and as he gave me half a smile, his features went from gruff and surly to heartbreakingly gentle.

My heart leaped into my throat. *Oh no,* I thought with a dawning realization. *Don't you dare fall for him, June. He's not attachable. He's mercury in your hands. He's pretty, but you can't hold onto him.*

Amos slid a coffee cup toward me. "Ready?"

"Yeah," I said faintly. "Oh, hey, thank you for the clothes. Where did you get these?"

"Shopping app," he said absently as he checked something on his phone.

How was this guy real? No wonder I was getting all twisted up over him. And then, suddenly, the idea that I'd already let myself become too attached to him hit me like a sledgehammer to my gut. *June, you softie. Detach. Pull back. You're going to end up depressed and jobless if you can't.*

"Avocado toast is in the bag," he said, motioning with his head toward a brown paper bag next to my coffee.

I took the warm cup, inhaling the rich brew. "Avocado toast, huh?"

He leaned his hip against the counter and gave me a perturbed look. "I don't have Sugar-O's or whatever."

"Did I say that?" I asked, feigning offense. "How dare you make assumptions about my diet, Amos Brady." I snatched the bag off the counter. "As it happens, avocado is my second favorite green food."

He smiled faintly as he grabbed his crossbody bag off the barstool chair and shouldered it. "What's the first one?"

"Green apple licorice."

"You'd better be joking," he said with a touch of exasperation. I wasn't. "Do you need water for your pills?" he asked.

I paused mid-sip, causing me to gulp loudly.

Amos halted on his way to the door, rotated, and then leveled a stern look my way. "June Ella Matthews, *please* tell me you've been taking your pills."

I coughed, wiping my lips guiltily. "I may have left them at my commission's house on Tuesday."

"It's Thursday," he pointed out. "You haven't taken them for two days? Why didn't you go get them? Or have someone take you, at least?"

"I, ah," I fumbled, wondering why those questions were so hard to answer. *Because he creeped you out and you don't want to go back.* "I don't know," I shrugged. "My lungs felt fine, so I figured I'd just get them Saturday."

Amos was pissed. "You have to take them every day or they won't keep the inflammation in your lungs under control." He approached me and set his coffee on the counter. "Pop quiz, Matthews. How will you know if the inflammation has come back?"

"Uh," I faltered, stepping back.

He leaned a hand on the counter, angling his body over mine. "They'll seize up and you'll *stop breathing.* Did you enjoy that last time?"

"No," I said, and my chest heated as my ire rose to match his. "You don't have to be an as—" I swallowed the word bitterly. "Jerk about it. I still have autonomy over my own body, *Doctor* Brady."

I could almost feel the tension in his shoulders mirrored on my own body. "Where is your commission's house? We'll get them before work."

"No," I said too quickly.

Amos angled a perceptive look down at me. "Why?" he asked slowly.

My thoughts scrambled and tripped like gladiator sandals on a rocky path. "It's—I can't just show up first thing in the morning."

"So, call them," he said, as if testing me. My brain went blank. And I knew in that moment that my poker face might as well be a projector broadcasting my thoughts into his head. Too-smart-for-my-own-good Amos Brady caged me in with his body and the counter behind me. "June," he said in warning. "What's wrong?"

His arm brushed up against mine, and the heat from his body nearly punctured my anger. But I tensed up instead, suddenly defensive for reasons I couldn't quite name. "It's nothing. I just didn't feel like going back before Saturday."

"Bull," he rumbled. He grabbed my nose and tweaked until I had to look up at him. "You suck at lying."

I swatted his hand away. "Fine, the guy who commissioned it is a *little* weird. So, I didn't feel like going back before I had to. Okay?"

His eyebrows crashed together. "Weird, how?"

"Like, I don't know," I shifted my shoulders uncomfortably. "He had some… creepy vibes, I guess."

Amos stepped away. "You're not going back there."

I groaned, letting my head fall back. "Amos. I said he was weird, not dangerous. I *am* going back because this is my first mural, and I'm going to finish it."

"Making a mural for your Instagram page isn't worth compromising your safety," he countered. He'd moved back toward the door like the matter was settled and his mind had made up the decision for me.

"*What* did you say?" I asked. Outrage swelled in my chest.

"I said, your hobby isn't worth your safety," he repeated. He tapped the digital pad by his front door, and behind me, the lights died, and the blinds lowered over the wall of windows.

"It's not a hobby," I said, aghast. "Are you for real? Amos, my life's goal isn't to be your *secretary* for eternity. I'm an artist. What kind of professional would I be if I stopped a job just because the person made me — because he was a little —"

Amos jerked the door open and turned furious eyes on me. "Go back to what you started to say. He made you feel what?"

I swallowed acrid anger. "I can't believe you just called my art a hobby."

Amos waited with the door open for me to pass through, his expression thunderous. "You're avoiding the real issue, here."

I stormed past him, my grip on my coffee cup so tight, I was worried I'd pop the lid off. "Piss off, Brady."

He followed close behind me and then punched the down button on the elevator panel with the side of his fist. "You're not going back. End of discussion."

I flared my eyes up at him. "Excuse me, but who gave you power of attorney over my life? Just because we screwed a couple—"

He hooked his pointer finger under my chin and pressed my lips closed with his thumb. His eyes had gone onyx black. "You're. Not. Going."

I wrenched my face away from him, and as the elevator doors opened, I jammed myself into the corner of the gilded box, clutching the coffee to my chest and glaring at him. He ignored me, and as the elevator dropped along with my stomach, he typed out a text to someone. It was on the tip of my tongue to say that he had better not tell Katherine to deny me a ride to Archer's house, but I didn't want to give him any ideas.

As we weaved through bumper-to-bumper traffic, I ignored my coffee and breakfast, and I stewed. The infuriating aspect of the whole thing was that Amos was partially right. I had clearly felt uncomfortable about Archer and his house, and if I were shrewd, I'd listen to my gut and back out.

But Amos was also wrong. Dead wrong. I was willing to bet that women in medical school faced the same discomforts if not worse when it came to their male peers. If women backed away from achieving their dreams every time a man tried to dominate them, intimidate them, or abuse them, then women would have remained as impotent as the past had forced them to be.

And no, my completing a mural wasn't the hill that feminism needed to die on. But it was *my* hill. It was *my* passion and my future, and it was the hill I was willing to die on. If I had been a biologist on the verge of a breakthrough, and my colleague had made me uncomfortable, Amos would have offered to help or talk to the man who made me feel that way. He wouldn't have *forbidden* me from finishing my work. But because it was art, he hadn't bothered to support me. He had tried to control me. That was his shortcoming, and it wasn't one I was willing to tolerate.

Katherine stood next to me, and with a wary glance, said, "He's going to fire you for this."

"Probably," I agreed.

"He's going to fire *me* for this."

"I won't let him," I told her honestly. "He won't. He's mad at me, but he won't blame you for being a good friend."

"Fuckin' hope so," she muttered.

We were standing beside her car, and she had an armful of paint quarts that we had picked up on our lunch break. I knew I needed to start the cotton candy sky and possibly some of the dark undertones in the background, so we'd stopped by the art supply store to grab the colors I would need. She already had the bulk of my other supplies in her car because I'd forgotten to grab them yesterday.

Ahead of us, the storybook manor rose up the hill and cast a shadow over us like a hungry giant. The air felt muggy today, full of smog from trapped emission gasses and thick with pollen. Amos had utilized the in-center pharmacy to get me new corticosteroids and an inhaler, and he'd literally stood over me while I took them. Like a fucking marshal. I'd wanted to kick him in the balls, even if he had been late to his first surgery to make sure I got my medicine.

Overbearing bastard. Which was why I had texted Archer and asked if I could paint this afternoon instead of over the weekend. He'd agreed quickly, and I ignored my twinge of discomfort at that, too. Because, I'd decided, I was going to be firm. I wasn't going to let this loon and his leering bullshit ruin my mural. I just had to be assertive. I could do assertive. I was feisty as hell.

I filled my lungs with empty courage and adjusted the strap on my oversized art tote. "Alright. Here goes nothing."

Katherine followed me through the gate, her full figure swaying her black, gypsy-style skirts around her. "Remind me why he doesn't want you to do this, again?"

"He's an ass, Kat. Why do you think?"

"Okay," she said, unconvinced. "Guess that makes... no sense at all."

When we knocked on the door, a young woman opened it. She blinked at us in surprise and adjusted a pair of round, gold-framed eyeglasses. She looked about my age, and she immediately contradicted her soft, sweet features by asking, "Fuck, seriously?"

I opened my mouth to say something, but nothing came out. *Wait, what?*

She sighed and twitched a lock of her short-cut, brown hair away from her dark eyes. "Let me guess—you're here to paint 'my' room," she said with air quotes.

I tried to make a sound. I really did. But I was too surprised. *This* was Bridget?

Annoyed, she opened the door wider. "Come in, I guess." She dropped a glance from my head to my toes. "I hope they're paying you well."

"Uh, yeah," I finally managed to get out. "You're... you're Bridget?"

"Unfortunately," she said in monotone.

"Bridgie?" Archer's voice called from beyond the foyer. "Was that the door?"

Still staring at me with hooded eyes, Bridget raised her voice to shout, "Yeah. Artist is here."

I suddenly felt really, really stupid. I had been commissioned to paint a fairytale enchanted mural for a, well… I gave Bridget a once-over. She had a knit cap over her pixie haircut, and a black hoodie over her short frame. Wireless, pink headphones blinked with a steady, blue light, and she had a laptop under her arm. Okay, so she was a full-blown, adult woman. I plastered a smile on my face. "I'm June. It's nice to meet you."

"Yeah," she said sardonically, but her tone softened some. She had a voice like warm chocolate syrup, and I hoped she was a musician or something. Every word out of her mouth was stunning. "Thanks for humoring them."

"Bridgie," Archer said, his voice gently reproving as he met us in the foyer. He had on a polo again—baby blue—and he'd swapped out the khakis for black cargo pants. Same socks and tennis shoes, though. He definitely had a look, and he was sticking with it. "Don't give the artist a hard time. Hi, June," Archer said with an eager smile. His huge, blue eyes shone with a film of perpetual moisture like he might cry at any second.

"Hi, Archer," I said. "Thanks for letting me come last minute."

A woman walked up behind Archer, and I realized immediately that it had to be Meg. She wore a peasant-style blouse with a cinched-up bodice under her ample breasts. Her skirt looked like straight out of a cosplay, and she wore a beaded scarf over her head. The only thing that didn't scream "Ye Olde Renaissance Faire" was the fact that she had half a makeup store's worth of product on her face. "You must be June!" she exclaimed, surrounding us all with a cloud of potpourri that made my nose itch.

I gave a weak wave. This was, without a doubt, the strangest family I had ever seen. "Hi."

"Well, I'm out," Bridget said, pulling her eyes wide like this was just as weird for her as it was for me. "See ya."

"Bye, sweetie!" Meg called after her daughter. "I'll send you pictures!"

"Uh huh," Bridget intoned as she shouldered her way out the front door.

Archer put a hand between my shoulder blades to lead me through the foyer. "Come on in, come on in. We're so excited to see what you do with your sketch."

I bobbed an annoyed look at his arm, and as I did, I noticed two things. One: Katherine did not like Archer. Two: Meg did not like me.

Katherine's eyes went squinty as she followed us down the hall, and Meg just about burned a hole through my skull with her suspicious glare. There was no way in Hell this could get more awkward... an opinion that was immediately debunked when Archer slid his hand along my shoulder and unhooked the bag from my arm. "Here, let me get that for you."

"Dear," Meg said tightly, "I'm sure June can carry her own supplies."

"I, uh," I wanted to agree with Meg, but Archer had already taken it in his clammy hand and gestured for me to go through the door to Bridget's bedroom.

"After you, honey," he smiled.

Honey? Gag.

Katherine made a sound in the back of her throat like she was choking on her own words. That made two of us. My instincts, which had been a low hum in my brain before, rose in pitch like a swarm of disturbed bees. *Cut your losses, girl. Cut your losses.*

But then Amos's voice drifted through my thoughts with a harsh "… hobby," and I clenched my jaw. No way. I was going to finish this damn mural, get paid an outrageous sum because I was charging them extra for the awkwardness, and then when I posted it on social media, I'd hopefully get a wave of business.

Katherine set my paints on the beautiful carpet, her blue gaze full of trepidation, and stood uncertainly, like she wanted to say something.

"Thanks Kat," I smiled. "I'll get a rideshare home. And… cover for me?" I asked meaningfully.

She sighed heavily, looking at me with pursed, bright red lips. "Okay," she said finally. "Text me," she added pointedly.

"I will," I promised.

"Nice to meet you both," Katherine said as she went to the doorway, even though Archer and Meg had pointedly ignored her existence.

"What are you starting with?" Archer asked, rubbing his hands and exuding a strange, giddy energy. Meg tilted her chin up, her sharp eyes on her husband.

Oh, boy.

At first, while I laid out a tarp over the carpet and poured paint into the paint trays, Meg managed to keep Archer entertained with her conversation about what they would do with the furniture and window dressings in the room. But then, eventually, Archer became fully engrossed in what I was doing.

As I tied my skirt around my waist to keep from tripping — and found depraved mirth at the idea of ruining the dress Amos had bought me — Archer's eyes had locked in on my legs.

He came to stand behind me and put a hand on my lower back as I climbed the ladder. "Here, hon, let me help you."

"I've got it," I assured him.

But the only way to get out of his reach was up, and he knew that. His hand trailed from my back, over my ass, down my thigh, and to my calf under the pretense of steadying me as I climbed.

What an absolute jackass, I thought acidly. *Is this his fetish or something? I bet his browser history is real "artsy."*

Even as I rose too high for him to reach, his eyes followed my every movement. I wanted to scream. How long was he going to do that?

I balanced the tray of pink, white, and lavender paint on the top of the ladder, dipped my brush in the viscous liquid, and tried to turn my mind to the project. As my brush worked in sweeping "X" shapes, dipping into each color in varying hue strengths, I crafted a sunrise sky so soft and feminine, I could almost smell the peony and lavender in its colors. I got lost in the work, manipulating the colors just right so they practically glowed.

"God, that looks amazing," Archer said suddenly from below me.

I jumped, nearly dropping the paint tray. I'd forgotten he was there. I looked down at him and found him standing with his hands in his pockets and his eyes feverishly bright. They were fixed not on my face, but on my breasts. My cleavage had wiggled partially out of the low curve of my sundress, and I resisted the urge to fix them, which would draw more unwanted attention to them. "Thanks," I said, my voice thin. *Focus, June. So, he's looking. Whatever. Instagram. New followers. Moolah.*

"You really are fantastic," Archer pressed on. "I'll bet you have all the boys drooling."

He had devolved from talking about my art completely and was getting bolder. That did it. I needed to leave and come back with someone who could buffer his crazy. It absolutely rankled my pride to admit that Amos had been right, but there was something off about Archer. I gave an awkward laugh. "Nah."

"Oh, no boyfriend?" he asked with interest.

"He's a doctor actually," I said suddenly. "My boyfriend." *June, you twit. That is completely untrue. Right?*

Archer chuckled like he'd caught a six-year-old telling a fib. "Ah, I see. Okay."

I gnawed on my lip. *I wonder how gracefully I can bow out of this circus. Probably "tripping over clown shoes" gracefully. If this wack job would just leave, I could slip out.*

Like I'd cast a magic spell, Archer sighed deeply. "Well, I'd better get back to it. I work from home," he added, like I'd give a fuck. "I'll come check on you in a bit." He pointed with a warning finger like he was joking. "You'd better have a lot done, pretty lady."

Nausea slithered down my esophagus.

He left, and I stared at my paintbrush. It was shaking in my hand, and I felt frozen by indecision and revulsion. Behind me, Meg's voice said to her husband, "I left you a snack, sweetie. It's on your desk."

"Thank you, baby," Archer said, and I heard them kiss loudly.

I swallowed bile. Gross. Just gross. What was with these two? Suddenly, Meg appeared below me, and she leaned against the wall, not even bothering to look at my painting. I still stood on the very top rung of the ladder, and even then, I had to reach above my head to reach the edges of the wall. I let my brush fall to the paint tray as Meg said, "You know, it's funny. You'd think I would learn."

I stared down at her, my mind already so rubbed raw with apprehension, I didn't have any polite phrases left.

"*I'm* the one who loves this decor," she said, lifting a gold-bangled arm to gesture around the room. "And yet, Archer, bless him, manages to make the most out of the hired help. I should hire them on my own and vet them ahead of time, but I just," she paused, shaking her scarf-draped head. "I think I have a hard time taking away his toys, you know? It makes him so happy."

I stared down at her in horror. Was she saying what I thought she was saying? Was she calling their contractors "toys?"

Meg glanced back up at me, her heavily lined eyes clouded with pure spite. "Relax, June. I'm not going to let you join the ranks." She pulled a face like she'd smelled something disgusting. "I'm not in the mood today."

So, this was a game for them. Hire a painter, harass her a little, and get their rocks off on infidelity with a splash of fetishized abuse.

I should have known that my art wouldn't be good enough on its own. They didn't want an artist. They wanted a plaything.

And I'd been stupid enough to think that my talent had presented me with an opportunity.

Way to go, June. You suck.

"The worst part," Meg said with a mirthless laugh, "is I actually really love what you're doing here." She sighed. "Shame."

I swallowed hard, finally finding my voice. "Do you want me to go?"

She scowled, snapping a look back up to me. "Hell no. If you go, he'll know I sent you away."

My mouth went dry.

Meg gave me a sympathetic look devoid of any true warmth. "I'm just sorry to hurt you. You could have been fun." She pushed away from the wall, and with strength I didn't see coming, she kicked the ladder out from under me.

TWENTY

Amos

I rubbed the back of my neck, trying to ease some of the soreness from my muscles. Days with back-to-back surgeries were brutal, but there was a reason I kept my body in top form. The stronger I was, the more patients I could help. And this was one of those days I'd skipped lunch and would likely end up with a late dinner.

Sighing, I returned my focus to the patient on my table. I'd already exposed the lamina and the spinous process, and I picked up the drill to start a laminectomy. The tang of disinfectant mingled with metallic blood and whatever goat's-milk-and-something soap my resident, Bennett, used. He lived in a van, and if I didn't know better, I'd think he was a complete moron based on the way he dressed and talked. But the kid was smart as hell, so I forgave him his bizarre taste in soap fragrances.

"Localizing," I said for his benefit, and dipped the drill down to make a divot that we could test with intraoperative fluoroscopic imaging to make sure we were in the right place before going any further.

"Penfield number four," he said, handing me the dissector.

I took it from him, and despite the seriousness of this surgery, which was to remove a three-centimeter tumor from a thirty-seven-year-old mother's spine, I felt a distracting niggle of worry that I hadn't heard from June since before lunch. I'd sent her a message before this surgery asking her to move up my discectomy from five to four because I was ahead of schedule, but she hadn't responded. The appointment had gotten moved, so I assumed she was still angry with me and giving me the silent treatment, but at the very least, she was doing her job.

Honestly, she had a right to be upset. I shouldn't have been a domineering ass, but I was human, too. In the face of fear, my reaction had been to remove her from the threat. But in doing so, I'd hurt her feelings, insulted her, and pushed her away. I would have to apologize after my last surgery. Next time, because I didn't doubt she would get more commissions, I would go with her if she felt uncomfortable.

I let the motions take over, and as we brought in the microscopic surgical equipment, I went over the procedure with my resident, asking him to lay out the process and walk me through the steps. I felt confident based on the imaging that we could remove the tumor entirely, and then we would send it off for biopsy to confirm my suspicions that it was benign.

But, as we exposed the tumor, and each microscopic cut revealed more and more problematic tissue, I realized with a sinking heart that the contrast MRI had either been incomplete, or the tumor had grown since then. It wrapped all the way down past the surgical field and to her L4 and L5 discs.

I felt tension radiating off Bennett, and I could hear his thoughts because they were mine, too. *Do we keep going or do we close up and regroup?* I cracked my neck, and over my shoulder, I said to a nurse, "Get June on the line, please."

He dialed June's direct line on the operating room speaker phone. Katherine answered. "Hello, June Matthew's line."

I paused, lifting my head from the oculars. "Where's June?"

Silence stretched on for a few seconds that felt like an eon. Then she said, "She just left for lunch. How can I help you, Dr. Brady?"

Dread writhed around my suspicions. "Tell her to call me when she's back at her desk. Immediately."

"I will," Katherine promised.

"Tell her to reschedule my four o' clock," I said. "I'm going to be here a while."

"I'm on it," Katherine said.

Shaking my head, I forced my focus back to the open spine beneath my equipment.

"You okay?" Bennett asked.

"Yes," I lied. "Go update the family, please."

It was a grueling two hours, and even though I managed to get a good portion of the tumor, it had clearly spread far past the limits of what was safe to operate on blindly. She needed updated imaging and an aggressive plan of care that assumed the opposite of my initial presumption that the tumor was benign. It was never good news to give to a patient or their family.

I let Bennett close up, and as he did, I tore off my surgical gown and gloves. I pulled my phone from my pocket and texted June another question about where she was.

No answer. No impending message dots. Nothing. I pumped hand sanitizer on my hands, and then I fast-walked down the surgical suite toward our clinical offices. If June wasn't there, then I would have to assume she had done something truly reckless. And if she had, I was going to give her the dressing-down of her life.

I shouldered through the connecting door from the nurses' station to the front desk and rounded on the secretaries. Maxine jumped out of her chair in surprise, but it was Katherine's reaction that pulled my focus to her. She jumped almost imperceptibly but didn't look up from her computer screen. In fact, she looked determined to pretend I hadn't arrived.

I went around to the front of the desk, grateful that it was past clinical hours, and leaned on it with my forearms flat against the granite surface. I glared down at Katherine until she reluctantly looked up to me. "Hey, Dr. Brady."

"Where's June?" I asked.

Katherine licked her red lips before rolling them between her teeth in an uncertain gesture. "I think she wasn't feeling well."

"So, you took her home?" I prompted. Maxine stared at us both from behind Katherine's back, her blue eyes huge.

Katherine scratched her neck with her long, coffin-shaped, black nails. "No, I didn't take her home. I think she was planning on getting a rideshare home."

Nice try. "A rideshare home from *where*?" I gritted out.

Katherine made a pained, groaning sound before giving up. "Dr. Brady, she begged me not to tell you."

"*Where*, Katherine?"

"She's working on her mural," she admitted with a guilty flick of her fake lashes up to me and then back to her computer screen. "She seemed pretty determined. Although," she paused, and then made a face like she was kicking herself.

"Although, what?" I asked.

"Dr. Brady," Carla said, popping her torso through the connecting door. "A word?"

I squelched the urge to kick the mahogany desk. I turned my attention to Carla. "Yeah?"

"In private," she added derisively.

Katherine looked like she was going to explode, and Maxine seemed like she wanted to be anywhere but there. I tapped the desk at Katherine's eyeline. "Don't go anywhere." I pushed away from the desk and followed Carla through the door, down the hallway, and to her office.

Carla, who had looked infinitely calmer since our retreat, now had concern pinched between her black brows. Her lipstick today bordered on violet, and despite her apparent concern, she looked as put together as always. Her heels clicked on the tile floors as she swept through her office door. "Have a seat, Amos."

I could count two times in my life I had felt antsy—once when June had been in a tree, and then this moment. It was like termites burrowing under my skin. "What is it?" I asked, ignoring the offer to sit. I leaned against the doorframe. Most of the employees were heading out for the evening anyway, so I didn't bother to shut the door.

"Are you in a relationship with June Matthews?" Carla asked, getting straight to the point.

I sighed, folding my arms and crossing one leg over the other. "Yes."

Carla looked pained. "Since when?"

I shrugged. "I'd say… the retreat."

Her brown eyes bugged. "Are you fu —" she stopped herself. "Are you for real?" I gave another shrug. "Are you telling me," she said slowly in a clear attempt to calm her voice, "that you engaged in a relationship of a *sexual* nature at a *company* retreat?"

"Yes." I shifted my gaze in question. "Was that against the rules?"

Carla's face went as purple as her lipstick. Narrowly avoiding a full conniption fit, she gritted out, "Did that need to be said?"

"Carla," I drawled, letting some of my annoyance slip out in my tone. "June and I are both consenting adults of commendable intelligence. I think we can be trusted to make our own decisions about interoffice romance."

"June," Carla said fiercely, "is not fair game. And you know that."

I felt a twinge of amusement at Carla's protectiveness over June. I wondered if June knew how our office manager felt about her. I was aware that most of the people in our center considered her something of an office sweetheart. They had jumped to her defense many times in the past when I'd made the mistake of complaining about her. But I didn't know Carla shared their sentiments. "You paired us together," I pointed out.

She brought two hands to her nose, closing her eyes like she needed to gather her composure. "Please tell me you aren't going to chase her away, Amos. We *like* June."

"I'm not planning on letting her get away," I smiled faintly.

Carla sighed, resigned. "Fine. As long as you know how I feel about this. Which is that I *do not support* anything that jeopardizes her position here."

"Got it," I nodded.

She regarded me suspiciously for a second more, and then she dismissed me with a wave. "Fine. Go."

I shoved off the doorframe and took long strides right back down the hallway. Maxine had left, as I assumed she would, but Katherine stood by the front door. Her posture shifted nervously, and she drummed her fingers uncertainly on June's white purse. As I approached her, she turned wary eyes on me. Round two of June's protectors, *ding, ding, ding.*

"Where is she?" I asked without preamble.

Katherine handed me June's purse. "I asked her to text me back, but she hasn't," she rushed to say, as if she'd been holding the words like a pent-up breath. "The guy was weird, Amos. I shouldn't have left her."

I took the purse with forced calm. "Address. Now."

TWENTY-ONE

June

I went weightless for one heart-stopping moment, and then in slow motion, my eyes assessed my impact before it hit. I had the presence of mind to feel the way my body had tilted forward, how the ladder had slammed into my shins as it pitched over, and how the wall and floor were going to collide with my body with no way for me to control the momentum.

But then that brief moment of awareness ended, and my vision tumbled with the rest of me. I felt the pain in my shins just before a sharp *crack* as my shoulder smashed into the wall. I landed heavily, half on the metal ladder and half on the carpet. The impact jarred my teeth and whacked my head against the floor with such force, I immediately saw stars, and then the world went black before my vision swirled back with muddy colors. Cold paint seeped under me and dripped off my throbbing limbs.

Meg gasped, stepping away from me with her hands to her mouth. "Oh my God!" she cried out with an Oscar-worthy performance.

Footsteps pounded, and as I rolled onto my back, gritting my teeth against agonizing pain along my right side, I heard Archer's voice. "What happened? Oh my God," he said, as he walked briskly across the floor. "June, are you okay?"

Tears clogged my throat as I struggled to sit. Archer reached for me, and I jerked away from him. Pain fired along every nerve ending on my right side.

"I'm fine," I choked out.

Meg gasped again. *"My carpet."*

I had managed to get myself into a huddled position, and cradling my right arm gingerly, I looked around me. The drop cloth had slid away with the ladder when it had toppled. Pink and purple swirled in soggy pools on their custom carpet. It had coated most of my legs and under my arms, causing my dress to stick heavily to my skin. *Well played, Meg.* This absolutely looked like a clumsy blunder on my end.

Archer groaned. "Oh, hell. Megs, lovie, I'm so sorry."

I shot a glare at Meg over my shoulder before I leaned forward. I attempted to get up, but the pain in my arm yanked me back down.

Meg started to cry. She sniffled loudly, and then like she was trying to hold back her emotions, blurted out a broken sob. Archer went to her and put an arm around her wide shoulder. "Meggy, it's okay. It's okay, we'll fix it."

I was finding it hard to think about anything but the searing pain in my side and how my shins were warm and wet in a way that I didn't think was just paint.

"Please leave," Meg blurted out, suddenly furious. That was real. That, I knew, was true emotion.

I struggled to my feet. Even stunned and in pain, I knew there was no protesting my way through this. Meg had not only made this look like an unprofessional accident on my part, but she'd caused me to destroy truly valuable property. I could deny it, but it was their word against mine. It looked like an accident. "I'm sorry," I mumbled. *You fuckers.*

Archer soothed his wife, giving me an apologetic glance. "June, honey, I'm sorry. You'd better go. Do you want me to call you a—"

Meg's sobbing increased fivefold suddenly, and she leaned heavily against Archer's chest. I felt my lip curl. "It's fine. I'll come back for my things later," I muttered.

Archer nodded, his attention clearly torn.

With my uninjured left arm, I slid my hand through the pools of paint to find my phone. It had flown off the ladder with the paint, and I found it covered in lilac goo. I didn't bother to look for anything else. I gathered my sopping dress to my waist and limped my way across the bedroom. My desperation to be out of that house propelled me forward despite the throbbing in my legs and in my shoulder.

As soon as I had the front door in my sights, Archer suddenly appeared beside me. I shrank away from him, but he clamped a hand on my injured elbow under the pretense of helping me to the front door. I cried out in pain, but with robotic indifference to my reactions, Archer continued on like he was helping a damsel to the window of his storybook tower. "June, honey, I'm sorry about that." I pulled against his hold, but he retained his forced ignorance of my struggle. "Let me help you to the door."

"I'm fine," I whispered harshly. Even to my own ears, I sounded pitiful and weak.

Archer looked down at me, his bug-eyes full of delusional chivalry. "You're hurt. I'm so sorry about this. I am." We had reached the door, and still holding my elbow and sending lancets of agony through my shoulder and down my ribs, he ignored my whimper of pain.

"Oh, look at you." He tutted, licking his lips. His other hand smoothed over me, as if to wipe away the paint on my dress. He lingered over my breasts and down my belly, and I shoved at him, but he was determined. He fondled me crudely, bending down to sniff my hair as I buckled under the pain in my shoulder.

"Poor baby. I'm sorry this didn't work out. I am. You take care, June."

Finally, he opened the door, and the second he released my elbow, I wrenched my body through the doorway and down the stairs. I didn't look back. I wanted to be brave, but tears blinded my vision, and in a haze of pain, I stumbled away from the towering mansion and into the blistering evening heat. As I limped away, I struggled to clear my phone screen with hands that shook so violently, I didn't know how I hadn't dropped it.

Not that it mattered. The screen had shattered so violently, a chunk of glass was missing from the front of it. I managed to get myself through their gates, and then I shuffled across the cul-de-sac. Angrily, I threw my phone to the ground and crushed my molars together to keep from giving in to the waterfall of tears I wanted to release.

I felt like some kind of zombie. The summer day shone bright and full of innocence. Kids played loudly on their front lawns, running through sprinklers and jumping into glimmering in-ground pools. Insects chirruped innocuously, and the savory aroma of smoked barbeque wafted through the air. And yet, despite the mundane rhythm of suburban life, I dragged myself through their neighborhood like some kind of misplaced ghoul.

I made it as far as an enormous boulder at the base of someone's grandiose estate that had been built up a steep hill. I stumbled into the alcove between the boulder and a Russian sage tree. I was a good three feet away from the street that curved down the mountain. As I sat heavily, I lifted my skirt with a shaking hand to reluctantly look at the damage.

I choked back a gasp. My right leg had a deep gash in the shape of a backwards "L" where the skin had been peeled back by the blunt force of my fall. It wrinkled like a sheet shoved to the end of a bed, and bright blood wept from the thick tissue, mixing with paint and swirling down my skin. My left leg looked bruised and was swelling, but it seemed like most of the impact had been along my right side. I didn't dare try to understand what had happened to my right arm. I got the sense that if I really knew what was going on with it, the adrenaline would desert me, and the pain would get worse.

Shock was a funny thing. I had a voice in my head, the sensible one, the creative one, the one that excelled at solving problems and pushing me to make good decisions. But as I sat there next to that boulder, slowly tilting to the left so I could lay myself against its cool surface, that voice had faded. It said things in the background, but it was muffled, like it was talking to me through a thick door.

It wasn't until I saw Amos' car drive past slowly, headed for Archer's house, that my awareness jolted back to the foreground. My heart thudded to life, and that voice that had been muffled suddenly shouted in my head like it had taken a pillow off its mouth. *Amos! I want Amos! Get Amos!*

I shook my head. That was nuts. He was going to be so pissed off with me—did I really need a lecture along with my bleeding leg and injured shoulder? He'd probably tell me this was what I got for being stubborn.

Bullshit. You know he'll help you. Before I really knew what I was doing, I stood uncertainly from my hiding place and dragged myself back up the hill where the road curved to the left before fanning out into the cul-de-sac. I stopped behind a wisteria tree at the spot where the circle of asphalt funneled down to the road. From behind the tree, I watched Amos' gray car stop in front of Archer's house.

He still wore his scrubs, and whether he realized it or not, he still had his green surgical mask tied around his neck. He poked the intercom button on the estate's gate, and his hands rested on his hips as he appeared to speak with Meg or Archer. As he talked, he leaned to the side to peer through the gate. I watched him pause, and then his head rotated slowly down the hill like he was tracking something with his eyes.

My paint footprints. God, he was clever. He followed them to my phone, which he bent to pick up and examine. His head jerked up, and even from a distance I saw the worry in his expression. "June?" he called.

I screwed my eyes shut and leaned my forehead against the rough bark. There were too many emotions eddying around my head and heart for me to pinpoint why I was standing there, hesitating, instead of going straight to him.

The sound of crunching sneakers on loose asphalt sounded behind me, and I looked over my shoulder. A fit couple in athletic wear marched fast up the hill, and the girl's long, blond ponytail swayed as she looked up at the handsome man next to her. They talked in low voices, and the man laughed.

I could ask them for help. I could ask to borrow a phone and call a ride or Katherine. Or my parents. Yes, I could call my parents, but then they'd be worried. They had a lot going on in their lives right now, and if they saw me like this…

"June!" Amos called again, his voice more panicked.

I turned away from him with my back to the tree trunk and closed my eyes again. I knew why I was hesitating. If I went to Amos now, then I'd have to admit what I feared the most.

I want him. I want to be with him, and I don't know what I'll do if I can't have him. If I admitted it, if I faced it, then I opened myself to the possibility of more pain. I faced the possibility that Amos wasn't looking for what I was. I couldn't play it casual anymore. I couldn't be with him and pretend that it wasn't the safest, most ambrosial joy I'd ever known. I wanted him to be angry that I'd gone to Archer's house against his advice. I wanted him to care for me as much as I cared for him, but what if he didn't? What if I reached for him, tumbled headlong into the abyss of feelings for him, and he just let the darkness swallow me?

The couple to my left were nearly parallel with me now. They were going to see me any second, and I had to choose.

"June!" Amos shouted louder. It was the desperation in his voice that made my decision for me.

I opened my eyes and turned around the tree so I could stumble out of its shade and into the cul-de-sac. "I'm here," I said.

It wasn't loud, but he heard it like I'd shouted. His head swiveled to me, and with his gaze locked on me, he closed the space like I'd hooked a winch to his body. "June," he said again, softer, and his arms reached for me. Sharp as always, Amos assessed my body language accurately, and he hovered his hand under my injured arm as he clasped my left arm in a warm grip. "What happened?"

My features crumpled. "I don't know," I whispered honestly.

"Okay," he said softly. His baritone voice filled me with soothing vibrations, and I leaned into him as tears fell from my lashes to the tight, dried paint on my cheeks. Amos circled my left side so he could pull me against him, still taking care not to touch my right arm. "I'm here, baby," he murmured. "I've got you."

"I really messed up," I mumbled, pressing my face to his chest and giving in to the feeling that I wanted to morph my body to his like modeling clay. He might not feel the same, but in this moment, in this space, he was everything I needed and so much more. And he held me so tight to his chest, I wanted to lock myself in that embrace and never leave. He was offering the strength I lacked. However long that lasted, I would take it.

"I'll fix it," he assured me. I choked back a laugh. What a promise. He didn't even know what had happened. "First," he continued, "let's get you in the car. Can you walk?"

I nodded. He supported me halfway across the cul-de-sac as I walked on two throbbing legs before he bent down, gently hooked an arm under my legs, and carried me the rest of the way. I let out a cry as it jostled my shoulder, but he crossed the distance so swiftly, I soon found myself in the passenger side of the car. The smell of leather, lemons, and Amos swirled around me, and I leaned my head against the headrest gratefully.

Amos bent forward, unnervingly silent about the whole situation so far, and his hands skillfully palpateds my arm starting at my wrist, pausing at my elbow as I sucked in a breath, and then moving to my shoulder. He barely touched it, and I wanted to scream. "Where else are you hurt?" he asked.

Reluctantly, I lifted the hem of my filthy skirt to reveal the gash on my right leg. He bent over and barely glanced at it before unlatching the glove compartment and fishing out the small, red first aid kit he kept in there. I felt a twinge of amusement over the fact that he had used that same first aid kit on the same leg not even a week before. Looking at the shape of the gash, it suddenly made some sense. The "L" shape was because I'd already had a vertical wound in the process of healing.

He pressed a square of non-adherent gauze to the cut, and I sucked in a harsh breath through my teeth. Ignoring my sound of protest, he secured the gauze pad with medical tape. "Anywhere else?" he asked. I shook my head, but he cocked his head, leaning further into the car to look at my left shin. He pressed around it and over the swollen bruise until I let out another yelp. "Okay," he sighed, straightening.

It was only then that I read the eddy of emotions in his eyes. Storm clouds before an F5 tornado had nothing on Amos Brady's expression. It was clear to me that he wanted to keep his expression neutral, but he hadn't succeeded. "Anywhere else?" he asked again.

"N—"

"Think, June," he interrupted me. "Did you hit your head when you fell?"

I frowned. "How did you know I fell?" He leaned his hand against the doorframe, waiting. I put my left hand to my head where it throbbed dully. "I guess a little."

He bent over me again, this time bringing his hands to feel around my head from the base of my skull and up. I closed my eyes. His fingers were so strong and sure of what they were doing. I couldn't help but enjoy it. I winced a little as he felt around my right temple, but he kept going. "Did it hurt right away? Did you lose consciousness?"

Reluctantly, I admitted, "I did see black."

"Were you confused? Nauseated?"

"A bit." I knew where this was going. He would want me to go to the ER again, but I wasn't going this time. Suddenly, I felt Archer's hands on my legs, on my breasts, going down my belly…

I pulled away stiffly. Amos froze in surprise, and then lowered his hands. "You might have a concussion."

"Good thing you're a doctor," I said thickly.

He leaned against the frame again, his gazed angled down to mine. "Babe, you have to go to the hospital."

I gripped my one good fist around crusty, drying paint on my dress. "Amos, I can't," I whispered, and my voice broke on the last word.

"Why?" he asked softly. He seemed to have tempered his rage and replaced it with reluctant patience.

I imagined all the people who would be there. The nurse who would touch me. The doctor I didn't know who would press their hands against my body the way Archer had done. Panic clawed up my throat like a deranged demon. I tried to swallow the hysteria away, and I stared at my fist. "I just want you," I said at last. It was the best way I could word it. I couldn't make myself tell him out loud. It was hard enough to let him see how pathetically I needed him.

I felt Amos's indecision from the way his posture shifted, and then finally, he straightened and shut my door. I watched him pace around the back of the car through the rearview mirrors, and he pulled out his phone to talk to someone as he kept pacing.

Finally, he slid back into the driver's side and zipped his seatbelt into place.

"Where are we going?" I rasped in the vacuum-like quiet.

He started the car. "Home."

Relief pulled my body into an exhausted slump. Thank God. Also, he'd said "home." Not "my home" or "my apartment." He'd said, "home."

I shouldn't have let myself love that, but I did. I really did.

TWENTY-TWO

Amos

June looked like she might nod off. I reached over to squeeze her good knee and said, "Stay awake, Matthews. We're almost there."

She nodded numbly, her eyes glazed over and far away. I hadn't noted any symptoms of shock, but the concussion had me worried. She also had a dislocated shoulder, a pre-tibial laceration that would need extensive debridement because of all the paint drying in the wound, and the contusions on her shin and elbow had the possibility of being fractures. I could hold her over at home for a while, but she needed to get to the hospital for X-rays, eventually.

As we crawled through stop lights, I asked, "What did you fall from?"

"Ladder," she said dully. At first, I thought she was annoyed, but no. It was something else. She didn't want to think about it, whatever had happened. It was unlike June to clam up and not spill her thoughts for the whole world to hear. That, more than anything, caused my pulse to skyrocket.

Several times, I'd been a furious heartbeat away from breaking down those gates and snapping necks. Those people in that tourist trap monstrosity had not only done something to June, but they'd watched a bleeding, severely injured girl limp out of their front door and down their lawn, and they had said nothing. When I'd asked, they simply said she had left. The fact that they hadn't called her an ambulance told me all I needed to know about them and how June had gotten hurt.

But the way June had shrank from my touch had changed things. "Tell me," I said, keeping the volume of my voice low. But the intensity of my words crackled through the air, and June turned to look at me finally. She had paint everywhere. On her face, in her hair, all down her side and the front of her dress. I hadn't missed the male handprints in that paint. I wanted to be wrong, but I knew I wasn't.

She sniffed and wiped the back of her hand under her nose. "I don't know. It happened so fast."

"Start with how you felt about them," I said. Our conversation this morning had scared me witless as it was. She couldn't know what I had seen reflected in her micro-expressions, but she hadn't felt comfortable with them even then. She'd been terrified to go back.

She looked forward again. "At first, I thought I was seeing things or overreacting. He… he just was… interested in me. And watched me a lot."

"Who?" I asked roughly. She opened her mouth, choked, and swallowed. "I need a name, June," I said seriously.

"Archer," she whispered. "His name is Archer Holmeyer."

"And when you got to Archer's house, what did he do?"

"Nothing at first," she insisted, but her voice sounded hesitant. She wasn't telling the truth. She was in too much shock to realize that the evidence of what he'd done was all over her clothing.

"Okay," I bit out, and I hoped my lack of patience might break through her reticence. "Let's be more direct. How and where did he touch you?"

Her gaze flew to mine, wide and reflecting her surprise. "I think it was a game for them," June said finally. "The wife, Meg, and Archer, too. He likes to bring women into the house, and she likes to play the victim when he inevitably," she paused, closing her eyes and swallowing.

I wanted to touch her again, but I didn't want to make it worse for her. "Rip off the band-aid, baby. Just be direct."

She drew in a breath. "When he would touch them or, I assume, abuse them, Meg would play the victim. He liked his wife begging for his attention, and she liked the power of sending the girls away. I think."

What a bunch of psychos. Girls, plural? I listened while June haltingly told me the story. How Archer had touched her going up the ladder and how he had watched her and grown increasingly bold. Then, she told me how Meg hadn't been in the mood for "the game" that day. And her solution, the crazy cunt, had been to kick the ladder out from under June so it looked like June had ruined their carpet and made an absolute mess of her job. Then she told me about how Archer had fondled her at the door before throwing her out.

I went from furious to homicidal in a snap. It was one thing to distantly assume something like that had happened. It was another to hear it from June's mouth. *My* June's mouth.

My hands clenched the steering wheel so hard that I thought I might tear the leather away from the thick stitching along the inside. June glanced over at me from where she'd been staring at her fist. She sighed, looking back down. "I know. It was stupid."

I didn't think I could get any angrier, but her words were like kerosene to a bonfire. "June Ella, are you seriously implying that my anger is directed at you right now?"

She flinched, hunching a look my way again. "You told me not to go."

"Yes, and I'm frustrated with *myself* for the way I communicated my worry for you." She sucked in her bottom lip. Unable to help myself, I reached over and tugged on her chin until she released her lip. "Cupcake, my anger with you is always surface-deep. You push back even a little, and you'll find that the only thing I want is to see you happy."

Her throat bobbed, but she didn't say anything. I turned into the parking garage, and as I'd hoped, Irving was there in the spot next to mine. I killed the engine and said, "I'll be right back," before meeting Irving at the door of his silver SUV. The lines on his face deepened as he glanced over his shoulder at my car and then back to me.

"How bad is it?" he asked with concern. I'd given him a brief summary when I'd asked him for supplies.

"Bad enough," I replied grimly. "They made it look like June's fault. It's their word against hers."

Andrews clicked his tongue as he reached for the black duffel bag in his passenger seat. "That won't be an enjoyable process to prosecute."

"Maybe," I agreed. "I'll call Azura and see what she says."

"Good idea," he said. "Please let me know if you need anything else. I threw in everything you said and a few extras, so you don't have to leave her. But don't hesitate to call me."

Andrews was possibly the busiest man alive. I'd felt bad enough calling and asking him to get medical supplies from the center on his night off. "I owe you one," I smiled.

"Perfect, you babysit?" he joked with a grin.

I tapped the hood of his car. "Andrews, you didn't pull me from a battlefield. Let's not be dramatic."

With a laugh, he rolled up his window, and I secured the duffel bag on my shoulder before going to my passenger door. Getting June upstairs wasn't going to be comfortable for her. Carrying her had been faster, but it had jostled her dislocated shoulder. She was better off walking, so we took it slowly. I held her tight to my right side while we made our way across the garage and to the elevator. By the time we'd made it to my front door, she had sweat beading her hairline and her breathing had grown ragged.

I scooped her up at the threshold, and a dim part of me found that horribly ironic. This was not the way I had intended to sweep June off her feet when I'd realized I was helplessly in love with her. I carried her to the master bedroom, figuring we might as well get the worst parts over with first.

I set her on the edge of the tub with her feet on the outside, and then with her curious eyes on me, I dragged the padded chair over to her and set the duffel bag between my feet. Irving had organized it nicely, and I found the Midazolam bottle and a syringe.

June gave me a worried look. I punctured the bottle with the needle and drew out five milliliters, sparing her a glance. "This is just to help you relax."

"I'm relaxed," she said tightly. I snorted. "I am," she insisted. "Your bathroom is very soothing."

I looked around the spa-like space and had to agree. It was usually relaxing. "Regardless, you're getting a few shots tonight." I stood and moved from her right side to her left, pinched the tissue on her arm, and punctured the skin. I pressed the plunger faster than it took her to open her mouth to argue with me. That done, I got her a water bottle from my fridge and had her take two Ibuprofen pills.

With her right arm held gingerly between her legs, June followed my movements with a worried gaze. I sat down on the chair in front of her, and my knees sandwiched hers. I bent to the side and scooped up a penlight from the bag. June shied away from the light, and after I held her chin still, I didn't get the pupillary response I wanted. Definite concussion, then. I dropped the penlight back into the bag. "Okay, now the fun part," I said with heavy sarcasm, and I took her right hand in mine gently. "Have you dislocated your shoulder before?"

"No," she demurred. She went rigid, and her left hand pressed on mine like she wanted me to remove my hand.

"You have to relax," I said, hoping my voice sounded more comforting than the tumultuous emotions inside of me felt. "Just relax and I'll give you a massage. That's it."

She gave me a dubious "yeah right" look.

Slowly, I brought her right hand to my right shoulder with her elbow down, so it crossed between our bodies. "The trick to this," I said, holding her gaze with mine, "is to trust me." I gave her a rueful grin. "You *did* say you trust me."

That pulled a smile from her. "True."

With her wrist braced on my shoulder, I used my right hand to pull down on her elbow and my left to massage up her sore arm and toward her shoulder. "I know it hurts. Dislocated shoulders are rough. But all that tension around your shoulder is keeping it out of place. So, relax." I massaged closer to her shoulder with firm, guiding motions. "Let it go. I'll guide it back into place, and as soon as I do, you'll feel a hundred times better."

She tensed away from me. "I've seen how they do this on TV. It's going to hurt."

I lifted my eyes to the heavens and prayed for patience. "Just because TV does it, doesn't mean it's accurate," I reminded her. "I'm on my own—I don't have the assistance of another physician, so we're doing this the slow way. Nice and easy." I massaged harder, pushing until I knew she was going to start feeling it. To distract her, I said, "What were you doing behind a tree?"

She let out a puff of a laugh. "I don't know. Hiding, I guess."

"From me?" I asked, offended.

"Yes."

Holding onto her elbow with my right hand, I tugged down a little harder while my left pushed the ball toward the socket. "Well, that's rude. I charged across the city to save you."

She winced, and through gritted teeth, she admitted, "I know you did. That's why I was hiding."

"Well, now I'm really offended."

"I don't know," she went on, her voice strained. "I guess I was just… afraid."

Her muscles were still tight, spasming around the dislocated joint and keeping it from sliding back into place. I applied a little extra pressure. "I thought we went over this," I reminded her. "You don't have to be afraid of me."

"I'm not afraid *of* you," she growled, gritting her teeth harder.

"Relax," I reminded her.

"It hurts," she shot back. "How am I supposed to relax when it hurts?"

"Take a breath and let go," I suggested. "A little pain is good. Especially if it means relief is coming."

June let out a bitter laugh. "Oh man."

"What?" I asked, quirking a brow.

"That's you," she said tightly. "What you just said—that's you. You want me to let go and risk the pain." She met my gaze reluctantly. "But I'm afraid of pain, Amos. Like," she paused, swallowing. "Not physical pain. I'm afraid of *you* pain."

I frowned, trying to understand her.

June blinked back tears. "I was hiding because I'm afraid of how I feel. I think I'm falling in love with you, and if you can't ever love me back," her voice broke, but she cleared her throat and finished with, "it will hurt."

I paused my massaging motions, and her green eyes locked onto mine with baleful resignation. Like she'd just realized the full truth of her own words. This was not a helpful conversation for my concentration, but I had a feeling that I might have the magic words to help her. "June, I already love you," I said softly.

She couldn't have looked more shocked if I'd told her green apple licorice was a vegetable. I pulled down and gave an assertive push with my left hand.

Pop.

"Ow, mother trucker," she hissed, leaning forward and clamping her hand to her arm.

I rotated her shoulder to make sure it was positioned well, and my lips pressed into a smile. Her substitute curse words were almost as cute as her sailor's vocabulary. I felt around the joint, making sure everything was where it should be. "Better?"

June sighed, and still hunched over, she leaned forward until her head rested against my chest. I reached around her, so much smaller than I was and achingly vulnerable. I slid her off the bath and onto my lap so her good shoulder leaned against me, and I could tuck her head under my chin.

"I think I hit my head harder than I thought," she mumbled.

"You didn't," I assured her. "I'm in love with you. I have been for a while."

She picked up her head and speared me with a needle-sharp stare. "Brady, you better mean that."

Smiling again, I cupped the soft angle of her jawline and tilted her lips up to mine. "I mean it, Matthews. I love you."

She closed the distance between us, sealing her lips to mine and arching her back to mold her body to my torso. I savored her mouth, licking along the bottom edge of her lower lip and then greedily devouring every glide and press of our kiss as it deepened. Her body was like putty in my hands. June had a way of fitting herself to every gap and crevice in my body and being, until I was convinced I could never be whole again without her there.

But then a disturbing *plop* sounded through the bathroom, and I reluctantly pulled away from her to look down. *Plop, plop, plop.* Blood dripped from her leg to the Italian marble floors. Her pulse had raged to life from our kiss, and now it was causing the laceration on her shin to bleed freely.

June followed my gaze and then groaned. "No, Amos. Let's just ignore it."

"This is why I get cranky with you," I said lightly, and ignoring her protests, I shifted her back to the edge of the bathtub and spun her around, so her feet dangled in the tub. "You make harebrained decisions that make no sense."

She looked down at herself, and I could see the "loading circle" swoop around in her head. "Wait. Does that need stitches?"

"Mhm," I said. I unzipped her dress for her and slid the strap off her good shoulder.

She whipped around and glared. "And *how* are you planning on getting the paint off my legs?"

"Water," I said placidly. "And soap."

"Death first," she said, and tried to slide away from the tub.

I hooked my arm around her left side and pinned her back in place. "Relax. We're just washing the paint off your legs. I don't want to mess with the clotting your wound has already done, so I'll leave it alone for now." I peeled her dress down her torso, exposing her black lace bra and, not surprisingly, more paint. It was everywhere, dry now and cracking like packed desert dirt. I tried not to think about how mouthwatering she looked in the underwear I'd bought for her this morning, but it was an impossible feat. She looked absolutely delicious.

"For now," she mocked, but she helped me with her dress and stood so she could shimmy it down her hips where it pooled at her feet. "I know what 'for now' means. It means poking and scrubbing and sewing."

"I don't know what I need a medical license for," I said dryly. "You clearly know what to do." I removed her dress, and because I'd somehow convinced this gorgeous creature to like me, I dropped a kiss on her neck for good measure.

"Shut up, Brady," June muttered, but there was no heat in it. "My arm hurts and my legs hurt, and you turned me on and left me with blue balls."

"You keep saying that, but last I *thoroughly* checked, you don't have testicles." I rotated the bath handle to a lukewarm setting, and June squeaked, shifting her feet out of the way.

"That's because society doesn't care about sexually frustrated women, so they didn't give us a term for it. So, I stole yours," she said primly.

I knelt behind her and reached my arms around her soft hips, steeling myself against how erotic every touch felt when I was near her. Never in my life had I been attracted to a patient I had to care for, but I'd had to do it for June twice now. I didn't think I'd survive another experience without spontaneous combustion. As the water poured out of the faucet, I gently splashed it on her legs and reached for the bar of unscented soap to my right, lathering it between my hands.

June craned her neck to peer down at me. "I can wash my own legs."

I knew she could. I wanted to do it. "I'm more careful than you are," I said, leaving no room for argument in my tone. I rinsed the paint off her legs, and because she was bleeding through the gauze anyway, I peeled off the tape so I could wash around it. Truthfully, I was grateful it was her leg. If she'd taken the brunt of her fall on her shoulder and her legs, then it had spared her head. Her slight concussion was nothing compared to what it could have been.

When I felt confident that her legs were clean, I kissed her good shoulder and murmured, "Okay this next part is up to you. Do you want to wash the rest of the paint off now, or do you want to sponge it off later? Once I stitch your leg, I want you to keep it dry for a few days."

"Definitely now," she said, although I heard the strain in her voice. She had to be in a whole world of hurt right now. But I helped her sit in the tub and remove her underwear, and then, careful of her contusions and most painful spots, I helped her rinse off the paint and wash her hair without fully submerging the gash in the bath.

Toweled-off and cleaned, I told her to lie down on the bed, and I tidied up the bathroom. As I did, I thought about all the ways this scenario could have gone worse. What if the wife *had* been in the mood for "games?" What if June had hit her head harder? Would those monsters have called her an ambulance, or would June have ended up a picture on a documentary about the crazy fairytale murderers from South Salt Lake City? I tried to banish those thoughts because they weren't logical or practical. But despite my best efforts, fury and fear mixed in my blood like noxious ammonia and creatinine.

By the time I made it back to June with the supplies I'd need to suture her wound, June was asleep in my bed. She'd wrapped her bath towel loosely around her leg, and with the sheets haphazardly draped over her body, she'd fallen into a deep sleep on her back. I couldn't delay her stitches any longer than I already had. Blood had already seeped through the towel.

Suddenly, June sat up with a gasp, first bringing her hands to her chest, and then crying out in pain as the sudden movement jerked her injured shoulder. Not knowing I was in the room behind her, she curled forward, and a broken sob shook her shoulders. As she held herself together, I knew what had woken her.

And I was going to fuck up that nightmare until he begged for death.

TWENTY-THREE
June

If I thought the shoulder thing was bad, it was nothing compared to Brady stitching up my leg. Apparently, paint had dried on the inside of the "tissue" and had to be "debrided." Also, the word "tissue" was disgusting, and I would be happy if it never came out of his mouth again.

Although Amos applied topical anesthetic all over the tender area (ouch) and injected local anesthetic under the skin (double ouch), I still writhed in agony while he flushed the wound and literally *scrubbed* paint off my bleeding hunk of flesh. It was 2023. We didn't have a better method of getting paint off a nasty wound than a sponge?

Actually, the stitching part was a relief, and I found myself able to relax again while he worked steadily, threading a curved needle through my numb skin and tying tight, precise knots along the jagged edges. I fell back into a fitful sleep, but I almost dreaded it. My dreams were uneasy and full of sharp anxiety, teetering on the cusp of adrenaline so that when I woke to darkness sometime later, I felt like I hadn't gotten any sleep at all.

I stared at the dark room, disoriented and fighting against the feeling that my eyes were permanently crossed. My head pulsed with slow waves of intense pain like I'd cinched it between a vice, and my shoulder screamed in agony. Amos had propped me upright on a mountain of pillows, and at some point, he'd secured my arm in a sling, but the pain medicine he had given me earlier must have worn off.

I looked around for him, but then I heard his voice, muted and talking to someone in his cavernous living room. I sat up gingerly, listening as his voice grew louder. "… isn't like it will help anyone if she has to testify about it in court." He paused, and I realized he must be on the phone with someone else. "That's what I'm saying. It's hearsay." He stopped again. Then, "Az, I don't care how *legal* it is, can you fix it, or not?"

Az must be Azura, his sister. I remembered him saying she was a lawyer, and suddenly, I wanted to catapult myself from the bed and stop him from doing whatever it was he was planning. I didn't want to prosecute the mother… ducker. I wanted to forget it had ever happened. I wasn't even going to go back for my stuff. I was done with art for a while, anyway. It wasn't worth it. Amos had been right.

I struggled to sit up all the way, fighting the stiffness in my shoulder, and I threw the comforter aside so I could slide off the side of the bed.

"Okay, I can type up her statement and I'll send it to you tomorrow. Thanks, I owe you one." He paused again as Azura said something. "Okay," he replied wryly, "yes, alright, I owe you *two* favors. How did that go, by the way?" Another beat of silence. "Good. That guy was an asshole… *don't* give me grief, Az, yes, I said asshole. You got this? Okay. Thank you. Goodbye."

I gritted my teeth as I shuffled across the room toward him. "Amos," I growled. "Whatever you just did, undo it."

He leaned into the room, and then his dark, slashing brows came together. "Cupcake, sit your butt down."

"I'm not a cupcake," I countered, "I'm a crème brulée and every inch of me is on fire. It's making me cranky, and if you don't call off whatever you just did, I'm going to—"

"You'll what?" he drawled, taking lazy, long-legged strides to me and standing like an iron wall to halt my progress. "Hit me with your best threat."

I tilted my head back, back, back, and realized without my shoes on, he was absolutely massive when he stood that close to me. I gave him my best perturbed glare anyway. "Forget pig Latin. I'm going to change all your patient names to Elvish."

"That's not a real language," he said dismissively, and putting his hands on my waist, pushed me back toward the bed.

"Yes, it is," I argued. "There's an app for it and everything."

"If you learn Elvish just to spite me, I don't think I'll have any choice but to be impressed," he said with amusement lilting through his words. "Come on, June. Back to bed."

I didn't feel like arguing with the bed part, but I wasn't done with our conversation. As I slid back under the blankets, I said, "Amos, I don't care about justice or whatever. I really don't. You fixed me, and I don't even have, like… a medical bill I'd want to sue them over. They're creepy. I'm over it."

"I know you feel that way now," he said, and sat on the edge of the bed next to me, hitching me against Mount Pillow with his hands on my waist, "but I'm not letting them move on with their lives from this. Besides, what about the next girl?"

That was a sobering thought. Not only the next girl, but what about the girls before me? Archer and Meg clearly hadn't been caught or prosecuted because they were still doing it. "I don't know," I admitted.

"Well, the beauty of this arrangement," he said, tucking the blanket around me and leaning over my body so his nose nearly touched mine, "is that you don't have to know. I know. And I'll handle it."

"What if I don't want you to handle it?" I countered, my voice barely above a whisper.

He kissed the tip of my nose. "Too bad."

"Brady," I glowered.

Amos got an obsidian glint in his eyes. "Not all good things are born of integrity, June. 'Do no harm' does not apply to the people who hurt what's mine." He leaned in close so his lips briefly caressed mine. Dipping his voice down low he said, "And you are mine."

My heart nearly exploded. I stared at his face, at the angles that were so hard and straight, and then at the heat in his gaze. I never would have dreamed I would see warmth like that in Dr. Amos Brady's stern features. He had admitted that he was in love with me, but I couldn't make myself believe it. I leaned into him, and my left arm smoothed over his shoulder and around his neck. I pulled myself against his firm torso to kiss him again. Suddenly, I was a starved woman, and Dr. Brady was milk and honey.

Amos chuckled, kissing me with smiling lips, but he unlatched my arm from his neck and pressed me down into the pillows. "Down, Tiger."

I growled, and it did sound suspiciously like an angry kitten. "That's the second time you've left me hanging."

He lifted my palm and kissed the center of it, sending tingles down my skin and straight to my heart. "Baby, if I could destroy that body of yours in unspeakably filthy ways, I would. But it's not happening."

I let my head fall back with an anguished sigh. "Fine." As he stood, I asked, "Okay, but what are you planning on doing? You said so yourself on the phone, it's hearsay. They could easily claim I fell on my own, and if I press charges, they'll sue me for ruining their carpet. It was *nice* carpet, Amos. I can't afford that."

"Oh, it was *nice* carpet," he conceded, like I'd given him a devastating revelation. "In that case," he paused, sliding his hands into the pockets of his black joggers and letting his expression darken dangerously, "I'm still going to fuck him up."

Stunned, I stared at him in the semi-darkness. "What?" I breathed, drawing out the word.

Amos' phone buzzed in his pocket, and he fished it out, pointing to me before answering. "Go back to sleep. Hey Az, what did you find?" He left the room, and as he did, I heard the evil satisfaction in his voice as he asked, "Oh, did she?"

A bizarre mixture of apprehension and relief tap-danced in my chest as I tried to calm my mind and find sleep again. Whatever Amos was planning, I didn't think Archer would see it coming.

Friday went by in a blur of pain. I woke up feeling like I'd been fed through a shredder and spit back out in bandages. My legs were so sore, I could barely get to the toilet. My brain smacked against my eyes with every heartbeat, and my entire torso was so stiff, the pain actually went down my left arm and to my fingers. Brady wanted me to go to the hospital for X-rays, but I told him in my firmest tone that the only place I would be going was his liquor cabinet for relief. He'd offered me acetaminophen instead. And then he'd reminded me that he had suggested the hospital in the first place.

Amos had tried to reschedule as many of his surgeries as he could, but he'd had to go to a nasty tumor resection that afternoon, and I'd assured him that his patients at the center needed him a lot more than I did. Fortunately, he had a TV in his bedroom, and he'd fired up the cell phone model he'd used before his latest one so I could download my data onto it and put my SIM card in it. Then, I ate snacks and watched garbage TV until he got home.

He'd declined sex. Again. The tool. But he had fed me zoodles with chopsticks and cuddled me against his heavenly body while we traded off watching each other's favorite movies. So, all in all, it was the best scenario after being attacked by two crazed cosplayers.

When I woke up on Saturday morning, I found Amos hovering over me with his arms braced on either side of my body and his black coffee eyes warmer than fresh brew. "Hey, Cupcake," he smiled.

"Hey," I croaked around a dry throat. After he'd seen me in so much pain that I couldn't maneuver off the bed, he'd given me a pill of the "good stuff" that made me feel like a hot air balloon. But it did make my mouth horribly dry.

"I just got paged to U of U. There was a pileup on 215, and they need the extra hands," he said apologetically.

"S'okay," I smiled. I made a shooing gesture. "Go away. You're smothering me."

He snorted, knowing full well that I had clung to him all night. "Your medicine and water are right there to your left. I'll be back as soon as I can."

I nodded. "You're so cool. Mr. Magic Hands."

"*Doctor* Magic Hands," he winked before kissing my cheek.

My God, was he ever. After he left, I took the pills he'd set out for me, took two puffs of my inhaler thing—the name Brady had used was way too long to remember—and then I staggered into the bathroom to brush my teeth. As I did, I looked over and saw that Amos had bought me three new outfits, and I cringed.

Okay, time to face some facts, I thought as I gingerly dressed myself in the loose, moss green jumper shorts he had picked for me. *One, Amos loves me. Or he thinks he does. Either way, he doesn't mind me being around, and the one time I had mentioned going home, he had laughed like it was the dumbest thing I've ever said. So, logically, the second fact is that I'll be here for a while. And if that's the case, I need my stuff.*

I looked at myself in the mirror and winced again. My hair had dried bristly and frizzy, and it clouded around my face in a wild, red mane. A bruise at my right temple had wrapped down to my cheekbone, and with my arm in a sling, I looked properly bashed up. Not to mention the huge bandage on my shin that smarted with every step.

Alright, so I looked horrifying. But I could still take a cab home and grab a few things. Clothing, for one, so Amos didn't feel like he had to buy me an entire capsule wardrobe just for our sleepovers. Also, my own deodorant, zit cream, blah blah blah.

I gasped out loud. My birth control.

June, you dumbass, I thought with a groan. *That's still in the day bag you left at the Medieval Times Horror House.* The indignity of having to ask Amos to write me a new birth control prescription did not leave me a lot of room to think. I pulled up the rideshare app and requested one to my house, and barely thinking, I slipped my feet into the pair of flip flops he'd bought me.

The whole way to my house, I kept kicking myself. *I don't use birth control for funsies*, I'd said. With *full* fucking confidence like I knew what the hell I was doing. My Mercury wasn't just in retrograde. It had left the orbit and was careening through space on a drunken bender.

I thanked the driver, who was an older woman who had chatted about her grandkids the whole time, and I gave her a tip like I didn't have the saddest bank account this side of the Salt Lake. At least Amos was feeding me free food. That helped.

I hobbled my way up the stairs to my apartment, and it was the first time I hated being the top apartment, because usually, I was grateful not to have upstairs neighbors. I paused.

My keys.

"Mother *trucker*," I growled. I couldn't remember if I had locked it. I was pretty sure I had, but I tried the doorknob just in case. It gave way.

With a sigh of relief that my stupidity had saved me from my airheadedness, I breezed through the door and made sure to lock it behind me. I pulled out my phone, and trying to be responsible, I texted Amos to let him know I was grabbing a few things, but I'd probably be back before he would.

A shape shifted to my left. I looked over, and a scream froze in my throat.

Archer stood from a crouched position. He'd been bent over a pile of my stuff—my paints, my art tote, my day bag—and stood with elated surprise in his Gollum-wide eyes. "June," he said, like *I'd* walked into *his* house. "Gosh, you're here." He looked me up and down. "Wow, I'm so glad you're okay. I was really worried about you. Have you been at the hospital?"

I frowned. "Archer?" Anger ripped through the hurt he had already caused me. I actually saw my curls tremble in my peripheral vision from my fury. "Get out," I snapped.

"Easy, easy," he said, holding out a hand. Something had changed in his expression. Where before, a placid mask had covered the crazy, now there was nothing filming his thoughts. They were plain to see, and whatever had happened after I'd left, it had exacerbated his unhinged thoughts. "I was just returning your stuff. I figured you might be too afraid of Meg to come back and get them."

My lungs seized as he approached me, and I hurried to the front door. But Archer was faster. He sidestepped, having positioned himself in just the right place behind my door so he could block my path. Like a vacuum seal bag, my lungs sucked in tight. They refused to inflate again. *Fudge*, I thought angrily. *Shut up, body. This is not a helpful panic response.* "Ge-geht," I wheezed. "Geht, ouht." Fear tickled over my thoughts like thousands of spiders.

Archer took in my retreating form with a growing, manic smile. "What's wrong, June? You look sick."

I closed my eyes briefly, trying to will air back into my lungs. But it was no use. I needed to relax. I needed Amos behind me and the birds chirping in a tree overhead. I needed to feel his warmth and know I was safe. I didn't have that here. What I had was fear so tight, it pulled me inward like a black hole at my center.

The Dracula theme song played over my phone suddenly, filling the air with ironically foreboding music. Archer waved a hand. "No, no, don't answer that, honey. Let's visit. I really, really am sorry about Meg. She's," he paused, laughing like he was lamenting the brown spots in his lawn, "she's a little crazy."

Black dotted the edges of my vision as I tried futilely to pull air into my lungs. The song stopped as Amos' call went to my voicemail. I took several steps back.

Archer frowned suddenly. "Come on, June, don't you want to at least offer me something to eat? A drink of water? I came all this way."

Sure, Archer, I thought caustically. *Let me just whip up an assault sandwich with a side of pickled stalker.* "No," I said rudely. I backed away to the kitchen, and when I reached it, my hands fumbled for the knife drawer.

"Oh, I got all those," Archer chuckled. He pointed behind me to my stuff where every knife and sharp object in my kitchen had been piled in the corner. I gave him an incredulous, terrified look. Edward Scissorhands had a homicidal stepbrother named Archer.

He pulled a knife from his back pocket, but held it up loosely, like I had him at gunpoint. "Relax, June. I just didn't want this to get ugly."

Air, I thought desperately. *I need air. I need air. If I can't breathe, I'm going to pass out and he's going to kill me. I'd so much rather the moose have killed me. At least she was protecting her baby. Archer is just a toad with mommy issues.*

Toccata and Fugue played again, insistently ringing through the small, quiet apartment. Archer narrowed his eyes. "Who is that?"

"B-boss," I gasped.

"Does he know where you are?" he asked suspiciously.

I nodded violently. "Coming," I wheezed. "To get me."

"Answer the phone," Archer snapped, lowering the knife. "Tell him you're at home resting."

I nodded again, and with trembling fingers, I answered.

"Speaker phone," Archer mouthed with a glint in his eyes.

I tapped the speaker button. "June?" Amos asked.

I didn't try to hide the painful sound of my lungs searching for air. "H-hi, Dr. Brady," I said formally. "Thanks for," I wheezed in, gathering so little air, I might as well have been in space, "calling back."

He paused. "Are you on speaker?"

"Yes," I puffed out. "I'm alone," wheeze, "though."

"Why aren't you at work?" he barked.

Jesus, Mary, and Joseph, he's smart, I thought gratefully. "Sick," I rasped. "Don't co-uh-um."

"You sound terrible," he griped. "Did you try cough syrup?"

"Syrup, yes," I gasped.

"Okay. I'll see you on Monday," he said briskly. Then he hung up, and I felt my whole safety line slither down a canyon far beyond my reach. My only consolation was that Amos knew. He knew I was in trouble, and he was coming. I wasn't sure I could ever use that "safe word" again, but at least he had thought to include it to be sure.

Archer laughed long and loud, leaning against the kitchen counter. He let out a loud sigh, like that had been the best laugh of his life. "You said he was your boyfriend. I knew you were lying."

I nodded, backing up to the sink.

Archer peered at the purple chef's knife in his hand. "You need to sharpen your knives, June. These are a mess."

I gave a nonchalant shrug like I knew, and I didn't care. Which was true. "Lazy," I said indifferently.

He tutted, slowly closing the distance between us. "June, sweetie, I've got to have you come over sometime. I have the best knife sharpener."

I'll bet you do, Voorhees. I tapped my chest. "Archer," I sucked in another breath, and alarmingly, black flashed over my vision like a strobe light. "Asthma."

"Oh," he drawled, pocketing the knife and nodded. "I thought you were being dramatic. But you have asthma. Do you need an inhaler?"

I nodded. "Bag," I rasped. "You brought," wheeze, "my bag."

"Wow," Archer said, flaring his eyes. "Oh, wow, you left your medication at my house this whole time?"

I nodded again.

He put a hand to his chest. "June, honey, you should have said something. You've needed me this whole time?" Archer backed away toward the bag. "I'm so glad I came."

"Me, too," I rasped.

As he moved toward the bag in the corner, I took my opening. I darted from the kitchen to my bedroom, slammed the door shut, and locked it. Darkness swallowed me for a moment, but I shook my head, clearing my vision to grab the corners of my dresser so I could tip it over in front of the door.

"June?" Archer called. "What are you doing? Don't you need this?"

I did, but I'd rather take my chances with my asthma than Freddy Krueger out there. I sat on the edge of my bed and closed my eyes, trying to force my lungs to calm down. It wasn't working. How had Amos done it in the woods? Fill the balloon. Let it out slowly. Relax my jaw and throat. I tried, but then my bedroom door shook so hard, it splintered around the hinges.

White had joined the black dots, and I felt my body teeter to the side as unconsciousness grabbed for me with spindly fingers. Gritting my teeth, I stumbled off the bed to my closet. Suddenly, I was grateful I had the world's smallest bedroom, and I fell more than lunged for the floor where I kept my paint supplies. I wasn't sure what I was looking for, but I didn't have any useful hobbies like archery or knife-making. Or baton twirling. A baton would have been nice.

The door shuddered again, this time moving the dresser aside easily. So much for that movie trick, too. I scrabbled with my hands, searching for something, anything I could use. My hands found a familiar object.

Archer finally blasted through the door, and panting, he stumbled inside with a "What the hell, June?"

Wheeze, wheeze, wheeze, *Come on June, one big breath. You got this.* I forced as much air into my lungs as I could, pulling hard and forcing my ribs to expand.

Archer put his hand on my shoulder. "Come here, you little—"

I turned and aimed a can of black spray paint at his face. I pressed the nozzle hard, aiming for his eyes, and I ended up coating his entire face, his open mouth, and his eyes, which he screwed shut. He batted the spray can out of my hand, but then he fell to his knees behind me, screaming, spitting, and clawing at his face.

My greatest masterpiece yet.

I struggled to escape again, but he reached out with a growl and grabbed my ankle. I kicked blindly, and to my surprise, I connected with something. It caused him to grunt, and I pushed my hands on the ground to stand, but I fell.

Air refused to get past my swollen airways. I lay on my side, gasping futilely like a dying fish, and I wondered dimly if I had at least broken his nose. I hoped I had. My world swirled like a palette under a running faucet, blending together and muddying until the colors converged into darkness.

I wasn't sure what miracle had happened, but Archer didn't reach for me. In fact, other than the desperate, rasping pull of my tortured breaths, I didn't hear anything at all. If I could just get to my bag…

But no. There would be no moving. My limbs didn't have enough oxygen to do anything. I was surprised my consciousness was holding on the way it was.

Thump, thump, thump. My front door pounded. "Police! Open the door!"

An inkling of gratitude shot through my dimming awareness. They'd made it here. Amos must have called 911 when he'd realized I was in trouble. I didn't hear them break my door down, but I had to assume they did because suddenly someone shouted, "Over here!"

Hands moved me onto my back. I tried to lift my hand to point to my bag, but I had nothing in the tank. How unfair was that? I knew what I needed, but I couldn't even tell them. "I've got a pulse," a female officer said.

So glad you do, I thought dimly.

"We're clear!" a man called. "Let him through."

Feet pounded, and then a familiar voice said, "Move."

Amos? Fuck, did you join the PD? I like you as a doctor. Oh wait, I said "fuck." Sorry.

My last thought was that Amos wouldn't look bad in uniform, actually.

TWENTY-FOUR

Amos

Dating June was going to give me high blood pressure. I had just scrubbed in when my pocket had given off a June-specific *ding*. I'd already been on edge about leaving her alone, so I had my nurse check the message, and never in my life had I wanted to throw something in my OR more than I had after she'd read that text out loud to me. I had very nearly grabbed the nearest instrument and broken it against the wall. What kind of woman, after being assaulted, took a damn taxi across the city to go back to her apartment alone? She couldn't have waited, what, two hours?

Fortunately, Bennett had been there, and whether or not he had felt he was ready to take over a surgery on his own, I knew he was. So, I'd given him my surgery as I'd called 911 and sprinted out of the hospital with my heart in my throat. I disobeyed a lot of traffic rules getting there, and the entire ride, I went through her call in my head. She'd sounded like she'd been in bad shape, and she was obviously being threatened by someone in the background.

I didn't ever want to hear the word "syrup" again.

I got there at the same time as SLCPD and before EMS. I prayed hard. I prayed June had her inhaler in there. I prayed she hadn't been hurt. I prayed, above all, that I would have the chance to give her a piece of my mind. Not a nice piece. The furious, vampire overlord piece.

They agreed to let me in once they had cleared the apartment, and it was the longest two minutes of my life. I waited at the doorway, just inside the living room, which they had immediately cleared as safe. I didn't miss the corner of June's belongings and the knives behind them. My blood ran cold at how quiet it was as the officers banged open doors and cleared the kitchen, the bathroom, and then finally, they shouted, "Over here!"

I ran forward before they'd given me the green light. June's bag wasn't in the living room, so I went for her bedroom. Just as I arrived, they yelled, "We're clear! Let him through!"

I ran past them, only barely glimpsing a small man's inert form handcuffed at June's feet. But my eyes weren't even on June with her blue lips and pale skin. I saw her bag near the man. I swiped it up, ripped open the main pocket, and pulled out the albuterol inhaler. I knelt next to June, shook the inhaler within an inch of its life, and administered four puffs of medicine while holding her lips around it. While I pressed the button on the inhaler, I inspected her for any evidence of blood or wounds, but she looked otherwise unharmed.

"Come on, June," I whispered. I saw her chest working hard to suck in air still, but her pulse fell under my fingertips and her respiratory rate was less than thirty. Albuterol wasn't working. "Where is EMS?" I asked angrily.

"Here," a voice said behind me. I didn't bother to move out of their way. Ordinarily, I would have. When June had gone to the hospital the first time, I had gladly stepped aside—but I wasn't taking any chances this time. "Ipratroprium, CPAP, and IV epinephrine," I said without looking away from her.

While the medics got a blood pressure cuff, oximeter, ECG leads, and IV started, I took the CPAP mask from the EMT first, placed it over June's mouth and nose, and then took the ipratropium and administered it through the airtight mask. "Epi?" I asked.

"I can't get a vein, switching sides," the nervous EMT said.

"Just give me the epi, I'll administer it intramuscularly," I said. I took the syringe, popped off the cap, and stabbed her thigh.

"Should we reassess airways?" the female EMT asked as she tried for another IV.

"No, I'll get a line in, and then we'll push hydrocortisone." There was no point in assessing her airways when she was non-responsive and blue in the lips. I took the IV needle from the EMT, who looked at me like "WTF are you doing here?" Understandably. I ripped off June's sling, and knowing full well she was going to feel this *when* she woke up—because there was no acceptable situation in which she didn't—I slid the IV in place on her hand and gave her the steroid that would hopefully help to open her airways.

"O2 sats rising," the male EMT next to me said. "Seventy-four, seventy-seven," he continued.

That was a good sign. June's chest rose and fell, working with the CPAP machine that pushed oxygen forcefully into her lungs. Her body exhaled it back out on its own, which was another encouraging sign. "Okay, transport her," I said. "We can stabilize her en route."

The EMTs knew the routine. We got her on a stretcher, and I followed along, checking her vitals and looking for signs that she was waking up. As the stretcher jarred and bounced to the ambulance, June cracked one eye open.

If my heart had had feet, they would have crumpled in relief. I felt my pulse slow down, although the adrenaline sharpened my senses still. "Pulse/ox?" I asked the EMT who had loaded her.

"She's tachycardic and O2 is seventy-nine," he said.

She was bound to be a little tachy with that many stimulants accelerating her heart rate. "We need to get her to ninety. Let's give forty of magnesium and repeat albuterol, but watch that tachy," I said, standing next to her and feeling some gratitude that we could look at monitors now that we were in the rig. She still had a capnography waveform that resembled a shark fin, but it was starting to even out.

June's eyes popped open fully, and she inhaled, wheezing audibly. That would be a nasty shock to wake up to a CPAP pushing air into your lungs and wires everywhere. "Ketamine," I said before leaning over her and taking her face in my hands. "June, relax baby. I'm here. You're safe."

She tried to take the CPAP off, but I blocked her with my elbows. "I know, it sucks," I said. "The more you relax, the faster we can take it off."

Her eyes hooded as the ketamine rushed through her veins, but I gave her the credit. "Good job, June. Keep that up. Work with the machine. It's pushing oxygen in, and you need to push it back out. Stay calm."

"Archer," she gusted out.

I shook my head. "You'll never see him again. I guarantee it."

She closed her eyes, and then screwed them shut as she fought against the CPAP. Feisty June. It was good to know she could be a pain in the rear even with her life on the line.

By the time we got her to the ER, she was looking better. She was maintaining her oxygen, and her breathing had become more deliberate. The bronchodilators and steroids were doing their job. She was also more alert, which was equal parts annoying and gratifying because she was mad about the CPAP. But that also meant she was okay, and for that, I could have cried.

I didn't, but I could have—and a vulnerable part of me recognized I would need to sit with that at some point. Until then, my focus stayed on June as she stabilized, my eyes on her monitors and my heart thudding along with the *beep, beep, beep* of June's. She woke up several times, and even after we took her off the CPAP, she wanted the oxygen mask removed, and then the cannula, and finally, I threatened to tie her hands to the bed if she didn't sit still.

Her eyes had hooded in desire, of course. The minx. My life was going to be one enormous jumble of stress and joy with June Matthews in it. And she *would* be in it. I needed that inevitability like I needed a vagus nerve. The question was, did June feel the same? She had said she was *falling* in love with me. And she'd said she was afraid of it. If what June had said about her struggles with letting herself connect with others was true, then she might not return the depth of my feelings. Hell, even I hadn't accepted the depth of my feelings at first.

They were illogical.

Anomalous.

Preposterous.

And yet, despite my intense misgivings about our sprint from animosity to infatuation, I couldn't deny how June made me feel. I couldn't imagine a single day without her capricious unpredictability. I didn't want to. On the drive to her house, when I had imagined a hundred ways she might leave this life, I'd had to face that possibility. I had decided that if I was given the chance to keep her, I would. I would grab on with both hands and never let ineffably luminescent June disappear again.

I'd also decided that if anyone dimmed her light again like Archer Holmeyer had done, I would personally snuff theirs out. Fortunately for him, the authorities had him in custody, and his brief bout of unconsciousness from June's foot smashing his nose up to his prefrontal cortex had not saved him from detention. Two officers from the incident had come to take June's statement, and she'd told them about finding Archer in her home and fighting for her life as he'd threatened her with a knife.

I had been equal parts proud and horrified to hear her version of events. And she'd told it with such matter-of-fact anger, like he'd ruined her plans and inconvenienced her instead of nearly killing her.

After they left, I stood from my seat by the window and reached for her hand. She looked up at me with fury and hurt mingling in the tears along her bottom lashes. "Amos, excuse my Goddamn French, but I'm glad that fucker is behind bars." Her voice sounded harsh like a cicada drone. The anticholinergic medications we had used to help open her airways dried up moisture in her body, and it made her voice dry and raspy.

I exhaled a short chuckle. "The audacity, Matthews."

"What did you have planned for him, anyway?" she asked with a little frown. "I mean, before I went Karate Kid on his face."

"What *do* I have planned for him?" I corrected with a half-smile. "There's plenty of damage left to accomplish. But don't worry about that right now. You've done more than enough today."

June sighed, leaning her head back against the pillows as her fingers drummed against the back of my hand. "Hospitals take forever to get people discharged. How much longer?"

I sat down on the edge of her bed and quirked an eyebrow. "You mean 'how many days?'"

"Haha," she said, rolling her eyes. I blinked at her pointedly. She gave me a round-eyed glare. "You *are* joking, aren't you?"

"Do I strike you as a comedian, Matthews?"

"You're hilarious if you're suggesting I sit in this bed for fu-fudging days," she glared.

A small smile pulled at the corners of my mouth. "Why did the vampire's queen end up in the hospital for three days?"

She glowered. "Why, Brady?"

"Her breathing sucked."

She threw a pillow at me and howled in pain. "Where's Archer? Tell him to come back and stab me for real. I'd rather die than live with someone who's jokes are that bad."

I caught the pillow, and laughing with her, I brought my eyebrows practically up to my hairline. "June Cupcake Ella Matthews, *what* did you just say? Live with whom, now?"

Her pale, freckled cheeks turned pink. "Uh…"

I leaned forward, my features mischievous. "Who do you want to live with?" She sucked her lips in, blinking once. I grinned and lowered my voice. "Use your words, June."

A slow smile crept up her delicate features. "I've been thinking about the merits of living with the vampire overlord."

I kissed her neck just above her racing pulse. "Yum."

TWENTY-FIVE
June

"You're doing *what*?" Liz screeched over the phone.

I pulled the receiver away from my ear, wincing. "Sis, decibels," I reminded her.

"You're moving in *with your asshole boss*?" she reiterated.

I waved goodbye to the mover as he left Amos' apartment after depositing the last of my boxes. "Well, kind of. But I told you, he's the good kind of asshole. He's an asshole to everyone else and, eh, different with me."

"What kind of different?" Liz asked dubiously.

"Like he has an addiction to cupcakes, and I happen to be the only edible cupcake in the entire world different," I said wryly.

"Oh *fuck*, you love him," she said.

I shifted my gaze around like someone would hear. But Amos was in surgery again, and the movers had all left after carrying all five boxes' worth of my stuff into the apartment from their pickup truck. "Yeah, I might," I admitted, leaning my head against the front door I still had propped open with my ass.

"I leave you for *two weeks*," she groaned. "Baby girl, you can't move in with a boy you just met."

"First of all," I pointed out, "he's a man. A really hot man. And secondly, why not? You going to get a different roommate in your empty apartment in the next two and half months?"

"That's a good point," she paused, as if thinking. "Yeah, okay. He probably has a bougee place anyway, right?"

I looked around the bright, modern apartment that was bigger than my childhood home. "It's pretty nice."

"Okay, but if he plays games, you be a big girl and bounce," she warned.

"Trust me. I can handle Big Bad Brady," I grinned. The elevator doors slid open, and speak of the sexy devil, Amos Brady walked toward me like I'd summoned my own personal demon. I gave him an up-down flick of my eyes as I took in his wide shoulders straining against the sage button-down shirt. Staring down at his phone, Amos scrolled through something as he strolled lazily toward his front door.

He stopped short when he realized I was holding it open. I gave him my sexiest smolder.

"Oh, I see, the virgin is talking a big game now," Liz joked, cackling.

I glared at her through the receiver. "I'm not a virgin anymore, thank you very much. Twice over. Although it would be more if *mister cranky pants* would stop coddling me."

Amos slid his phone into his back pocket and rolled his eyes.

"How are you, by the way?" Liz asked, sobering. "That was crazy. I saw it in the news and everything after you told me."

"Much better," I said, emphasizing the words with a flare of my eyes for Amos' benefit. He gave me a perturbed stare in return. "Seriously, I don't even notice my shoulder anymore."

Amos stood toe-to-toe with me, his eyes sparking with dark humor. He circled my right wrist with his thumb and forefinger and lifted slowly.

"Agh," I gasped. My arm hadn't even made it parallel to the ground before the pain had pulled him up short. Amos smirked.

"June?" Liz asked. "You okay?"

He leaned down, and in my other ear, he whispered low, "Stay on the phone. Keep her talking on speaker phone." He brushed a kiss against my jaw before straightening again.

Giving him a questioning glance, I brought my phone between us and tapped the speaker icon. "Yeah, I'm here," I said distractedly. My eyes were on Amos as he loosened his tie and burned me to cinders with his stare.

"Bedroom," he mouthed. My eyebrows zipped up.

"Well, I'm glad you're feeling better. That must have been crazy," Liz said.

"It was," I answered slowly, my mind doing the rumba. The bedroom had better mean games. If he made me lie down and watch TV again, I was going to scream. But if we were playing games, why did I have to stay on the phone with Liz? "Tell me about your DJ."

While Liz launched into an overly detailed diatribe of her DJ's best qualities, I sat on the edge of the bed and set the phone on the bedside table. I leaned my weight against my left hand, lounging with my eyes on the doorway expectantly. "He did what with two cherries?" I asked Liz.

"Knotted both the stems at the same fucking time," she screeched happily. "Oh my God, it was so sexy."

Beyond the windows behind me, a blazing July sunset had set the city on fire with an orange glow. Lights blinked on one by one, slowly dotting the deepening night like fireflies. When Amos entered, the evening light filtered over his skin like sepia tone. He'd removed his tie and undone the first two buttons on his earthy green shirt, and with his tie wrapped around his fist, he motioned for me to stand with two fingers.

My pulse galloped to life, and I stood with my eyes glued to the angles of his body and the devious smirk curving his lips. He made his fingers twirl, motioning me to turn around. "Oh my God," I whispered, smiling.

"Huh?" Liz asked.

"I, uh, just… that's crazy," I stumbled.

"Right?" she agreed. "Wait, wait, shit, did I tell you about nineties night?"

"No," I said, facing the wall of windows now and drumming my fingers against my sweatpants. I had to wear the ugliest, loosest clothing to accommodate the aches and pains from my fall. There were bandages on my legs and kinesthetic tape on my shoulder to help keep it in place. Not a sexy look, but I didn't care anymore. It had been days since I'd been discharged from the hospital, and sleeping next to Amos' roaring hot body every night was doing things to me. Deliciously awful things.

Liz launched into a long explanation of her club escapades, and then I felt Amos behind me. He slid his hands under my baggy T-shirt and carefully lifted it, grazing my skin with his knuckles. I drew in a sharp breath.

He pressed his lips to the sensitive spot under my ear, inhaling before pulling away and shimmying my shirt forward so it looped down my front and didn't require me to lift my arm. He pinched my bra clasp and let it fall open.

"… it was like, wait, you want me to get *in* the cage?" Liz went on.

I gave Amos a questioning glance over my shoulder, but he gently rotated my gaze forward with a grip on my chin. I smiled with cat-like satisfaction. He finished undressing me, dropping kisses along my sensitive skin as he went. His fingers brushed up my legs slowly, trailing goosebumps as they went.

When I was naked, Liz asked, "And do you remember the cheetah chick?"

"Yeah," I said, trying to hide a laugh.

"She was fucking *there*. While I was like ten feet in the fucking air in a cage, she started some loud shit about my fat ass…"

Amos nuzzled my neck, and I leaned my head to give him better access as he fondled my breasts from behind. "Stay here," he whispered.

Then he was gone, and I resisted the urge to do an antsy dance in place. I shot an uneasy glance at the phone. How long was he going to keep Liz on the other end? "What did you do?" I encouraged.

"Oh, girl, you *know* I didn't just let her fuck with me like that," Liz raged.

I heard Amos return from his closet. He walked up behind me, and then he set a black, triangular pillow on the bed in front of me. It was impressively big, covered in velvet, and the tallest angle reached my navel. Still standing directly behind me and pressing his body to mine, Amos reached around me to pile pillows on the wedge pillow. Just as I had a twinge of disappointment that he was still fully clothed, he slid his right hand down my right arm, pressed my forearm against my stomach, and then put pressure on the back of my neck with his left hand. He bent me forward, angled over the wedge and pillows, adjusting them as I went.

I ended up bent over with my hurt arm comfortably cushioned between my body and the pillows and my left arm cradling the rest of the pillows under my head. Amos put his hands on my hips and hitched me up until my tip toes barely grazed the hardwood floor.

This left my ass completely up in the air, and cold air hit my exposed pussy. He tickled his fingers up the back of my thigh, over the globes of my ass, and along my spine. I gritted my teeth to keep from sighing happily.

"… those fucking mouth breathers let the winch slide, and *crash*," Liz growled. "They dropped me right in the middle of the club."

"Oh my God," I said as Amos' fingers slid dangerously close to the places I wanted them to. "Wha — were you okay?"

"No," Liz said angrily. "I mean *yes*, but let me tell you…"

Something colder than my body temperature pressed against the entrance of my pussy. It was slick and smooth, and Amos braced his left hand against my lower back as he pushed something inside my vagina with excruciatingly slow, twisting movements. I realized it was a little larger than an egg, but the same size, and I got an inkling of what he planned on doing while I was on the phone with my best friend. The egg slipped the rest of the way inside of me, and he gave the loop at the end an experimental tug to make sure it was secure.

Amos bent over me, his arms braced on the bed. "Your safe word is green apple," he murmured, so low I barely heard him.

"Not licorice?" I quipped with a whisper.

He licked just under my jaw and then nipped my skin. "Too close to 'lick this.'" He lifted his hand so I could see the small, black button between his fingers. He clicked it with his thumb. The vibrator hummed to life and sent a shock of pleasure straight to my clit. I bit down on a groan.

Amos straightened and left again as the vibrator buzzed against my G-spot.

"June, you there?" Liz asked, slightly annoyed.

"Yeah," I said, my voice strained. "Sorry I'm... making dinner."

"Oh, I got you. Do you need me to call back?"

I lifted my head to find Amos, and he caught my eyes as he walked around me to the other side of the bed. He shook his head.

"Uh, no," I said tautly.

"Good, because I'm just getting to the good part. That *bitch* has the fucking audacity to crack a joke about my weight because of the falling cage shit…"

Amos reached the other side of the bed and stared at me with one hand in the pocket of his black dress pants and the other in front of him, still holding the tiny remote. He locked a dark gaze with my surprised one and pressed the button again.

The vibrator increased in strength. I swallowed back another groan and pressed my head into the pillow.

"… has some serious balls to come at me like that with her tits falling out of her tacky-ass, cheetah print jumpsuit. Like, I think a porno from the seventies called, sweetie, they want their linty costume back."

"For real," I agreed tightly, scrunching up my face.

Amos pressed the button again. The vibrator went haywire and lit my pussy on fire. I bit the pillow to keep from screaming.

Suddenly, it stopped. Already breathing heavily, I looked back up at Amos. He lay on his side on the bed, propping his head up with his elbow and fist, and gave me a placid smile. I gave him crazy, "WTF" eyes. He spun the remote on its loop around his forefinger and raised his eyebrows at me.

"And what do you think that crazy bitch did after I pointed that out?" Liz asked.

"What?" I asked breathlessly.

"She yowled, June. Like a fucking cat."

I laughed, suddenly diverted by Liz's story. "Wait, for real?"

Click. Click.

The vibrator inside of me revved up to the second setting and I made a silent choking sound before letting my head fall forward again. Who made this vibrator from Hell? NASA? It was more intense than anything I'd ever used on myself.

"I shit you not," Liz laughed. "She is certifiable, I'm telling you."

I turned a desperate gaze on Amos, but he just gave me his lazy half smile with chestnut eyes that traveled from my open mouth to my butt in the air, and back again.

Click. Click.

I let out a strangled sound.

"Exactly," Liz laughed loudly. "She is sick. And she keeps fucking showing up at these clubs."

"No way," I gritted out.

"What are you making? It sounds like you're on the struggle bus, sis," Liz said with some amusement.

"Uh, eh," I fumbled. The vibrator stopped, and it was everything I could do not to sigh in relief and exasperation in equal parts. "Lasagna," I puffed. "It's… it has all these steps."

"Brave," she mused. "Okay, well I gotta go. We're hopping to lower Miami tonight. Good luck with your domestic bliss," she sang.

I laughed, "Okay, sounds goo—"

Click.

"—ooohhh my God," I moaned.

Silence pulled taut on Liz's end. Then she barked, "Are you *fucking* him right now June Matthews?"

"No," I groaned honestly.

"Gross," Liz grumbled.

I laughed, slightly manic. *Click. Click. Click.* My laugh turned high pitched and staccato, and Liz sighed disgustedly before she hung up.

I lifted a crazed glare to Amos. "Brady, what the actual fu-huhhh," I moaned loudly as the vibrator went space engine strong before abruptly stopping again.

He laughed.

"Oh, this is funny, is it?" I panted.

Amos gave me a vampire overlord blink. "I'm just waiting."

"Waiting for *what?*"

Click, click, click, click.

I let out a high-pitched shriek and my toes pointed as every nerve at the apex of my thighs coiled tightly around the vibrations. Amos got off the bed, and turning the vibrator on and off, did mundane things around the house like loading the dishwasher, pulling something out of the fridge, and walking around behind me in and out of his closet. On, off. On, off. The vibrations ratcheted up tightly only to fall and leave me gasping and clutching the pillow to my face.

"Amos!" I screamed as he revved it up to the highest setting and left it there for a good minute while he tossed a condom onto the bed next to me.

"Yes?" he asked, his voice low as he bent over me again. His warmth sent shivers down my cold, sweat-dewed skin.

"Oh my God, you *know what*," I groaned, my toes starting to cramp from pointing in tortured ecstasy.

"Not sure I do," he mused, kissing my shoulder, my neck, my jaw.

"*Please*, Amos."

"Please what?" he whispered in amusement.

"Please, just fuck me," I begged.

He chuckled low and suddenly the vibrator stopped. "If you insist. Why didn't you just ask?"

"Oh, you *dick*. That's it," I started to straighten, but he put a strong hand against the center of my back and slowly forced me back down.

"I don't remember hearing a safe word. Did you say a safe word?"

"No," I grunted with my face in the pillow.

"Then stay still, Cupcake." He hooked a finger through the loop on the vibrator, and slowly, far too slowly, he removed it. But instead of tossing it aside, he shifted it so the latex egg slid through my slit and lay directly against my clit, held in place by my legs and the pillow.

"Oh fuck," I whispered. I trembled all over, knowing exactly what he was about to do.

Click.

I jumped as agonizing pleasure teased my clit with such force, I was sure I would come right then and there. But he stopped it again, and that time, I felt him press against my pussy with the head of his cock. I moaned in response, begging him wordlessly to do it. He slid in easily, and with perfectly timed strokes, he filled me and retreated, slow enough to stretch me, but fast enough to bring me relief. As he picked up his tempo, he smoothed his hands over my ass and took hold of my hips. I felt the remote between his palm and my skin.

My orgasm climbed fast, and I gasped, pressing my forehead against the pillows. "Amos," I groaned.

Click.

I screamed again, this time in pure ecstasy as Amos filled me from behind and the vibrator shocked my clit straight to an orgasm. I gave myself over to it as Amos pistoned in and out of me fast and hard, giving me the most exquisite combination of pleasure and pain imaginable. As my waves of release pulsed around his cock, Amos huffed hard, pulling himself against me as he turned off the vibrator.

I rode the waves with him inside of me, my fingers still clenching the pillow and my body unraveling in gratifying ripples. Amos caged his sated body over mine, breathing hard against my skin before kissing between my shoulder blades. "Christ, June," he gritted out.

I popped up a heel and looked over my shoulder at him with a contended grin. "Christ, Brady."

He blew out a breath, righted himself, and went to the bathroom to get rid of the condom, I assumed. Then he gently lifted me off the pillows with his arm around my middle. When he'd stood me in front of him, he turned me to face him, and I saw then that he'd removed his shirt and pants, but he had on a pair of sporty black briefs he preferred. He placed one hand on my injured shoulder and pivoted my sore arm with the other. "You okay?" he asked with concern tilting up his inky brows.

The muscles in my shoulder pulled with a slight twinge, but it was well worth it. I gave him a loopy smile and leaned into him. "So good."

He rolled his eyes, but indulgently bent to kiss my lips. "I really should know better than to fuck an injured woman." He took both my shoulders and pushed them back, so my posture straightened painfully. "Do your PT exercises while I start dinner."

I winced. "I hate those things. Let's watch true crime instead."

"You can do both, and you know it," he drawled as he walked away.

I heard him wash his hands in the kitchen, and I scooped up my baggy T-shirt so I could slip it back on. As I hinged my arm out and in, doing the exercises Amos had given me, his phone buzzed on the nightstand. I glanced down at it and saw the name "Cade" with a message that caused my heart to squeeze. It was only the first part because his phone privacy required the phone to be unlocked to see the full text, but I saw enough.

Cade: Got a lead on Meg…

TWENTY-SIX

Amos

I had to amend my earlier conviction. Dating June Matthews wasn't going to give me high blood pressure, but fucking her was. I had never, in my life, seen a more tantalizing thing than June bent over for my display with her perfectly round ass in the air while she danced in ecstasy on the very tips of her toes. The sounds she made were enough to make me feral. Combine her husky voice with her pleading expression? Jesus wept.

It had been against my better judgment to give in and have my way with her, but truth be told, I'd been just as desperate as she had. June had taken to walking around naked in the morning before I went to the surgical center just to tease me into fucking her. And, in true June fashion, it had worked. But although I had given her exactly what she wanted (okay, fine, it had been what *I* wanted), she didn't sit back and relax after we'd had sex.

June rounded the corner of the hallway and media room with my phone in her hand. In a furious display of red curls and rumpled T-shirt that barely covered her generous ass, June marched up to me and pointed the phone in my direction. "Who is Cade and why is he getting leads on Meg?"

Ah. That explained it. I extended my hand for the phone. "Cade is my research partner, and don't worry about it."

She pivoted the phone away from me, her lips tight. "Brady, *I* told *you* to forget about it."

I went back to cutting cucumbers. I was curious what Cade's brother, Remington, had turned up when he'd looked into Meg and Archer, but I wasn't going to let June know that. "It's not what you think," I replied honestly. "I started off looking for leverage through Azura, but she tipped me off to some charges in their past that made me curious. Actually, they made all of us curious."

"Who is 'us?'" she asked, stalking closer to me with the phone still clutched in her hand.

As soon as she was within reach, I set down the knife and lashed out a hand lightning quick. I pulled her to me and trapped her hard against my body. With her expression still shocked, I swiped the phone from her fingers. "Azura is interested in their illegal activities, Remington, Cade's brother, is interested in the cyber nature of their prior convictions, and Cade is nosy."

June scowled. "So, this isn't some revenge scheme?"

"It was," I clarified. "But Azura has a personal interest in them, now. If they end up getting caught doing something dirty, well," I shrugged nonchalantly. "All the better."

"I don't believe you," she said with a suspicious squint of her eyes.

I bent down close. "What are you going to do about it, Matthews?"

She stood on tip toes and brought her lips just below mine. "I'll unsort your darks and whites."

"Have mercy," I grinned. I slid my hands around her waist, and that action alone sent a surge of desire through every cell in my body. Clamping down hard, I lifted her suddenly and sat her on the counter, her wild hair framing both our faces and her dark-lashed, forest green eyes angled down to mine. "I thought you were going to say you'd paint every inch of my walls in neon colors," I teased.

The joy in her eyes dimmed a touch.

I laid my hands on her thighs and smoothed her soft skin with my thumbs. "Hey. Remember what I told you, June Bug."

"Stop daydreaming while you're talking because it makes you feel like that teacher from Peanuts?"

I squeezed playfully above her knees, making her jump. "No. The other thing."

She rolled her eyes. "Yeah, yeah. I know."

"I want to hear you say it," I pressed.

In monotone, like she was reciting the lunch menu to her fifth-grade class, she droned, "Their crazy doesn't get to steal my love of art."

"And?" I prompted.

"And I'm," she paused, holding up two thumbs, "the best."

"June," I glowered.

"I know," she relented, leaning her head forward to rest on my shoulder. "I know. And I got another commission today."

"I knew you would," I said honestly. "You don't get to give up just because two psychos took advantage of you."

"It's a small commission," she admitted.

I took her face in my hands and forced her to look at me. "Good. Keep going. Brain surgeons don't perform hemispherectomies in their first year of medical school. Everyone has to start somewhere."

She pulled a face. "Your job is gross."

"Better than a podiatrist," I pointed out, releasing her.

She made a "gag" face, but then smiled softly. "Thanks. I'll get over it. I know I will. But it stings."

"Yeah, well. You wouldn't be sensitive June if it didn't," I smiled, leaning into her. "I can replace it with another kind of sting. All kinds, actually."

She brought her left hand up to tickle her fingers over the five o'clock shadow on my jaw. "That's unfair."

"What is?" I murmured with a smile.

"The whole supportive boyfriend deflection thing. You can't seduce me into forgetting about your illicit activities with your sister and wanna be best friend detective."

"Can't I?" I challenged. I pulled her tight against my stomach with her legs straddling me.

She swallowed visibly. "I don't know. I forgot what I was saying."

I chuckled. "Do you trust me, June?"

Her eyes bounced between mine as a little pucker of worry formed between her brows. Finally, she smoothed her hand along the back of my neck, scratching deliciously along my skin with her nails as she threaded her fingers through my hair. Suddenly, she jerked my head close to her, her lips grazing mine as she whispered, "I do. But if you mess up my heart, I'm going to butcher you."

I kissed her softly, smoothing my hands up the curve of her spine. "I'm an MD, Matthews. Your heart is in good hands."

My phone buzzed on the counter next to us several more times, but I ignored it because June was busy devouring me, body and soul. She didn't know yet, but I'd been able to finish the poem I had started in confusion weeks before. The words that had stuck fast behind fear and reluctance had finally found their way to the surface, and it was June who had unearthed them. I might have been the doctor, but June had the expert touch.

The simple way you smiled,

How it crinkled up your nose,

The complicated way you're brilliant,

And your mind keeps me on my toes,

The effortless way you dance like dust in sunbeams

warms me to my core.

The pining way you're the

missing piece

I couldn't bring myself to look for.

EPILOGUE
June

I fidgeted nervously in the back of the luxury car, pulling the gap in my long, maroon coat closed and swallowing a wave of nausea. Amos was going to kill me. Either he was going to kill me, or he was going to fuck me like I wanted, and there wasn't a whole lot of gray area in-between.

It was worth the risk.

The car slowed to a stop, and speaking of the vampire overlord himself, Amos opened my door for me just outside the event center. He had an umbrella in his hand and held it over the car door opening to keep us both from getting drenched in the sunset rainstorm. "Hey, gorgeous," he said with a silky smile.

I bit down a groan. My God, he was perfect. His wavy, black hair had been combed to the side and flicked over his left ear, and his dark eyes smoldered with heated promises as he dragged them from my glossy curls to my red pumps. "Where did you get that?" he asked, looking at my coat.

"Uh, the mall," I hedged. Although, in a minute, the coat I'd bought would be the last thing he noticed. He had sent a car to take me to a charity ball a local non-profit was holding for Children's Primary Hospital, and in mid-October, I was definitely putting myself out there with the dress underneath the coat.

But drastic measures had to be taken.

He extended a hand, which I took gratefully because heels and I didn't get along. Like he knew this, Amos kept a tight grip on my hand and threaded my arm through his. "Well, you look amazing. Thank you for agreeing to come to this thing. They're horrifyingly boring, but the food is good."

Like I cared. I mean, it was true that I was way out of my element with these people, and I'd never been to a ball where wealthy patrons pledged the equivalent of my yearly salary to hospitals like dropping change in a Ronald McDonald box at the drive-through. But I'd leaped at the chance to enact my evil plan:

The slow, decadent persuasion of Amos Brady.

I followed him up the stairs and into the posh event center, which had been decorated like a gilded fall gala, with gold pumpkins, glittering leaves, and dancing candlelight. I followed Amos through a tall foyer and to a smaller reception area, and we wove through a sparse crowd. Amos stopped to talk to his colleagues, introducing me and garnering me more than a few interested looks. I was ten years his junior, and I looked possibly younger than that, I knew. It was the whole big-eyed, lost doofus vibe I had going for me.

When we reached the dining room, it was my moment of truth. Either I kept the coat on and avoided the wrath of Amos, or I went big so we could go home. I unbuttoned my coat, slid it off my shoulders, and handed it to the attendant at the door who would take them to some mysterious, fancy-person coat room.

Amos handed his coat to the young guy — probably a college kid earning some hefty tips — and turned back to me. He froze. Ice-sculpture, marble-monument, stunned-into-silence froze.

I tugged my bottom lip between my teeth and gave him an innocent blink. "What?"

There wasn't anything remarkable about my dress, really. It definitely screamed "sex" with its red lining and black lace top layer, and it ended mid-thigh, which was just this side of slutty. But the black leather bralette I'd paired under it swooped over my cleavage, crisscrossed up my breastbone, and circled my throat. If my dress screamed "sex," then the bralette hollered, "spank me, Daddy."

Amos looked entirely lost for words, so I looped my arm through his again and led him into the crowded dining room. "I wonder what they're serving," I mused.

He turned us right back around, snatched our coats from the coat kid, who looked like he'd seen Amos rise from a coffin, and marched us right back out the foyer. He shoved my coat back over my shoulders. "What in the name of *God* are you wearing, June?" he hissed.

I bit my lip again, fighting a laugh. "It's a dress, Amos. I know I don't wear fancy ones very often, but I thought—"

"That is not a dress," he snapped. "That is… I don't know."

"Sexy?" I offered. Another surge of nausea threatened to overcome me, and I swallowed back the bit of bile that had sloshed into my mouth. *Keep it together*, I thought with consternation.

He stopped in the middle of the foyer, his eyes hard obsidian. "That is the understatement of the century, Matthews."

I gave him my best doe-eyed look. "Are you telling me to cover up, Amos? I thought you were a feminist."

A muscle in his jaw ticked. "What are you playing at here, June?"

"Nothing," I said, splaying my hands out in front of me. "I mean, I wouldn't consider it a *game* so much as a *message*, and since you've been firmly ignoring said message for several weeks, I figured, hell… why not shout it?"

He considered me with ember-dark eyes, his straight brows drawn together infinitesimally. Finally, he looked away, smoothing his fingers over his mouth. "June. We've been over this."

"Oh, I know we have," I quipped and turned back around to go into the dining room. "And since you can't *make* me leave with you, I think I'm going to set the terms. Either we go home," I continued, even as he hooked his hand around my elbow and dragged me over to a huge marble column to tuck me into the shadows, "or I stay here."

He pressed me against the hard column, his long body pinning me in place. I gave him a pointed look. "Either you treat me *exactly* the same way you treated your other girlfriends, or I'm staying here and showing off my interests."

"They're not *your* interests," he bit out, bending over me and leaning his forearm against the stone beside my head. "They're *my* interests, and I don't think they're fitting for you or our relationship."

"Why?" I challenged, some of my ire leaking out around the word. "Why not? Why don't I measure up to every other woman you've been with?"

He sighed through his nose, letting his head hang a moment. His cologne surrounded me, heightening my emotions and compelling me to nuzzle my nose against the base of his throat. I heard him swallow.

"It's not that you don't measure up, June." Amos lifted his head, his shadowed gaze capturing mine. "It's that I… I treasure you. I can't do those things to you. I don't want to." He bent his lips to my jaw. "You've given me a sweet tooth, Cupcake."

I let out a little growl. "I don't want to be treasured. I want you to fuck me the way I *know* you want to. You're holding back because you think I'm weak."

"Fragile," he corrected, angling another look my way. "And precious."

"I am not," I scowled, pulling away.

Amos chuckled softly. "Imagine being told you're precious and getting angry about it. Matthews, you defy logic."

I gagged, suddenly coughing on another bit of vomit that threatened to escape from my throat.

Amos gave me a concerned, assessing look. "Babe, I think you need to sit down."

I resisted the urge to stomp my foot. "Play dirty, Amos. I'm asking you to. I'm insisting on it."

He rolled his eyes. "Well, considering that you played dirty first," he responded, hooking me with one of his glares that sent goosebumps skittering down my arms. "I'm not sure I have much of a choice."

I shrugged, giving him a falsely hopeless look. "I guess so."

Amos narrowed his eyes. "You want me to punish you, June?"

"Mhm," I hummed, my gaze flicking up and down his hard features.

He hooked a finger through the collar of my leather bralette and yanked me so our lips nearly touched. "Then take off that coat and walk into the dining room."

I frowned in confusion. "Uh... okay. Seems like the opposite of what you wanted me to do ear—"

"Did I ask your opinion?" he asked, his voice quiet but razor sharp.

I swallowed, drowning in his fathomless eyes. "No." I handed him my coat and turned toward the dining room.

Amos leaned away from the pillar and swatted my ass. "Go once around the dining room perimeter, but don't stay too long. I'll be counting."

"Counting what?" I asked, clacking across the spacious foyer that reminded me of a museum with its four-story ceiling and echoing floors.

Amos just gave me a simmering look with his hands in his tux pants pockets as he watched me cross into the dining room. I shivered. Turning my attention to the packed dining room decorated with vases of wheat stalk things and glittering leaves, I let my hand trail along deep orange tablecloths, and stared in wonder at the beautiful gowns and glittering jewels on the laughing guests at the fundraiser.

I didn't know a single one of them, so no one stopped me to talk, but plenty of eyes followed me. I cupped my elbows, feeling more and more as I walked around the room that I'd been an absolute moron. This whole thing was massively uncomfortable. Of course people were staring—I looked like the bawdy entertainment.

I turned and found Amos leaning against the door, his eyes bouncing from me to the guests with quiet observation. What was he doing? When I finally reached him, he held out my coat wordlessly, and I shrugged it on, cocking my head in silent question. "Let's go," he said softly, his gaze still on some of the occupants, and then he turned to leave with my hand in his.

What the hell?

Amos held an umbrella over my head, and magically, our black luxury sedan was there waiting for us, so I slid into it. I was immediately grateful that there was a partition between us and the driver because I already wanted to jump Amos and find out what his idea of a dark sexy time looked like. He'd been holding out on me since we started dating. He played fun games, of course—he was still Amos. But I knew he'd been holding back, and I honestly couldn't stand the thought that he'd been with other women more experienced than I was.

I could be kinky. Probably.

Amos got in the car after me, and after the driver took off, I turned to him with a sly smile. "So?" I prompted.

"Eight," Amos said, shrugging out of his tux jacket.

"Eight?"

"That's your number," he continued, not looking at me. He unclasped the cufflinks around his white button-down sleeves.

I made a comical thinking face. "Hm."

Amos rolled up his sleeves. "That's how many men fucked you with their eyes while you walked around that room."

I opened my mouth, but no words came out. "Uh… "

"So, eight is your number:" He turned his coal-black eyes to me. "Get over my lap."

My eyes went round. "Oh my God."

He sat back, stretching his legs out as the car stopped at a stoplight. "You know your safe word."

I unbuckled my seatbelt, shucked off my coat, and darting uncertain glances his way, I put myself on all fours, bridging over his legs. I twisted to look up at him, and my curls fell heavily to one side. Amos pushed down on my back and I fell to his lap, covering my mouth with my hand and smothering a grin.

Dr. Amos Brady was about to spank my ass.

Amos tugged my tight dress up my thighs until he exposed the red thong I wore underneath, and cold autumn air hit my cheeks. "I'm tempted to double your eight," Amos muttered, smoothing a hand over my cheeks and causing me to sigh with pleasure.

I was pretty sure no matter what he did, he wasn't going to really *hurt* me, so I gave him a saucy look over my shoulder. "Whatever tickles your funny bone, Brady."

Smack.

I gasped as the sharp sting of Amos' slap against my ass sent a shockwave of pain over the middle of both cheeks. I reared up, gripping the leather seat. "What the *fuck*?"

"Count it," Amos said, his voice dark.

I rotated a shocked look up at him. "That *hurt*, Brady."

His gaze narrowed slightly. "I know."

Oh shit. I swallowed hard, suddenly extremely unsure of what I'd gotten myself into, here. "Uh, one?" I squeaked.

Smack. He cracked a second slap over my left cheek, and I shrieked, looking at the partition to the driver uncertainly. I couldn't see who they were, but they *had* to have heard that.

Don't think about that, June, I thought as my thoughts sprinted from worry to the distracting burn on my bum. *Kinky girls don't care who hears their ass slapping or whatever. Probably. Fuck, who am I kidding? I have no idea what the hell I'm doing.*

Smack. "You're behind, June. Count them."

I reared up again, but Amos held me down, and my cheeks were on *fire*, tingling and burning in a horribly unpleasant way. "Fuck," I hissed. "Two, three. Wait, Amos, does it always hurt like that or are you just super piss—"

Smack.

"Ow!" I growled, gritting my teeth and gripping the seat. "*Brady.*"

"I'm going to start adding slaps if you can't follow directions," Amos warned.

"Oh my God," I moaned. My butt stung so badly, I thought it was probably redder than the maple leaves passing by outside our car window. I pressed my head into my hands. "Four."

Amos rubbed my ass, and it felt good and chaffed my sore skin at the same time. Somehow, I'd imagined all those spankings I'd read about or watched online as vaguely satisfying? But Amos didn't seem interested in satisfying me at the moment. He seemed like he was doing exactly what I'd asked him to do. He was punishing me.

Smack.

I groaned, wiggling my ass and contemplating shouting "green apple." Instead, I gusted out, "Five."

Amos rubbed my singed bottom again, this time dipping his fingers between my cheeks and finding my sensitive, aching pussy. To my shock, his fingers found slick heat, and he rubbed up and down the length of my wet slit. He made a sound low in his throat. "Fuck, June."

My body was responding to this insanity? A cocky smile tugged at my lips. *I knew it. I knew I was Brady's kind of cupcake.*

Smack.

My smile melted and I let out a shriek. "Ow! Brady you fucking—"

Smack. Smack. "I'll do you a favor and count you to eight," Amos interrupted, his voice rough. He caressed my flesh again, dipping back down into my pussy and slipping two fingers inside of me.

I huffed, going limp over his legs. "Jesus," I gritted out. My cheeks burned and my core ached for more of his touch as he slowly moved his fingers in and out of my wet pussy. The tingling pain on my cheeks was spreading in warmth, and like a heating pad, it seemed to reach all my most sensitive places and heightened my arousal. Goddamn, I could see the appeal, actually.

He kept moving, sawing his fingers in and out until a blush suffused my cheeks and my breath caught in my lungs. His thumb found my clit, and I knew I was a goner. Amos knew my body by now. He knew the perfect way to press and hook his fingers to get me worked into a frenzy in seconds.

I moaned, rolling my forehead against the leather seat as he pushed me straight to an orgasm. Relentlessly, he worked me until my legs shook, and with a shuddering cry, I tensed before sweet release broke through me and my orgasm clenched around his fingers. Breathing hard, I went limp on his lap. *Fucking hell.*

Amos removed his fingers, trailing the moisture along my burning ass, and then he lifted me upright to straddle him. His hands burned through the fabric of my dress at my hips, and I pressed down against his erection, leaning down and framing his face with my hands. "Okay, that *was* a little hot," I admitted.

"Hm," was all he said, his gaze going from my eyes to my mouth.

I grazed my lips against his. "Is this the part where you fuck me senseless?"

His teeth flashed as he grinned. "No."

I pouted, pulling back to hook him with a glare. "What do you mean, 'no?'"

The car stopped just outside our apartment building, and Amos kissed me on the lips softly. "Eight is your number. Get out, June."

I gaped. *What?*

Amos set me aside, slid out of the car, and held out a hand for me. Frowning in confusion again, I adjusted my dress, grabbed my coat, and we dashed through the rain to the apartment lobby. As we rode the elevator up, Amos gave me occasional glances full of dark, silent promises. I shifted my weight from foot to foot, my butt rubbing uncomfortably against the fabric of my dress. I needed ice or something, damn.

When we got to the apartment, Amos unlocked the door. He scarcely had it open before he hooked his finger under the collar portion of my bralette and tugged me inside, slammed me against the closing door, and slanted a hungry kiss over my lips.

I sighed into him, clutching his button-down for support while I melted into his kiss. Amos dipped his tongue into my mouth, flicking it along the back of my teeth while I pushed myself onto my tiptoes and devoured him with desperation.

He broke the kiss, breathing heavily, and I wondered if he'd lost his composure when he hadn't meant to. His lashes flicked down and then back up. "Okay. Bedroom."

"Yay," I grinned.

"Don't get cocky." He pushed off the door and smacked my ass again as I walked away. It burned like a son of a bitch, and I skittered away from him.

"Ow," I growled, giving him a glower. "That was nine."

"That's for looking so fucking tasty," he shot back, scowling and following me.

I snorted and grabbed my dress by the hem, peeling it off as I sashayed across the open apartment. Rain pelted the windows, and the city faded into a misty darkness beyond them. I walked straight to our bed in my bralette and thong, and fully anticipating the best sex of my life, I flopped onto the bed and stretched out on my side. I winced as the comforter rubbed against my sore butt-cheeks.

Amos breezed past me like he didn't care that his gorgeous goddess of a girlfriend was displayed on his huge bed, and he went for his closet. My teeth gnawed uncertainly on my lower lip. It wasn't new for Brady to keep his cards close to his chest, but I didn't know what he had planned.

I shifted onto my knees and watched as Amos brought out a velvet packet of some kind. He put it on the bedside table, and undoing the buttons on his white shirt, he went back into the walk-in. The closet was basically another room, and I hadn't really explored it much, but I knew it was huge and had unlabeled leather boxes along the top shelves. The Mysterious Curiosities of Brady's Smut Closet.

When Amos came back out, he had an entire piece of furniture. It was the bench he kept in his closet, and I had always assumed the black leather, curved couch was just artistic and had been put there for the hell of it, but now I looked at the bench with new eyes. Eyes that found little silver rings on leather loops and a set of leather cuffs along the rounded edge.

My mouth made an "O" before I scrambled off the bed. "You have a *sex bench*?"

"It's a chaise, technically," he said, leaning two hands against the higher curve of the S-shaped lounger.

"Oh, a chaise," I said in a fake British accent, skipping up to him. "How fancy."

Amos folded his arms over his broad chest, his shirt halfway unbuttoned and teasing me with a peek of his smooth pectorals underneath. "I don't think I spanked you hard enough."

My teeth clacked shut.

Amos took a step forward, crowding me with his warmth and his scent, and my eyes fluttered as his fingers brushed against the leather straps that dipped over the curve of my breasts. "I could get used to this, though," he murmured. He slid a finger beneath the leather and pulled me toward the chaise. "Over the top part," he instructed.

I draped myself over the bench, and Amos helped position me, kneeling on the flat wedge in the middle and bent over the hump with my fingers kissing the floor. It put my ass in the air, and Amos slid my thong down my legs before tossing it aside.

I gave him a giddy grin, and he broke his stern demeanor, snuffing out a laugh through his nose. Then, he bent down around me so his lips dropped a kiss on my shoulder. His hands skimmed my arms, searing a heated path from my shoulders down to my wrists, and then he attached a pair of padded leather cuffs around them. He tightened the straps, putting my hands down to the ground and my ass high in the air.

Nervousness and excitement swooped in my belly and fell to my pussy. I clenched my thighs together in anticipation of what Amos had in mind.

He started off by turning on a vibrator, but I couldn't see what he was doing behind me because he'd faced me toward the rainy windows and dimmed the lights. I jumped when he slid the vibrator through my folds and right up against my clit. But it didn't feel like any vibrator I'd used before. It hooked inside of my vagina and right up against my G-spot, and then a vibrating, suctioning sensation clamped around my clit.

I gasped loudly, my stomach tensing as I shot straight toward an orgasm. "What the—?"

Amos bent around me again, his chest bare and pressing against my back with simmering warmth. "Remember that number?"

"Eight?" I asked, my voice strained as the toy pulled me closer to an orgasm.

Amos held out a set of anal beads at my eye level. They were *way* bigger than I was used to seeing. And there were ten balls on the flexible toy, starting out small and growing in size with each one. Eight. He was going to stick eight of those up my ass. "Oh fuck," I whispered.

"Ready?"

I let out a harsh breath, my body already shaking as the insane toy revved me up toward an easy orgasm whether I wanted it to or not. I nodded.

Amos rubbed his fingers with aching tenderness along my trembling core and then around my ass, lubrication on his fingers as he eased it around each opening before pressing the first bead against my slick entrance. I let out a choked sound of pain and pleasure as he slipped the first bead into my ass and my body fought against the orgasm that threatened to rip through me.

"One," Amos whispered, and his other hand rubbed down my back and over my sore ass.

I whimpered as he pressed the second round bead inside, stretching my opening and causing my pussy to clench around the vibrating toy.

"Two."

I came after he slipped the third bead inside of me. I let out a tortured breath and hunched forward with my hands clenched in their manacles as my muscles loosened with an intense orgasm unlike anything I'd had before.

Amos pulled the vibrating toy away from my clit as I came down from the orgasm, and the fourth bead slipped through my lubricated entrance, which stretched and then relaxed, as the ball was buried in my ass. Literally nothing could have prepared me for the intensity of these sensations, and I immediately knew why couples craved this.

Then I felt Amos' cock at the entrance of my pussy, and I welcomed him with another low sound of arousal, my eyes screwed shut and my body alight with new sensations. He pushed inside of me as he slid another, larger ball in my ass. "Five."

I choked, "Oh my God, Amos."

I was impossibly full, and as Amos slid in and out of me slowly, my toes curled with pleasure. "You can take it, baby," he murmured, and as he slowly, languorously fucked me from behind, he pushed the sixth ball, stretching me to the point of pain again before I relaxed around the bead. Every time he pumped inside of me, he pushed against the anal beads, pressing the next, larger sphere against my entrance.

I shuddered as my body tensed, heading toward another orgasm. "Amos, please," I pleaded.

"Not yet," he warned, low and harsh.

As his dick pumped me full, he pushed the seventh ball inside of me, and I gasped from the pull of it. "Fuck, fuck, fuck," I gritted out.

"Seven."

My breathing picked up again, and I heard a familiar slight wheeze on the inhale. *No way my boyfriend fucked me so thoroughly that I need an inhaler,* I thought with caustic despair.

Amos paused, his hand between my shoulder blades. "June…"

I forced my breath to fill my lungs calmly. "I'm fine," I assured him. That would be just my luck. I'd prove Amos right and set myself up as too "fragile" for fun sex. No way. I wouldn't let that happen.

Amos increased his tempo, fucking me hard and drawing little gasping moans from me as he slowly pressed the last, largest anal bead against my entrance, and I lost myself in the sweet torture of the whole thing.

"Eight."

I shook with the effort to keep myself together. There wasn't anything on my clit, no vibrator or fingers, but Amos was sliding against my G-spot just perfectly, and I was so *full*, I thought I would explode.

"Come on, baby," Amos encouraged, bending over me and whispering a kiss against my neck. "Come for me."

I did, shattering and splintering as I gave myself over to the lack of control. My fingers tightened around my restraints and my sore, thrumming body tensed into waves of mind-numbing bliss. As I came, hard and fast, Amos pulled the beads out of me slowly. I was so distracted by my orgasm, I hardly noticed.

Dimly, I was aware that Amos had collapsed over me, breathing just as fast as I was, and our bodies clung together, sweaty and spent. He reached down and undid the restraints around my wrists, rubbing the skin gently.

As I turned on the bench, Amos lifted me and carried me to the bed, pulling us both heavily onto the mattress. I laughed as we collapsed, and he cradled me against him, tucking my head under his chin. "June," he rumbled. "You're a terrible influence on me."

I wheezed a laugh, pulling away to look up at his handsome, hard features. "Am I?"

"Horrible," he reiterated solemnly. But then a smile pulled at the corner of his mouth. "But you're gorgeous."

I smiled, all sunshine and happy glow. I sighed, letting my head fall back. "That was amazing."

He exhaled loudly, echoing me and going limp like I had, and we both stared at the ceiling. He slanted a look my way. "Was it?"

"Yes," I replied quickly, giving him a surprised look. "Couldn't you tell I liked it?"

"Uh, I don't know. You made a lot of sounds I haven't heard you make before," he admitted. "You're sure you're okay? I kept thinking you were going to use your safe word."

"Well, I didn't," I said with a stubborn tilt of my chin. "So, hah. Suck it, Brady."

His eyelids went half-mast over dark cola eyes, hooding with desire. "Gladly, Matthews."

I bit my lip, tamping down a grin. "You can punish me anytime."

"Hm, don't tempt me," he half-laughed, his voice husky. "You deserve it way more than you get it."

"True," I agreed seriously. "Although, I'm not sure I would really call that a punishment. You're so gentle with me."

Amos gave me a loaded look. "You know why."

I groaned, rolling over and then sitting up so I could remove my bralette and head into the shower. "Not this again."

"If you would just take a *test*, you'd see that I'm right, you stubborn little—"

"Nope," I cut him off, standing from the bed and vaulting toward the shower. Nausea sloshed around in my stomach like he'd conjured it with his inane theories. "I told you, it's the meds."

"Albuterol does not give you nausea," he insisted, following me with his toned, perfectly muscular body. "Your breasts and areolas are bigger—"

"Gross." I scrunched my nose and gagged.

"—and you literally haven't had a period since we've been together in July."

"Yes, I did," I argued, stopping, fully naked, to face him and point my finger at him. Then I poked him in the bare chest as he stopped in front of me. "I know I messed up my birth control pills or whatever, and that screwed up my cycle, but I did have one."

"June," he glowered, folding his arms. "Yes, you had a one-off period because you *missed your birth control pills,* and your calculations are way off because of it. And you *kept missing them* even after we refilled it. It's no wonder you got knocked up."

"I'm not pregnant," I insisted, turning on my heel and marching to the open shower.

"Matthews," he groaned. "You're killing me. You're probably more than two months along at this point. You can't keep ignoring it."

Yes, I could. Because of course he was right. Amos was a doctor. He wasn't stupid—he knew what he was talking about, and realistically, I was pretty sure he was right. Once you miss a few birth control pills, it throws things off. And then I missed a few more, and who the hell knew where I was at with my cycles and with a possible… *that.*

But I couldn't face that possibility because I was twenty-two, and it was horrifyingly reckless of me to get pregnant that young while living with too-good-to-be-true Amos Brady. This bubble was going to burst eventually, and I couldn't face that possibility.

My nerves suddenly jangled uncomfortably, and as I reached the shower, my stomach turned sour. Coughing, and giving up all pretenses completely, I fell to my knees in front of the toilet and heaved up bile and breadsticks from my lunch earlier.

Sighing indulgently, Amos kneeled beside me. He'd put on his boxers and T-shirt, and he rubbed my back in soothing circles. "This feels familiar," he mused.

It was *not* familiar. I didn't like it at all. I'd had random bouts of it, but lately, the nausea had been getting so much worse. I moaned, leaning my head on the sparkling clean seat of his toilet. "Amos," I groaned.

"I know, love," he murmured, still rubbing my back.

"I don't want to hear it," I growled.

He sighed again. "June. There's only so much I can do from the sidelines to keep you and the baby safe. You're going to have to admit it and see an OB at some poi—"

"Shut it," I muttered.

I saw him wring his hands in my peripheral vision, and I assumed he was mimicking strangling me. "Okay, fine. Let's get you in the shower at least. Then you can lie down and I'm making you some toast."

"Okay," I grumbled, and he helped me into the shower.

As I rinsed under the hot water, leaning my forehead against the Italian marble wall, I tried to quiet my stomach. But it lurched and heaved like that one bout of vomiting had opened the floodgates. It felt like it wasn't going to let up for a really long time, and that terrified me more than anything else.

I toweled off and slipped one of Amos' gray T-shirts over my head before climbing into the clean, crisp sheets and lying back on the pillows with a groan. Amos had already cleaned up after our lovemaking session, and he brought me a plate of toast along with a banana and strawberry smoothie.

"This should help with the *not morning sickness*," he offered dryly.

I plucked the plate from his hands. "Thank you very much." I didn't want the smoothie, though. The thought made me gag.

"You're getting thin, June," he warned, sitting on the bed next to me. "There are medications we can get you that will help."

I took a bite of toast. "I'm just busy at the school," I said around a mouthful. Which was true. I'd landed a huge commission painting a mural in a hallway of an elementary school, and it would take me a few months at least. They paid me hourly for my work, and it was the closest I'd gotten to a full-time art profession. Good thing my boss didn't mind splitting my time between the medical practice and the school.

Amos speared me with a hard look. With an intake of breath, he reached up and smoothed his thumb along my cheek. "June, sweetie, you know I'm here for you, don't you?"

I stopped chewing, swallowed dry toast down my scratchy throat, and stared at him. My shoulders sagged. "Yeah, I know."

"And you know even *when* you admit what's really happening here, I'm not going anywhere, right? You're mine,

Cupcake," he said, his tone turning light. "You're not going anywhere if I have anything to say about it."

I bit the inside of my cheek before answering, "I think I know that."

"Okay, then." Amos leaned forward and kissed me on the forehead. "Come around to it when you're ready."

God, he was perfect. How had I gotten so lucky? Amos Brady had every millimeter of my heart, and there wasn't any room for doubt. So, I didn't know why I pretended like I didn't already know what was so plainly apparent. That he was mine and I was his, and we weren't going anywhere.

Which meant it might not be the end of the world to acknowledge a few hard truths. I opened my mouth to say the unthinkable.

Suddenly, Amos' phone rang, and he turned, picking it up from the bedside table. He frowned as he stared at the caller ID.

"Who is it?" I asked.

"It's Zev. That brat never calls me," Amos muttered, half to himself. He answered it. "Hello?" He listened for a few seconds before abruptly standing. "What? Say that again."

I put my plate aside, suddenly worried for Amos. He looked stricken with fear as he paced away. "Amos?" I asked.

"When? How do you know?" Amos asked. He listened again, already going into his closet for clothing. "Yes, she texted me the location. I'll catch the next flight. No, don't call the police, it'll attract the wrong attention, and we don't know what she's been up to. I'll text you before I take off."

Dread gripped me with sharpened claws. "Amos?" I breathed out. Whatever it was, it had to be bad. He was rushing to get dressed, and I joined him, my toast forgotten and my nausea threatening to take over again.

"Get dressed," he said simply, already in a pair of jeans and throwing clothing into a weekender bag.

I found a pair of overalls and one of my shirts and dressed, worry slithering through my veins. When Amos came to stand in front of me, he dropped the bag he'd packed and took my upper arms in a gentle grip. His eyes had gone summer-storm dark, and he looked like he might be on the verge of tears.

"Whatever it is, I'm here," I assured him, cupping his face with my hand.

Amos nodded, leaning into my touch. "I know."

"Then, what is it?"

His throat bobbed. "Azura's been kidnapped."

Read Azura's Story Next! Coming **January 2024**

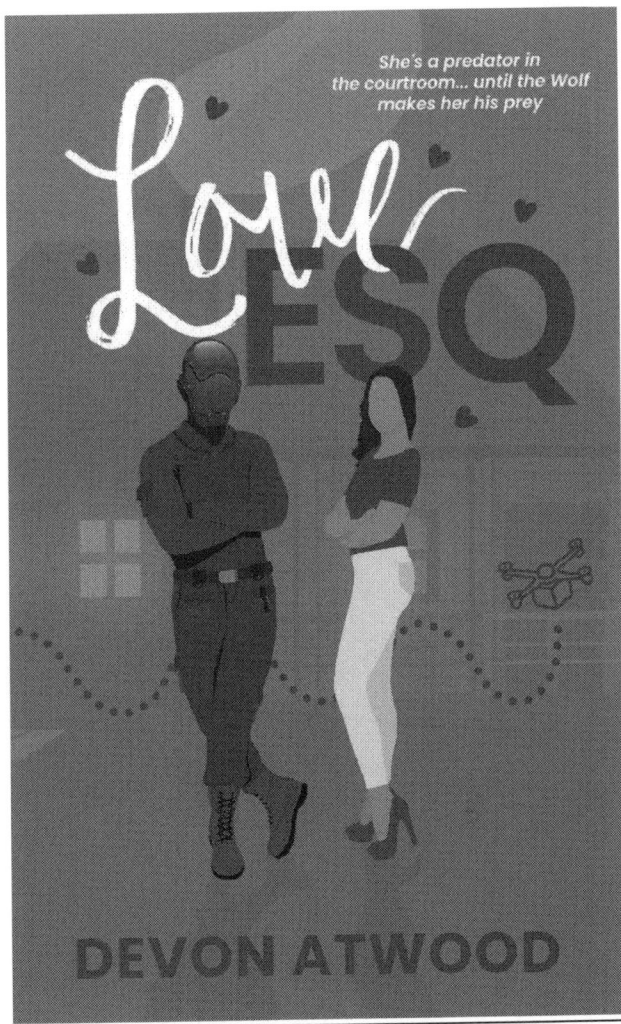

<u>Other Books by Devon Atwood</u>

THE FAIE KING'S MORTAL TRILOGY

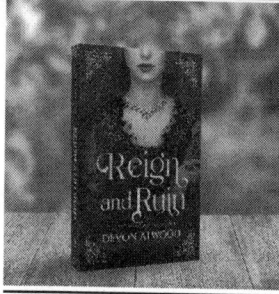

Acknowledgements

First, a HUGE thank you to the poet who spoke for Amos. Everyone *please* go find and follow **Christian @scruffylookinbookherder** for more of his amazing poetry. I told him about Amos, and he graciously created the most beautiful poems for me, and I could not be more grateful. He has a dreamy voice to listen to, and his talent with the written word is unparalleled.

Secondly, I want to thank my readers... yes, you! All of you have supported me and catapulted me through every book. I write for you, and I truly hope you've found joy in Love MD.

This book has my whole heart. I don't know what it is about June and Amos, but they had me in a chokehold the moment they popped into my brain. There's something about them, something about their chemistry and their story, that felt *so right* when I was writing it. I had a serious book hangover with them before I started Love Esq. I hope you have loved them as much as I do, and don't worry — you'll see them again!

Thank you to my husband, my family, and those closest to me. Your patience with my crazy author brain appears to be an endless well, and for that, I am eternally grateful. Thank you to my mother for cheering me on and giving me the DNA to do this in the first place, and thank you to my "street team" for your voracious support of everything I do.

Here's to many more books to come!

FOLLOW ME
@DEVONATWOODWRITES

Made in the USA
Middletown, DE
12 September 2024